Forever Glimmer Creek

STACY HACKNEY

Simon & Schuster Books for Young Readers
NEW YORK • LONDON • TORONTO • SYDNEY • NEW DELHI

SIMON & SCHUSTER BOOKS FOR YOUNG READERS
An imprint of Simon & Schuster Children's Publishing Division
1230 Avenue of the Americas, New York, New York 10020
This book is a work of fiction. Any references to historical events, real people,
or real places are used fictitiously. Other names, characters, places, and events are products
of the author's imagination, and any resemblance to actual events
or places or persons, living or dead, is entirely coincidental.
Text © 2020 by Stacy Hackney
Cover illustration © 2020 by Jennifer Bricking
Cover design by Krista Vossen © 2020 by Simon & Schuster, Inc.
All rights reserved, including the right of reproduction
in whole or in part in any form.
SIMON & SCHUSTER BOOKS FOR YOUNG READERS
and related marks are trademarks of Simon & Schuster, Inc.
For information about special discounts for bulk purchases, please contact
Simon & Schuster Special Sales at 1-866-506-1949
or business@simonandschuster.com.
The Simon & Schuster Speakers Bureau can bring authors to your live event.
For more information or to book an event, contact the
Simon & Schuster Speakers Bureau at 1-866-248-3049
or visit our website at www.simonspeakers.com.
Also available in a Simon & Schuster Books for Young Readers hardcover edition
Interior design by Hilary Zarycky
The text for this book was set in Goudy Old Style.
Manufactured in the United States of America
0321 OFF
First Simon & Schuster Books for Young Readers paperback edition April 2021
2 4 6 8 10 9 7 5 3 1
The Library of Congress has cataloged the hardcover edition as follows:
Names: Hackney, Stacy, author.
Title: Forever Glimmer Creek / Stacy Hackney.
Description: First edition. | New York : Simon & Schuster Books for Young Readers,
[2020] | Summary: When future filmmaker Rosie, age twelve, decides to make
a documentary about the miracles in her town in hopes of connecting
with the father she never knew, she discovers what true magic is. Includes recipes.
Identifiers: LCCN 2019004388 | ISBN 9781534444843 (hardcover : alk. paper)
ISBN 9781534444850 (pbk) | ISBN 9781534444867 (eBook)
Subjects: CYAC: Documentary films—Production and direction—Fiction. | Community life—
Fiction. | Mothers and daughters—Fiction. | Friendship—Fiction. | Miracles—Fiction.
Classification: LCC PZ7.1.H1516 Mys 2020 | DDC [Fic]—dc23
LC record available at https://lccn.loc.gov/2019004388

For Gail Marie Landis,
who told me I could do anything and made me believe it.

There wasn't a right way or a wrong way to get a Miracle.

As far as everyone in Glimmer Creek knew, there wasn't a way at all. Each Miracle was as unpredictable as the river itself. Sometimes it tiptoed into a hospital room. Other times it burst out of the water. Once it even blew into town on a hurricane of shrieking winds and needles of rain. Though the Miracles never arrived in quite the same way, they all lingered afterward like an echo in the quarry at the edge of town.

Mama always said real magic was forever.

CHAPTER ONE

Rosie Flynn raced toward the figure across River Bend Park, trampling the orphaned leaves along the path. She recognized that particular hitch in the step and the halo of marigold curls. Even better, she spied the bulky tote bag underneath her arm.

Rosie skidded to a stop beside a tree that twisted and turned upward like ropes of licorice, her stomach fluttering. *Please, please, please let the bag be for me.*

Betsy Broome held out the bag. "I've brought you some—"

"Rope!" Rosie reached for the tote in Betsy's arms and opened it to reveal a neat coil, the perfect length to loop around a tree. It was the same rope she'd forgotten at home, which wasn't a surprise. After all, Betsy usually remembered what someone forgot—ever since her Miracle.

"Thank you! I'm filming my biggest scene right now, and this rope is crucial for establishing my lead's motivation," Rosie said, beaming at Betsy.

"I saw it on your front porch and knew I had to bring it here right away. I would never have guessed it was for one of your movies though," Betsy said.

"You're a lifesaver. Want to come see the set?" Rosie looked up as a breeze tickled her arm. Puffs of clouds slid across the sky and from behind the trees, silver-tipped water glinted on the horizon. It was a perfect day for filming.

Betsy looked down at her watch, her wrists jangling with gold bracelets. "Can't. I'm late to senior choir. I missed half our practice last week because I was returning a ring to Miss Matilda. My choir teacher said he's going to take away my solo if I can't make it to practice on time."

Rosie gave Betsy a quick hug. "Thanks for bringing the rope. Sorry I made you late."

Betsy flashed a smile. "I'm used to it. Good luck with filming."

Rosie skipped back across the park, swinging the rope above her head in triumph. "You'll never believe it," she called out. "Betsy brought us the rope, so now we can film the scene."

Henry Thompson's pale hair stuck up around his head in at least four places, and his skinny shoulders hunched over his chest. The script called for him to climb ten feet to the top of a tree limb and shimmy down the rope in a dashing, adventurer-like manner. Instead, he was pacing the ground and muttering something about unsafe working conditions.

Rosie sighed. Actors were so dramatic.

"Maybe I can wear a helmet. At least then I'd have some protection against skull fractures. You know head injuries can cause subdural hematomas, right?" Henry knotted his hands together. "Think about Betsy. She was selling peanuts to raise money for new band uniforms when she fell off the Landon High bleachers. A Miracle was the only thing that saved her from permanent amnesia."

"You're not going to fall," Rosie said.

"I've already got an anxiety rash." Henry thrust out his freckled arm.

Rosie tried to be patient. She gave Henry an encouraging smile.

"Henry, on our *best friendship*, I need your help. Sheriff Parker could show up at any minute, and he'll tell us to stop filming because I don't have a permit. How am I going to win an Academy Award someday if I never practice directing?"

Henry hesitated and then expelled a long breath. "Fine. I'll do it. But you owe me."

"You have my blood vow," Rosie said in a dramatic voice.

Henry looked alarmed. "There's no need for blood."

Arms crossed and black braids quivering, Cam Abbott stomped over from the sidewalk. A cyclone of dust swirled around her feet. "Please tell me this is almost over. I have soccer practice in twenty minutes. Leila says we've got to improve our ball control."

"Don't worry. We'll finish in fifteen," Rosie said. She watched Henry attempt to swing a leg over the lowest limb, lose his balance, and tip over. Maybe she and Cam could somehow throw him onto the first branch like a professional stuntman.

Cam peered at the base of the tree and pointed to a notch in the trunk. "If you stick one foot there, you can hoist yourself onto the first branch. It's like when we went to that ropes course for my birthday last year."

"It took me a half hour longer than everyone else to finish," Henry mumbled.

"But the instructor said you were the most careful person he'd ever seen," Cam said brightly.

Rosie was pretty sure the instructor hadn't meant it as a compliment. Still, Henry beamed at the memory.

"That's true. Okay, I'm ready." Huffing out a breath, Henry used the notch to anchor his right foot and clamber onto the lowest branch.

Rosie gave Cam a little bow. "Great save. Now we're finally getting somewhere. This could be our best film yet." She hurried over to where she'd set up the tripod and camcorder.

"You told me last month's film was the best one yet when you made me dress up in that green monster suit," Cam said, following behind Rosie.

"And I will never forget how convincing you were as a swamp monster," Rosie added.

"Neither will Sheriff Parker," Cam said darkly.

"Sheriff Parker shouldn't have shut down our production because we scared a few kids. I've had to put the filming of *Monster Town: A Most Frightening Epidemic* on hold indefinitely. It was my homage to *King Kong* and *The Bride of Frankenstein* and all the old horror movies of the 1930s, and he ruined it."

"Well, we can't get caught this time. Dad said he was going to wake me up at five a.m. to run laps if I got in trouble with the sheriff again. He's started calling himself SDA—Strictest Dad in America." Cam rolled her eyes, but her lips curved up at the same time.

Rosie stopped adjusting the camcorder and swallowed hard. Longing unfurled inside her and rose like smoke off a summer campfire. "You're lucky. I'd take an SDA over nothing."

Cam grabbed Rosie's arm and squeezed it tight. "You'll meet him someday. I know it."

Rosie managed a small smile and bent back to her camera lens. An image of her father flickered in her mind: tall and handsome with blue eyes crinkled in laughter. She imagined him swinging her around in a circle as the sun set behind them and painted the sky a brilliant shade of tangerine. Panning the scene in a slow sweep, she saw matching smiles on their faces and the hint of a breeze ruffling their hair. Nodding to herself, she straightened and ignored the ache in her chest. Of course Cam was right. She *would* meet her father someday.

"Come on," Rosie said, handing Cam the voice recorder. "Let's get this scene filmed before Henry chickens out."

"Having a little trouble with your friend there?" Charlie Blue asked. All three Blue brothers had wandered over. They leaned on identical ivory canes and gazed upward at Henry, their matching blue eyes squinting.

"We have it totally under control," Rosie huffed, using her best professional director voice.

"I don't know about totally," Cam said.

"Branch doesn't look too steady," Arthur added.

"Reminds me of the mast on the *Blue Dolphin*," Bill chimed in.

"That mast tore right off in the wind," Arthur said. "We shouldn't have dared each other to take the *Blue Dolphin* out in that hurricane."

"It was a big hurricane too, the likes of which Glimmer Creek hasn't seen since. It was a Miracle we got back to shore alive," Charlie finished.

"Yeah, we get it," Cam muttered. "You were Miracled a million years ago."

Arthur squinted up at the sky. "Expect it will rain in the next hour. Best get this movie business done quick."

Rosie's pulse hiccupped. Rain would ruin everything. "Henry, can you please hurry? We've got to get this rolling," she yelled.

Cam pulled Rosie out of the Blue brothers' earshot back beneath the tree. "Relax. It's not going to rain." She gestured to the patches of blue between the leaves. "There isn't a cloud in the sky."

"The Blue brothers are always right about the weather," Rosie protested.

"Do you honestly believe that?" Cam asked, shifting on her cleats. "Maybe they just watch the weather radar every day."

"The Channel Four weatherman uses a radar and gets the forecast wrong all the time. The Blue brothers never do. Mama said Mayor Grant only calls out the snowplows when they tell him to expect a couple inches," Rosie said.

Cam shrugged. Why wasn't she agreeing with Rosie?

The air around them thickened as if a dense fog had seeped beneath the canopy of leaves.

"Hey, guys," Henry whisper-yelled from above. "Did you ever think you're both right? The Blue brothers could watch the radar and have Miracled powers. It's like how beetles have wings same as other bugs but are also different because they only use their hind wings to fly since their forewings form elytra." Henry closed his eyes. "Oh wow, I'm a little light-headed."

Cam and Rosie looked at Henry, then at each other, and grinned. It was impossible not to smile when Henry used his weird bug logic to convince you of something.

Cam nodded up at the sky. "Rain or not, the movie is going to be great. I don't know anyone else who could think up this cool of an opening scene except for you."

Rosie's cheeks warmed at Cam's praise. "Let's get the set ready."

Rosie and Cam jogged back to the camcorder. Eight of the nine Nelson children were also gathered nearby and pointed at the tree, bouncing around like grasshoppers. Mr. Willis, who ran the Glimmer Creek Museum of Extraordinary Artifacts, and Mr. Waverman, the postman, had stopped walking and stared up at Henry. The Blue brothers readjusted their canes to get more comfortable.

"Can you please move out of the way," Cam said in a loud voice to the crowd.

"That's the problem with an open set," Rosie whispered. "Ignore them."

Henry inched his way out on the limb and grasped the rope, which he had looped and knotted around the tree. His skin had taken on a distinct greenish cast.

"Ready?" Rosie called to Henry.

"You're sure this will hold me?" Henry said.

"Ropes don't always hold," Arthur said unhelpfully.

"Rope on the *Blue Dolphin* was triple knotted, but it still blew off," Bill cautioned.

"Miracle we ever survived," Charlie said.

"Oh brother," Cam exclaimed a bit too loudly.

"Quiet on the set," Rosie bellowed.

The murmuring of the makeshift audience ceased. Rosie leaned down and switched on the microphone and audio recorder. This was it, her big opening scene. Finger hovering over the record button, Rosie called out her favorite word, "Action!"

Henry pushed off from the limb, the rope gripped in his fists. For a second he dangled above them, not moving. His hands started to slide as the limb buckled. With a giant crack, the limb split off from the trunk.

"Ahhhhhhhhhh!" Henry screamed as he plummeted and crashed into the dirt with a terrific *bang!*

Rosie rushed over to Henry, her heart pounding. The fallen limb had cracked the seat of a nearby bench but luckily missed Henry entirely. He was already sitting up. Rosie would have breathed a sigh of relief if she hadn't caught sight of a determined figure in a lemon-colored dress and a matching turban coming up the left-hand side of the park. She was moving slowly, but she was moving right toward them. It was Henry's mama, Miss Betty.

"Henry George Thompson, what exactly is going on here?" Miss Betty screeched from halfway across the park.

Henry buried his head in his knees.

Miss Betty on a tear was bad enough, but it was about to get worse. Barreling straight at them from the right-hand side of the park was Sheriff Parker, his expression grim. Rosie considered the enormous tree limb and the damage to the bench and the filming without a permit (again). Her breath constricted as if someone had tied a bowline knot around her lungs.

"Oh no." Cam groaned. "My parents are going to kill me."

Rosie had to do something. She jerked her chin at Cam and Henry. "Run! You can still escape. I'll handle this. Mama has plenty of practice in dealing with Sheriff Parker."

Miss Betty was yards away but laser focused in on Henry. "Do I need to remind you that growth-plate fractures can cause crooked bones for the rest of your life?"

Henry shook his head at Rosie. "It's too late for me."

"Anyway, we're not going to leave you here alone," Cam said, tugging Henry to his feet. They took their places on either side of Rosie.

Sheriff Parker glared in Rosie's direction. "Rosie? Care to explain?"

Rosie plastered on a smile. "Would you believe this branch just fell out of the sky and we happened to get caught beneath it?"

"No, I would not believe that. I'm getting tired of this movie business." Sheriff Parker looked from the nearby tripod to the frayed rope to Rosie. "I think it's time we had yet another talk about the appropriate use of town resources."

"Don't blame Cam and Henry. This was my fault."

"Why am I not surprised?" Sheriff Parker said.

Miss Betty swooped in. She was clucking over Henry's torn pants and lecturing about a "perilous situation."

The littlest Nelson boy was crying, and the Blue brothers began examining the bench and shaking their heads in sorrow. Deputy Cordell, whom Rosie guessed had been immediately radioed by the sheriff after he saw them in the park, showed up and offered to take official statements on account of the destruction of town property. Sheriff Parker rubbed one hand along the top of his head, looking as if he wanted to scream.

Rosie gazed out at the endless sky, which was beginning to darken at the edges with ashy clouds. Arthur Blue was right. A storm was blowing in, and it looked like a big one.

CHAPTER TWO

B ut, Mama," Rosie said. "There's no way I could have known the tree limb was going to crack."

"That's exactly right. There's no way you could have known that limb was sturdy enough to hold Henry, which is why you should never have attempted that stunt. You're lucky Henry didn't break a bone or need stitches or sprain his wrist or bruise his tailbone or develop a concussion or something worse," Mama expelled in one long stream of words.

Henry was fine except for a few bruises. Rosie, however, was not at all fine. Sheriff Parker hadn't listened to a single one of her explanations. When she'd finally informed him it was all part of the artistic process, he'd told her she best stop talking and marched her down to Mama's office in the town hall.

Mama was the town manager, which meant she made sure the roads were fixed and people got permission to build stuff on town property. Though she always said her job mostly involved listening to folks complain about pot-holes on Magnolia Street.

Rosie slumped down into one of the two chairs across from Mama's desk. A bookshelf along one wall was filled with books, photographs of Rosie, and jars of colored pens. A bronze lamp cast a yellow haze over the papers strewn across the wood surface. Behind the desk, a large window framed the edges of River Bend Park and the shops in the center of town, all of which were now blurred by rivulets of water. The storm had arrived, and it was a doozy. Rain lashed against the windows as if the sky were spitting bul-lets. Inside the office, things weren't much better.

"I'll pay for all the damage," Rosie said, propping her elbows on the desk.

Mama raised one eyebrow. "You bet you'll pay for the damage. You'll need to work here in the office filing, and you'll have to use that money you've been saving."

Rosie bolted up straight. "But that money is for a new tripod light fixture. I've been saving for months. If you'll loan me the money, I'll pay you back in no time."

Mama was already shaking her head. "Sorry, sugar. The town needs the repair money now. You're lucky I con-vinced Sheriff Parker not to press charges. It took some doing. This is the third time in as many months he's had to call me. I can't keep the law off your back forever. I practically had to beg him not lock you up and destroy your bright future. Recall how last summer you broke the window of Hardaway Market."

"Another set accident. These things happen all the time in Hollywood. Who would have thought the sword-fighting for *Knights of the Pyramidal Table* would get so aggressive?"

"Yes, well, Sheriff Parker mentioned something about how if these 'set accidents' keep happening, he'll be forced to take some action. I assured him your next film would take place outside the town proper." Mama leaned over the expanse of wood and cupped Rosie's face in her hand. "I do not want a jailbird for a daughter. Despite your criminal tendencies, I'm fond of having you around. Got it?"

"Got it." Rosie slumped down. She'd have to continue to use natural light without the tripod, which meant no shooting at dusk. Plus, she'd have to rewrite all the town scenes in her latest film, assuming Miss Betty ever let Henry out of the house again.

"You'll earn the money back," Mama said.

Rosie pressed her lips together. It wasn't right. Mama was punishing Rosie for something that wasn't entirely her fault, and she had no one else to talk to about the unfairness of it all.

"I bet my father would support my filmmaking if he were here," Rosie mumbled.

Mama stared down at a pile of papers, fingering the gold locket she always wore around her neck. If only Rosie's father were around, surely he'd take her side when it came to small mistakes like ruining a bench no one cared about.

"I *said* I bet my father would support my filmmaking," Rosie said in a louder voice.

"Your biological father has nothing to do with your crime spree." Mama tapped her pen against the desk and muttered under her breath, "He wants nothing to do with anything."

Rosie flushed.

Mama usually avoided talking about Rosie's father, but she'd also never said anything bad about him . . . until now. Mama's mouth pinched in along the sides, and her clear brown eyes went cloudy. She always got this look when Rosie mentioned her father—a worried, sad kind of look—and then she'd change the subject or offer to get Rosie a slice of pie or suddenly remember she needed to pay the bills. But Rosie had so many questions Mama wouldn't answer. Questions like whether her father agreed with the ending of *Citizen Kane* (she didn't), or whether he liked chocolate chips in his oatmeal cookies (she did). Now she had another—did Mama not want to talk about him because she didn't like him?

Mama sighed. "I didn't mean that. It's been a long day." She pulled a Tupperware container from her desk drawer, opened it, and set it in front of Rosie, offering up a weary smile. The homemade popcorn glinted with bits of cinnamon and sugar—Mama's special recipe. "Here, you must be hungry. Cinnamon-sugar popcorn has a way of making most things better, and I've heard criminals are starving after they commit a felony."

Forcing her own smile and swallowing down her questions, Rosie scooped up a handful of popcorn. "I should probably take the whole container, then."

Mama and Rosie snapped together like the two halves of Mama's locket. They laughed at the same jokes and liked the same old classic movies and the same special foods, like bacon-chocolate-chip cookies and cinnamon-sugar popcorn. Together they made a perfect whole, one that wasn't worth breaking over a few questions.

Anna Lee burst into the room and flopped down in the seat beside Rosie. She worked as a part-time clerk in the mayor's office and attended night school at Gloster Community College. She made a habit of changing her hair color on a weekly basis. Today it was purple.

"I'm heading out," Anna Lee said. "I finished typing up that ridiculous report Miss Matilda made about sanitation showing up ten minutes late to collect her garbage."

"It's our job to take these complaints seriously," Mama said, her mouth twitching in a way that meant she was trying not to laugh.

"Fine. But that doesn't mean I have to like it." Anna Lee turned to Rosie. "Did I see you walk in with Sheriff Parker?"

"Yep," Rosie said. "A small set problem came up today."

"One that resulted in hundreds of dollars of damage to a poor, unsuspecting bench," Mama added.

"The bench wasn't even in the frame," Rosie said, leaning on her elbow.

"So it *was* the bench's fault. I knew that bench had a bad attitude," Mama said.

"The real problem is that Sheriff Parker has no imagination," Anna Lee quipped.

"I know," Rosie agreed.

Anna Lee rolled her eyes. "If he'd stop bothering Caroline every five seconds, maybe he'd actually have time to expand his perspective and appreciate real art."

"Exactly. I told him he needed to—" Rosie stopped and frowned. "What do you mean he's bothering Mama? Did he close down Poplar Lane again without telling anyone? What a mess that caused last month."

"No, he didn't. And he's not bothering me," Mama said hastily.

"He's in here three times a day," Anna Lee said.

"He's the sheriff, and I'm the town manager. We have business matters to work through, and he's only trying to be friendly," Mama said, her cheeks flaming strawberry red.

"But—but he makes your job harder," Rosie said. "People complain about how he's mean when taking police reports. He even made Mrs. Green cry when she questioned a parking ticket. He's the opposite of friendly. You said so yourself."

"He barely says hello to me," Anna Lee huffed. "If you ask me, he has a crush on Caroline."

Rosie's chest tightened as if a fishing line had gotten tangled up inside her. Mama couldn't possibly like Sheriff Parker. For one thing, he never smiled. For another, he'd given Rosie three separate lectures for the minor, accidental damage that sometimes happened on her film sets. He was much too serious. Mama and Rosie's favorite romance of all time was *Roman Holiday* with Audrey Hepburn and Gregory Peck. Sheriff Parker was not as fun-loving as Gregory Peck. He wasn't fun-loving at all.

"Sheriff Parker is old," Rosie said.

"He's not that much older than me," Mama said, laughing.

Rosie clenched her hands. "I heard his former wife disappeared under suspicious circumstances."

"His ex-wife lives in Richmond," Anna Lee said.

"He also has bad taste. I asked him who his favorite movie director was, and he said Michael Bay. Who says that? He didn't even know who Michael Curtiz was." Rosie's eyes widened.

"I don't know who Michael Curtiz is," Anna Lee said.

"He's only one of the most famous directors of all time. Ever heard of *Casablanca*, *White Christmas*, *Mildred Pierce*, *We're No Angels?*" Rosie asked, leaning forward.

"I'm not obsessed with old movies like you two," Anna Lee said, waving her hand.

"We prefer to think of ourselves as enlightened," Mama replied.

"That's right," Rosie said. "We appreciate the classics, unlike some people."

"Though maybe some people don't know where to start with the classics," Mama said.

"Or maybe some people don't care," Rosie challenged, lifting her eyebrows innocently.

"Anybody still here?" The deep voice came from the lobby.

Anna Lee didn't get up but yelled, "In the back."

Mayor Grant and Miss Matilda swept into Mama's office, arguing as usual. Mr. Waverman trailed behind, his mailbag slung over his shoulder. All of a sudden, the office was like a puddle crowded with too many minnows.

Mr. Waverman pushed his way past Mayor Grant and Miss Matilda and placed a bundle of envelopes on Mama's desk, then held out a letter to Anna Lee. "Got something for you. Didn't want you to have to wait on this. Best open it now. It's not good news."

Anna Lee looked at Mr. Waverman suspiciously. "Did you read my letter?"

Mr. Waverman straightened up to his full height of five foot four inches. "I certainly did not. Postal workers are not permitted to open another person's mail. I can't help it if I have a gift for knowing whether the mail is good or bad."

"So you're always telling everyone," Anna Lee said, rolling her eyes.

"Young lady, I was nearly killed ten years ago while carrying out my duties for the postal service. I was rushing to get Mrs. Lawler her social security check before the bank closed and never saw that Buick coming. The Miracle was the only thing that saved me. Dr. Bentworth himself called me extraordinary." Mr. Waverman sniffed.

Anna Lee snatched the letter from Mr. Waverman's hands, tore it open, and yelped. "My rent is going up again! I'm going to murder my landlord." She shot Mr. Waverman a chilling look that could have frozen over the river before stomping back to the lobby.

"Some people never learn." Mr. Waverman tipped his hat to Mama. "Nothing too bad in your mail. Y'all enjoy your afternoon. I've got to deliver a humdinger to Mrs. Gooch. I suspect her divorce is final."

Rosie waved good-bye to Mr. Waverman and his bulging mailbag. She sure was glad she didn't have to knowingly deliver bad news to all her friends. Why, she'd never want to leave her house again, not even for a double movie feature in Gloster.

Mayor Grant heaved himself over to Anna Lee's empty seat and ran a hand over his shirtfront. "Caroline, I know you're fixing to head home, but we've got something to discuss before the city council meeting tonight. Is that popcorn?" He reached across the desk and grabbed a handful. "I could use a snack."

Mama opened her hands wide. "What's the problem this time?"

"Marvin Blandstone is the problem. He's petitioned for a booth at the festival based on another one of his theories, even though we all voted no to his alien reptiles last year," Miss Matilda said, her dark skin gleaming against one of her signature blue dresses. She was the owner of Sook Diner and the longest serving member of the city council.

"You have to admit the train treasure is an interesting

story though Marvin may be climbing up the wrong tree with his ideas on where it is," Mayor Grant said.

"It's barking up the wrong tree, not climbing," Miss Matilda said.

"Now, that doesn't make a lick of sense. Why would I bark up a tree?"

"It's a saying," Miss Matilda said.

"It's a silly saying," Mayor Grant retorted.

They were now turned toward each other, faces outraged and red. From behind them, Mama pretended to stick a knife in her chest. Rosie giggled.

Mayor Grant chewed his popcorn, swallowed, and promptly turned back around to grab another handful. "If Marvin wants to set up a booth about the train treasure legend, we should let him do it. Folks are interested in the treasure, and it could spice up the booth lineup. It is our hundredth year of Miracles, and my last year as mayor. This year's festival needs to be bigger than ever."

Every year, one person in Glimmer Creek got a Miracle. The Festival of the Fish was a celebration of all those good fortunes. Mama also said it brought in tons of money because everyone in Glimmer Creek and the surrounding towns came out to support it. Businesses shut down early, and there were games and music. Rows of booths filled with crafts and food lined the streets, and the town decorated River Bend Park with silver-and-blue banners and twinkle lights. The festival always took place on October twenty-first, the date of the very first Miracle, when all the fish had returned to Glimmer Creek after dying out from a massive flood.

"What do you think about the train treasure?" Mayor Grant asked Mama.

Mama smiled. "What's not to like? It's the ultimate mystery."

Rosie lowered her voice, trying to imitate the narrator voice-over in film commercials. "It was a train robbery gone wrong. Only one thief escaped. His name"—dramatic pause—"was Lonnie Garrett."

Mama took up the deep voice. "He stole a fortune in gold and was never heard from again. Legend has it he hid the gold somewhere in the sleepy town of Glimmer Creek."

"A fortune worth millions," Rosie continued.

"A town shrouded in mystery," Mama said.

"Who will find it?" Rosie ended.

Mama and Rosie grinned at each other. The train treasure *would* make a great film. It had all the elements of a classic crime drama—robbery, suspense, and an antihero people secretly loved.

"What on earth are you two talking about?" Miss Matilda said. "We should not be telling our youngsters the story of a common thief."

Mama cleared her throat, her mouth twitching again. "From what I know, deep down Lonnie wasn't a bad kid. He only got involved with that Butler Gang after his parents died."

Miss Matilda harrumphed. "Well, no one can prove Lonnie Garrett came back to Glimmer Creek after the robbery."

"No one can disprove it either," Mama said, raising one eyebrow.

"That settles it," Mayor Grant said. "I'm voting yes to Marvin's petition."

Miss Matilda heaved out a sigh.

Mayor Grant leaned toward Rosie. "I heard about the bench."

"That bench was real rickety," Rosie said, suddenly absorbed with a stray pencil.

Mayor Grant patted her shoulder. "Bless your heart; you still want to be a movie star."

"Actually, I want to be a director," Rosie said.

"I get it. You want to be on camera," Mayor Grant said.

"No, a director is behind the camera—"

"Sheriff Parker was mighty frustrated today," Mayor Grant interrupted. "When he gets like that, I can't talk to him about anything productive. A sweet girl like you should have a less-destructive hobby, like sewing."

"Or fishing," Miss Matilda offered.

"Now, hold on one minute," Mama said. "Rosie might have a minor destructive streak when it comes to filmmaking, but she's also incredibly talented. I'm sure you aren't suggesting she give up her dream of becoming a director?" Mama was talking in her serious voice, the one she used to tell the city council to simmer down.

Mayor Grant looked chagrined. "We'd never stop Rosie from following her dreams."

"'Course we wouldn't," Miss Matilda said.

"Well, good," Mama said, her voice dipping in volume. "Glad we got that settled."

Miss Matilda and Mayor Grant went back to arguing. They didn't even notice when Mama double winked at Rosie and Rosie double winked right back.

Rosie snuck a piece of popcorn, savoring the salty-sweet taste on her tongue. Mama always knew what to say to make people listen. Rosie was lucky to have Mama on her side even if she did make her pay for a silly old bench.

CHAPTER THREE

Days later, Rosie sat at her desk with its flaking white paint and stubborn drawers. Staring ahead at the rippling blue-gray water, her fingers hovered over the keyboard of Mama's laptop. The house was silent except for the usual whispered creaks from the floorboards. Beyond her bedroom window, tall trees with gilded coral leaves still clinging to the branches bordered the backyard sloping down to Glimmer Creek. The creek was a half mile across here, and the houses on the other side were dots along the horizon.

Looking down, Rosie made herself type the letters—*Michael Weatherton*—into the search bar. After a moment's hesitation, she pressed enter. Pages of information on her father filled the screen.

Her father was a professional actor. Mama had told her at least that much about him and that he held small parts on different television shows and films. He lived in Los Angeles, all the way across the country. Between that and working on film sets all over creation, he'd never had the chance to come to Glimmer Creek and meet Rosie.

Rosie looked Michael up every few months to see what new thing he was working on. She always deleted her search history afterward. It wasn't as though Mama had forbidden her from finding out about Michael, but Mama wouldn't like it either.

Scanning the computer, Rosie clicked on a new article dated last week. The screen filled with a large photo of Michael himself. His lips turned up in a slight smile. Rosie studied every picture, searching to find herself in the slope of his nose or the tilt of his eyes, but she could never see it.

Leaning closer, Rosie scrolled down the page and read the last few lines from the Hollywood trade magazine:

> A last-minute replacement, Michael Weatherton has signed on to a supporting role in Heartland Pictures' Revolutionary Threat, the untold story of female spies in the Revolutionary War. Jack Relian will direct the period piece, and Julia Laverne will star as the spy who saved George Washington. Filming began last week in Richmond, Virginia. Revolutionary Threat is scheduled for a spring release.

Rosie sat back.

Richmond was two hours away. Two hours! That was

shorter than most movies—maybe not *Gone with the Wind*, but definitely most others. Her father could be here by supper if he got in the car right now.

But—but if Michael was only two hours away, why hadn't he called? Why hadn't he asked to visit? Wasn't he curious about his very own daughter?

Rosie's shoulders curled over her chest, and a thickness coated her throat. Her lip quivered, and she bit down hard to stop it. There was nothing to cry about. She was certain there was a good explanation for why he hadn't called. Maybe he was busy with rehearsals for *Revolutionary Threat*. The article said he was a last-minute replacement, so he must have a lot of catching up to do. After all, movie sets weren't like going on vacation.

Sunlight poured through the small round window above her bed and slashed across the bookshelf. There was the porcelain doll Michael had given her for her eleventh birthday, and the elaborate makeup kit for her tenth, and *The Complete Works of William Shakespeare* that had come one Christmas. None of the gifts was quite right, but at the very center of the bookshelf was the one present that was completely perfect—her camcorder.

The gleaming Canon XA30 had built-in Wi-Fi, HD recording, and a high-def optical-zoom lens. Mama had looked up the price after Rosie opened it and nearly hit the floor. She'd wanted to send it back, but Rosie had begged to keep it. That was three years ago, and Rosie had used that camcorder every day since. She had never once spoken to her father, but somehow he'd known to send her this perfect gift for her ninth birthday. That had to mean something, didn't it?

Opening her bottom desk drawer, Rosie rifled through the tangle of papers and discarded markers until she found the crumpled stack of cards that had accompanied the gifts. She opened them one by one. Michael had taken the time to choose and sign them all.

The final card was especially ornate, with swirling pink clouds, flying angels, and gold raised letters. She remembered it nestled in the cream-colored tissue paper of the camcorder box. Rosie flipped it open and stopped. She peered closer. There, beneath his signature, was a single sentence in her father's cramped handwriting: *When you use this to make your first movie, I'll be sure to come see it.* Inhaling sharply, she read the sentence again. She'd forgotten all about it. If only she could tell Michael about her movies, he'd want to meet her. This card proved it.

Rosie deflated as she remembered one problem— Mama.

Whenever Rosie received gifts from Michael, she asked to call him, but Mama wouldn't let her. Mama claimed he was out of the country on a film set or in between phone numbers or—worst of all—he wasn't quite ready to talk to Rosie. Mama always said it wasn't the right time for them to meet. Though lately Rosie had started to wonder if Mama really knew when the right time was. Maybe Mama never wanted them to meet.

"Rosie, darling? Where are you?" Miss Lily's voice drifted up to her.

"Coming," Rosie called, tucking the cards into her desk drawer.

Miss Lily waited at the bottom of the stairs. Her snow-white hair was pulled back into a low bun, and she wore a long poppy-colored dress. Rosie galloped down the steps and gave her a quick hug.

"Darling, I've missed you. Ever since school started back up, I hardly see you anymore. It's been weeks! Come along. I've brought all the fixings for a lamb curry," Miss Lily said, heading into their kitchen. She lived next door and made supper for them on nights when Mama had a city council meeting.

Rosie followed Miss Lily down the hallway. Mama and Rosie's house was nearly a century old and had all the creaks and dents to prove it. The rooms were filled with battered chests and sloped wooden floors. The outside had a chipped curlicued porch and arched windows dusted with dirt. The white siding needed a good paint job, and the floorboards on the front porch bowed like a hammock if you stepped on the wrong one.

"I heard about last week's bench catastrophe," Miss Lily said casually while she unpacked ingredients from a grocery bag.

Rosie collapsed into a stool beneath the counter. "Sheriff Parker was furious, as usual."

Miss Lily hauled out a large pot from the depths of a cabinet and set it on the stove burner. "Well, artists must suffer for their art, and if that means a bit of accidental vandalism, so be it. I certainly had my share of difficulties. I recall putting on performance after performance despite catching a dreadful case of pneumonia one winter."

"How could you sing if you had pneumonia?" Rosie asked.

"Pure will," Miss Lily said. "And my understudy was a horrible girl who was dying to steal my role. I couldn't let her take it, now, could I?"

"I guess not," Rosie said, grinning.

Miss Lily opened a cabinet, removing several glass jars of spices. "Tell me what you've been doing inside on this beautiful afternoon."

"Oh, reading and doing homework and—" Rosie stopped, struck with the sudden urge to tell someone what she'd discovered. "Actually, I was researching my father."

Miss Lily raised both eyebrows. "Indeed, and what did you learn?"

"He has a new role, and the film is shooting in Richmond."

"Ah." Miss Lily was silent for several seconds. "I'm sure he's quite busy. Rehearsals go day and night on film sets. It wasn't any different for a Broadway show." Miss Lily had been a famous Broadway actress before she retired and moved back home to Glimmer Creek.

"You're probably right," Rosie said, staring at a scratch on the counter but picturing the words written inside the card all over again. "Only—my father has no idea I want to be a director. He might come see my movies in person if he knew about them."

"Perhaps you should talk to Caroline about this," Miss Lily murmured.

"I can't. Mama doesn't like to talk about him."

"I'm sure that's not true. She's told you all about his career and where he lives and—and . . ." Miss Lily's voice trailed off.

"Exactly. She's told me the most basic stuff. That's all." Rosie remembered Mama's comment from last week; she'd said Michael wanted nothing to do with anything. "She never admits it, but she must hate him for leaving."

Miss Lily stopped mixing the spices and set down the wooden spoon. "Now, that's simply not so. Your mama and daddy were very much in love. Caroline could never hate Michael. I can promise you that."

"I know they met when Michael was working in Gloster in a summer stock theater, but I don't know much else," Rosie admitted.

Miss Lily glanced beyond Rosie's shoulder toward the door. "Caroline is truly the one to ask about this."

"But couldn't you . . . ? Well, couldn't you tell me something about him?" Rosie asked.

Miss Lily hesitated. "I suppose it won't hurt." She rubbed spices into the meat in front of her before choosing her words. "It was love at first sight. Michael saw Caroline in the audience during one of his performances, chased her down afterward, and demanded her phone number. She couldn't help but give it to him. They were wonderfully happy together. Michael even delayed leaving Glimmer Creek after the summer. But he couldn't sit still for long. He finally got a role he couldn't turn down. It was quite sad. I think the entire town missed him. He was only here a few months, but he'd gotten to know so many people."

"Really?" Rosie had never heard this part before.

"Oh yes. Michael had lunch at Sook Diner every day and spoke to all the patrons. He was fascinated with the town Miracles and would often visit with the Miracled themselves, asking questions about what happened and how it affected them." Miss Lily smiled. "Thinking back on it reminds me of the summer you spent cataloging every single Miracle."

Rosie gasped. "I forgot about that. I wanted to write a movie script about them. I still think it's a great idea." Even more so now that Rosie knew her father was fascinated with the Miracles just like her. She shivered. This proved they were alike in more ways than they even knew yet.

Miss Lily reached across the counter and patted Rosie's hand. "I'm glad you believe in the Miracles, darling. I know some young people don't anymore. I suppose I understand it. After all, there's no accounting for the Miracles. No one knows what causes them."

"I'll never stop believing," Rosie said fervently. The Festival of the Fish was coming up in a few weeks, and the whole day was all about believing in the Miracles.

"Good," Miss Lily said. "Because Miracles do exist."

"Will you tell me your story again?" Rosie asked.

"Come now, you've heard it a hundred times." Miss Lily waved a hand in the air. Her emerald ring caught the light and flung green sparkles across the counter.

"But it's one of my favorites," Rosie said. "Please."

Miss Lily's face softened, the lines smoothing out and

her eyes turning misty. "My first memory is of my mama talking to me, begging me to say something. Her green eyes filled up with tears, and she gripped my arms so tight. I tried to make a sound. I tried over and over, but I couldn't. And, oh my, I hated to disappoint her."

Rosie always felt like hugging Miss Lily at the start of the story.

"My parents took me to every doctor they could think of, but there was a problem with my vocal chords, something about improper vibration and my trachea. I'm not completely certain, but I was unable to make a sound from birth. I felt like a burden on my family."

"You never could be a burden," Rosie said, outraged.

"It was a different time. We had six children in our family, and no one knew how to handle disabilities. We heard about a treatment center in Boston that could help children like me, but my parents couldn't afford it. I began selling oysters, pulling weeds for the neighbors, anything I could to earn enough money to send myself to Boston. But it wasn't enough, so I decided to run away." Miss Lily gazed off into the distance, falling silent.

"And then?" Rosie prompted.

"And then, the night before I left, I went to the Fishing Well, tossed in a penny, and made my wish. I wished with every fiber of my being that I could find some way to make my mama proud and stop my family from worrying about me. When I woke up the next morning, something was different."

"How did you know?" Rosie whispered, even though she knew the answer.

"There was a tingling in my throat and a sweet taste on my tongue like sugared roses. I opened my mouth, and it happened. Words burst out of me as if someone had shaken a bottle of champagne and uncorked it all at once." Miss Lily clasped her hands together. "It was a Miracle. My parents were overjoyed, though it wasn't until that night that I began singing."

"And your mama said it sounded as if angels had come down to earth," Rosie said.

Miss Lily smiled gently. "That is what she said. Soon I was singing in the choir, then on the radio, and finally I made my way to Broadway, where I became a brilliant star and won a Tony Award. Twice. Well deserved, too."

Rosie then asked the same question she always did when Miss Lily was finished. "What if the Miracle happened because of your wish?"

Miss Lily shrugged. "Maybe it did. Who can say for certain? But it always did seem to me as if fate had taken over my life that night. Perhaps it was the Fishing Well or perhaps it was simply divine intervention."

Rosie smiled, her heart filling with warmth like a cup of chocolate and cream. Just imagine—magic, fate, and a true happy ending, all tied up together. If it could happen to Miss Lily, it could happen to her. Surely Michael's new job was its own kind of fate bringing them together. They were just one hundred miles apart. This was her chance to finally meet him, and there was only one thing to do. She had to find a way to get her father to Glimmer Creek.

CHAPTER FOUR

The following afternoon, Rosie hurtled toward River Bend Park. Henry had called an emergency HenRoCam, and she couldn't waste a second.

HenRoCam was the best combination of Cam, Henry, and Rosie's names. It was also code for their official meetings to discuss filming or fishing plans or the neighborhood talent show or anything, really. But an emergency HenRoCam was rare. The only other time Rosie could think of Henry calling one was when he found out his mama was sick. She hoped this meeting wasn't about that.

But even as she rushed down Magnolia Street and worried about the HenRoCam, Rosie's mind turned back to her father. She had thought about him nonstop since yesterday and started to come up with reasons—good reasons—why Michael hadn't ever called her. What if he believed Rosie wouldn't want to see him because so much time had passed? What if he knew Mama wouldn't let her see him? What if he thought Mama hated him? Rosie should call him first, but Mama wouldn't let that happen.

It was all so frustrating. Rosie couldn't figure out how to get her father to Glimmer Creek even though they were meant to meet. Cam's father attended every one of her soccer games, and Henry's father was the first person at his science fairs. Rosie wanted a father to show up for her. They already had so much in common: their love of movies and believing in the Miracles and probably loads more. If he came to Glimmer Creek, surely he'd see that.

Cam waved from across the street, and Rosie stopped to let her catch up. Throngs of people streamed into River Bend Park. Rosie stared at the growing crowd congregating around the Fishing Well up ahead.

"What's the emergency?" Cam asked.

"I don't know," Rosie said, gesturing to the people hurrying past them. "But something is up. Henry asked me to bring my camcorder."

"As long as it's not about Miss Betty," Cam said in a worried voice.

"It can't be. She only has two treatments left, and Henry said the chemotherapy is working," Rosie said, even though she had thought the same thing.

Cam twisted her mouth to one side. "I saw Henry's dad helping her out of the car yesterday. She could hardly walk."

Rosie wrapped her arms around herself and squeezed.

She would never forget Henry's face when he'd first told them Miss Betty was sick last year with breast cancer. He had swallowed over and over, his eyes had gotten huge and misty, and he'd blinked about fifty times. Rosie had never felt worse for anyone in her life.

Though Miss Betty could still boss Henry around like nobody's business, things were different at their house now. It was quieter, the curtains were often drawn, and there were medicine bottles lined up along the kitchen counter like soldiers guarding against the illness upstairs.

"I'm sure she's okay," Rosie said, hoping it was true.

"Well, Henry wouldn't tell me anything on the phone, though I didn't have much time to talk. I was in the middle of a meeting," Cam said.

Between the three of them, Cam was the only one with a cell phone. Mama kept saying Rosie didn't need a cell phone because Glimmer Creek had plenty of pay phones, which was ridiculous because no one used pay phones anymore.

"I didn't know you had a meeting today," Rosie said.

Cam shrugged, but her eyes sparkled. "Leila and some of the other eighth graders on the soccer team wanted to meet in the Lounge to talk about who should start in Saturday's game. I don't know why they asked me. This is only my fourth game."

"You were in the *Lounge?*" Rosie asked in disbelief.

The Lounge was strictly eighth graders only. It had its own vending machines with the best sodas and chips, a few tables, and beanbag chairs. It was loud and noisy and filled with kids who starred on the sports teams or ran the student government. One time a seventh grader walked in as a joke, and two guys from the baseball team put him in a trash can. Upside down.

"Did anyone threaten to put you in a trash can?" Rosie whispered.

Cam laughed. "No. Leila said it would be okay, and I trust her. No one is going to mess with her, you know."

Oh yes, Rosie knew. Leila Sellers sat at the first table in the cafeteria, boys were always talking to her, and she had a group of girls who walked beside her in the halls and all wore their hair in the same long French braid.

"It's not a big deal," Cam said, but she was almost skipping alongside Rosie.

"It makes sense she wanted you in the meeting," Rosie said loyally. "You're the best forward on the team."

Cam was also tall and pretty and had flawless bronze skin. Every kid in Glimmer Creek started off playing soccer when they were little, but Cam was one of the few actually good at it. She had a determined attitude and the right genes. Her daddy had played basketball in college. Cam was good at that too.

Cam smiled big and wide. "Leila said that too. She wants me to spend the night at her house in two weeks."

Rosie tried to smile back, but it was stiff and unnatural. She and Cam were always invited to the same sleepovers in elementary school. But this was seventh grade and middle school, and there was no chance of Leila inviting Rosie to spend the night. Leila didn't even know Rosie existed.

"Sounds fun," Rosie said, wondering what she would do on that Saturday night. She definitely wasn't playing Truth or Dare or FaceTiming boys, which was what eighth graders did. She would probably watch a movie with Mama and go to bed by nine o'clock.

"Come on, I see Henry up ahead," Cam said, taking off at a jog into River Bend Park.

The weathered gray rock and shingled roof of the Fishing Well rose from the clearing, looking as if it too had grown straight out of the ground, like the trees around it. There were clumps of people scattered around, and Mayor Grant paced nearby. A group of workers dressed in gray coveralls and orange vests pointed at something on the ground: a long, lean shape covered by a black tarp. For no reason at all, Rosie shivered.

Henry stood off to the side, his eyes fixed on the Fishing Well. He waved as they approached. "Great. You're finally here. I call an official HenRoCam to order."

"Subject?" Rosie asked, almost too nervous to ask.

"You won't believe it." Henry lowered his voice. "I heard Mama talking on the phone, and she said they found a human skeleton at the bottom of the Fishing Well."

Cam and Rosie stared at each other. Miss Betty knew the Sook Diner had changed its crab cake sandwich recipe before Miss Matilda sold the first one. If she said there was a skeleton, there was definitely a skeleton.

"Who is it?" Rosie asked in a hushed voice.

"I don't know," Henry said. "I told you to bring the camcorder because I thought we might want to get whatever happens next on record."

"Good thinking," Rosie said.

"No one in town is missing," Cam said.

"It could be a really old skeleton. The human body decomposes at different rates, but it takes at least eight years to become a skeleton," Henry said. "Sometimes scientists use bugs to determine the decomposition rate."

"Gross," Cam said, shuddering.

Rosie leaned in close, nodding her head at one of the nearby workers. "We should try to pick someone off to question. That one in the blue hat looks like he might crack under pressure." Instantly, Rosie pictured a long trench coat wrapped around her while she peppered the man with questions. The camera focused on her face in a classic over-the-shoulder shot.

"They aren't going to tell us anything," Cam said.

Rosie held up her camcorder. "We could say we're from a news station like that time we told the school crossing guard we were doing an interview for the *Gazette* to find out why the carpool lane closed."

Cam raised her eyebrows. "That got us nowhere, remember? The crossing guard threatened to report us to Principal Bradley. You know I'm usually up for your plans—"

"And you always make them better," Rosie added.

"Not this time, though. I don't think we should mess around with a skeleton. We're not in a mystery movie," Cam said.

"Obviously," Rosie said, fumbling with the strap of her camcorder bag. "I guess I should save my battery life anyway."

"I'm sure Mayor Grant will tell us what's going on any minute. You know he can't go long without making announcements," Henry said.

The Grants did abide by declarations. When Mayor Grant's son, Billy, proposed, he spray-painted MARRY ME, LINDA right across the middle of the grass in River Bend Park. He called it a romantic gesture. Sheriff Parker called it vandalism. It took three weeks to grow out.

All at once the voices in the crowd dimmed. Sheriff Parker stepped into the clearing and headed straight for Mayor Grant. Rosie glared at him, remembering how he'd yelled at her last week.

Sheriff Parker and Mayor Grant huddled together. Piles of gray brick and white buckets of mortar were strewn around the grass. The tarp-covered object seemed to have a huge bull's-eye target on it, and the eyes of everyone in the park were the arrows.

Rosie got out her camcorder and held it up, focusing on the activity around the well. She didn't care what Cam said. The mysterious tarp and possible skeleton felt like the beginning of a suspense film like *Rear Window*.

"Rosie Flynn!" Sheriff Parker barked from the front of the crowd.

Rosie lowered her camera, her cheeks warming as everyone's eyes swiveled in her direction. "Y-yes, sir."

"Put that camcorder down. This is not the time for that," Sheriff Parker yelled, running a hand over his head and glancing down at the tarp.

"Last I checked it was a free country," Rosie whispered to Henry and Cam, but she shut the camcorder off anyway.

"He sure is touchy today," Henry said, giving Rosie a sympathetic look.

"Don't worry about him. He's a jerk," Cam hissed, and glared at anyone still looking at Rosie. "He should be flattered that someone talented wants to film him anyway."

Rosie thrust the camcorder into her bag, wishing she could hide under the tarp herself. Sheriff Parker had managed to embarrass her in front of half the town. She wasn't even doing anything wrong!

Mayor Grant stepped forward. "Folks, I'm sorry, but Sheriff Parker wants y'all to clear out of here. The boys from the police department need some space."

"Why do we gotta leave?" Shane Rodgers called out. "This park is public property."

"This park is a crime scene," Sheriff Parker snapped.

"Now, I wouldn't call it a crime scene. We found one dead body," Mayor Grant said.

The crowd gasped.

"But it's a very old body," Mayor Grant said hastily.

"We deserve to know about a dead body in our town," Frank Rodgers said.

"We can't discuss any details right now," Sheriff Parker said, frowning at Mayor Grant.

Donna Davis pulled her two daughters close. "Was there an actual murder in Glimmer Creek or not? I don't want my girls out in public when there's a killer on the loose."

Mayor Grant gave Sheriff Parker an apologetic look. "Donna, there is nothing to worry about. It just so happens we found a journal on the body. It sustained some water damage, but it had the name of the deceased engraved inside so we can identify the body, and I can say for certain that any murderer—not that I'm saying this was a murder, mind you—but any *alleged* murderer is long dead."

Sheriff Parker leaned over and began whispering furiously in Mayor Grant's ear. Mayor Grant waved him off and continued. "Best if everyone hears it from me first. The body belongs to Lonnie Garrett. And before you ask, there was no gold in the well. Trust me, we looked."

The crowd erupted. People shouted out questions. Sheriff Parker tilted his head up to the sky, looking as if he wanted to throw Mayor Grant down the well. Rosie, Henry, and Cam all stared at each other, their eyes locked and sparking.

"I cannot believe this," Rosie said, pulling them away from the crowd. "Mama and I were talking about Lonnie Garrett last week. He's the man who stole the train treasure a hundred years ago."

"I bet everyone with a metal detector starts searching the woods first thing tomorrow," Cam said.

Henry paced beside them, his face set and pale. He did this whenever he was thinking about a mission for the

Lego robotics club or studying for a big test in his advanced classes.

"Henry?" Cam asked. "What's going on?"

"I'm just—just thinking," Henry said, not ceasing the walking back and forth.

"About?" Rosie asked.

"Treasure." Henry stilled, and his face lit up in a wide smile. "If Lonnie Garrett's body is here, the legend is true. The train treasure really is in Glimmer Creek. We should be the ones to find it."

"You want *us* to find it," Rosie said slowly.

"Why not? We have as much of a chance as anyone," Henry said.

"Except we're twelve, and we have no clues," Cam said.

"And we're in school all day. This isn't an Indiana Jones movie." Rosie eyed Henry. "It's not like you to go on a treasure hunt. What's going on?"

Henry hesitated. "Well, I—I bet I can get a ton of extra credit for American History if I find the treasure. It's a historically significant artifact, and um, if I present it to the class, Mrs. Collier will probably give me an A-plus for the whole quarter."

Cam narrowed her eyes. "You already have straight As."

Henry blinked rapidly. "Yes, but I bet it would also get

me into college. Colleges are really competitive these days, and a treasure hunter qualification would help me stand out from the pack. Besides, think about what we could do with all that money. I'm dying for a new . . . telescope." He looked from Cam to Rosie, his expression open and hopeful. "Come on, this could be our greatest adventure, even better than when we climbed Devil's Leap last summer."

"You hated that climb," Rosie said.

"And the jump into the river after," Cam added.

"That's why this is better," Henry said.

Rosie and Cam exchanged a look. Henry couldn't be serious. It reminded Rosie of when they'd convinced each other there were jewels in one of the streams near their street. All they'd found was a lot of shiny rocks, but they were sure they would become zillionaires. They had spent hours splashing each other and shouting every time one of them found a particularly sparkly specimen. That time was fun, but they were old enough to know they weren't going to find a real treasure in Glimmer Creek.

"I think it's a long shot. Like, a really big long shot," Cam said, but not in a mean voice.

Henry's face fell. "You're probably right. It was a dumb idea."

Rosie bit her lip. "It wasn't dumb."

"Only unrealistic," Cam said.

"It's okay," Henry said, thrusting his hands into his pockets.

The three of them headed out of River Bend Park. Cam was talking about the movie they were going to see on Friday, and Henry was nodding his head, seeming interested. He looked back at the tarp one final time.

Maybe it was the fading light of the October sun or maybe it was the dappled shadows from the trees, but for a single instant Henry looked exactly like Indiana Jones reaching for the Holy Grail; he looked like he would do anything to solve the mystery of Lonnie Garrett. Rosie couldn't help but wonder if this was really the last they'd hear about the train treasure.

CHAPTER FIVE

Rosie waved good-bye to Cam and Henry, who were heading toward Willow Lane, and stopped in at Sook Diner to pick up crab cake sandwiches for supper. Sook Diner was almost empty at this time of the afternoon. The black-and-white-checkered floor was spotless, the red vinyl booths were polished up, and the Blue brothers sat at the counter, since they took the early-bird special seriously and started their supper in the four thirty time frame.

Rosie ordered the sandwiches. Miss Matilda said it would take a few extra minutes, but she offered to throw in a couple of her Miracle cookies. Miss Matilda baked her sugar cookies every day in the shapes of different Miracles. There was a fish for the first Miracle, a music note for Miss Lily, a boat for the Blues brothers, and a mailbag for Mr. Waverman.

Charlie Blue peered down at the menu. "How much sugar is in the limeades?"

"The right amount," Miss Matilda said, scrubbing at the counter harder than seemed necessary.

Charlie pursed his lips. "Now, do you make the barbecue with vinegar or brown sugar?"

"Charlie, you eat here every day. You know how I make my barbecue," Miss Matilda snapped.

"I'm only asking a question," Charlie said. "Seems as though you don't want my business."

"I don't," Miss Matilda said.

"Well, I'm not leaving," Charlie said. "It's gonna rain in the next hour."

Rosie spotted Mayor Grant and his wife in a booth midway down the row. She slowed when Mayor Grant and Mrs. Grant's voices got louder. They were in the middle of a serious talk. It wasn't right to eavesdrop, but she couldn't help being curious after the skeleton. She slid into the booth behind them.

Mayor Grant sighed behind her. "The timing couldn't be worse."

"Honey, you're getting all riled up for nothing," Mrs. Grant said.

"I've already got twenty messages from concerned citizens asking about the murder investigation, wanting to know if I'm going to enforce a curfew at night, and questioning what I'm doing to solve our crime problem.

Glimmer Creek does not have a crime problem. For hollering out loud, this isn't even a real criminal investigation," Mayor Grant said, sounding as if he were about to burst through the buttons on his shirt.

"Didn't you say the sheriff thinks the dead man was shot?" Mrs. Grant asked.

Rosie leaned further back toward Mayor Grant, straining to hear every word.

"That skeleton is a hundred years old," Mayor Grant said. "Sheriff Parker said Lonnie was most likely shot by the FBI during the failed robbery. Now the *Gazette* will be chock-full of a murder investigation instead of the festival, with folks running around, pitching a hissy fit, and digging up half the town for some gosh-darn treasure.

"Some of the people who e-mailed me said they don't feel safe in River Bend Park anymore. What if they don't come to the festival? The Miracles are part of our town heritage, and I spend all year planning the festival to celebrate them. With this being my last one, it just has to be perfect! I need to come up with a way to make it even bigger, even better, so people forget about this skeleton and I don't end my tenure as mayor with a failed festival." He sighed again. "I need a milkshake."

Suddenly, Rosie sat straight up. The most brilliant, most amazing, most perfect plan popped into her head. It was a plan that would get her father to Glimmer Creek and solve Mayor Grant's problem all at the same time.

Rosie leapt out of the booth. "Hi, Mayor, Mrs. Grant."

Mayor Grant cradled his bald head in his hands, but Mrs. Grant smiled at Rosie.

"How are you, Rosie?" Mrs. Grant asked.

"I'm fine, ma'am," Rosie said. "But I couldn't help overhearing Mayor Grant, and it just so happens I have an idea to help."

"We'd love to hear it," Mrs. Grant said. "Wouldn't we, Harold?"

"Huh?" Mayor Grant said, looking up, his eyes bleary.

"What if I film a documentary about the Miracles and premiere it at the festival?" Rosie asked.

Mrs. Grant looked confused, and Mayor Grant looked miserable.

"What does a documentary have to do with helping the festival?" Mayor Grant asked.

"Don't you see? It will get people excited about the Miracles, which are what the festival is all about," Rosie said.

Mayor Grant started shaking his head and opened his mouth to respond.

"I know what you're thinking," Rosie said, holding out her hands to stop him. "I don't have the experience. I've never filmed a documentary before. That is true, but I have made at least twenty other films, and some of them have more than five hundred views on YouTube." She paused to let this sink in. "Mayor Grant, that's a lot of views, and they weren't all just me rewatching."

"I'll admit I really enjoyed your movie about the junior detective finding the cat," Mayor Grant said.

"That was a good one," Mrs. Grant agreed. "What was it called again?"

"*Creek Confidential*," Rosie said. "That was my first attempt at the police procedural genre. I watched *The Big Sleep* and *Chinatown* to prepare for that. They're also about private investigators solving crimes. It goes to show you I can learn how to make different types of films, like documentaries."

"Unfortunately," Mayor Grant said, shaking his head, "and I mean no offense here, Rosie, but I don't think a student film is going to solve my public relations problem. Besides, how would we premiere the movie without a movie theater?" Mayor Grant looked past Rosie's shoulder. "Where is Miss Matilda? I'm starving."

Rosie considered Mayor Grant's frown, hunched shoulders, and complete lack of interest. She had to come up with some way to convince him.

"You raise some great points. We could . . . we could—"

The solution hit Rosie like Miss Matilda's flyswatter. She snapped her fingers. "We could borrow the outdoor movie screen and projector from Gloster. I know they have one because Mama and I saw an outdoor movie there last year."

Mayor Grant tented his fingers and looked more interested. "I forgot they had an outdoor movie contraption."

"If Gloster loaned it to us, we could screen the documentary . . . and—and another movie too after the sun went down." Rosie watched Mayor Grant perk up. "Last year, when Gloster showed that outdoor movie, it was packed. People love to watch movies outside. You could show something everyone would like—something like *Singin' in the Rain* or *E.T.*"

"Not a bad idea," Mayor Grant said. "It could be another big attraction for the festival, make it a whole family affair."

Rosie was almost there.

"You can show the movie after my documentary," Rosie said. Her muscles bunched up with nerves. He had to say yes. "No one is going to be thinking about a skeleton when they have a movie to distract them."

Mrs. Grant turned to her husband. "Honey, I think it's a great idea."

Mayor Grant eyed Rosie for several long seconds. "All right, Rosie. Let's do it."

Rosie let out a small yelp of triumph. "You will not regret this."

Mayor Grant held up a finger. "I am going to need to see that documentary in advance."

"You bet," Rosie said, unable to stop smiling.

"And you only have seventeen days until the festival," Mayor Grant added.

"I'm great at working on tight deadlines. It's good practice for the real world too. Hollywood producers are notorious for riding directors on film schedules," Rosie said.

"I can't wait to see it," Mrs. Grant said warmly.

"I'm going home to start my storyboard right now, and I already have a ton of ideas. With all the research I have to do, I might even figure out what causes the Miracles," Rosie said, clasping her hands together. If she made a documentary and solved the town's greatest mystery in the process, everyone would be so impressed. Her *father* would be so impressed.

Mrs. Grant chuckled. "I don't know about that. No one knows what causes the Miracles."

"Well, someone has to figure it out," Rosie said. She scooped up her to-go bag from the counter and skipped out of the diner before Mayor Grant could change his mind.

Outside, the chrysanthemums on the Lawler front

porch looked redder, the leaves on the ground sounded crunchier, and the air all around was crisper. The sweet smell of caramel scented the air. Rosie waved to Mrs. Lawler and Mr. Willis. She smiled at Mrs. Green and Mr. Waverman, both of whom were holding metal detectors and walking down opposite sides of the street, already searching for the train treasure and glaring at each other across the pavement. Rosie wanted to shout out her news to the entire world. Not only was she making a documentary the entire town would see, solving a hundred-year-old mystery, and proving to everyone she was a real talent as a filmmaker, she'd found a way to get her father to Glimmer Creek.

Her plan was simple. Michael had promised to come see her first movie, so it was only natural for her to invite him to her big premiere. How could he possibly turn down the invitation to come to the festival when he was only two hours away? According to Miss Lily, he was fascinated with the Miracles too, which meant he'd definitely want to see a documentary about them. All she had left to do was ask him to come. Finding his address shouldn't be too hard.

Rosie wriggled, unable to keep her happiness inside. She imagined the look on her father's face when he walked into Glimmer Creek. He would pull her into a hug—an actual, real hug. If she was shooting it with her camera, the lens would zoom in on his face, a little craggy but still handsome. One tear would slip down his cheek; Rosie would look up at him, and they would both know everything in their lives had changed forever.

CHAPTER SIX

The next morning, Rosie wished she were still curled under the covers of her warm bed. Instead, she was filing papers at the town hall before school to earn enough money to pay back Mama for the new bench. The walls were a drab beige, like the underside of a moth's wing. Black metal filing cabinets lined each side of the hallway, crowding the narrow pathway and darkening the hall. She'd walked up and down the same stretch of gray carpet for an hour with an endless stack of papers to file. Rosie yawned. If only she hadn't stayed up so late thinking about her plan to get Michael to Glimmer Creek.

Unable to find a listed phone number or address, Rosie planned to search Mama's laptop for Michael's e-mail address after school today. Her stomach churned as she thought about what Mama would say if she found out Rosie had contacted Michael without telling her. Would her mouth turn down in that disappointed look she got when Rosie forgot to empty the dishwasher? Would she think Rosie had betrayed her? Rosie couldn't even think of the right way to tell Mama about the documentary because she was too afraid of blurting out the real reason for the film.

Mama burst into the hallway, her long skirt swirling around the high heels she wore for work. She held a muffin in her hand. "I present the cherry-chocolate muffin baked by yours truly. It's good for all manners of insomnia, including unrequited love, academic concerns, artistic dilemmas, reality-television malaise, and monetary distress."

Mama's words ran together in one long mix of letters. Sometimes she talked as fast as Katharine Hepburn in *Bringing Up Baby*, and Rosie had to watch that film three times before she got most of the dialogue.

Rosie snatched up the muffin and took a bite. The tart cherries and smooth chocolate mingled together in perfect harmony. She might work at the town hall, but Mama was still the best baker in Glimmer Creek.

"Well?" Mama asked, her eyes twinkling.

"Well what?" Rosie said around a mouthful of muffin.

"My room is beside yours, sugar, and I could hear you pacing half the night."

Rosie turned to throw the muffin wrapper away, searching for a trash can and stalling for time, unable to explain the real reason she was awake last night. "If I was awake, it was only because someone else in the house kept me up with their snoring."

"Impossible! I was the only other person in the house, and I'm much too dainty to snore. If you heard anything, it was probably a nearby train."

"There aren't train tracks in Glimmer Creek anymore."

"Well, maybe it was a buzz saw."

"At midnight?"

"It's the only explanation," Mama said.

"Besides you snoring," Rosie said.

"Like I said, impossible."

"You're impossible," Rosie said, smiling at Mama.

Back and forth, teasing and laughing—this was what she and Mama did best. Mama wouldn't yell at her like Henry's mama or snap at her like Cam's mama did sometimes. They had their own special communication. Rosie's smile faded as she thought about her plan to meet Michael, a plan that couldn't involve telling Mama. There was nothing special about lying.

"Does this mean you're not going to tell me what's wrong?" Mama asked, slinging an arm around Rosie.

Rosie pulled away, feeling as if a crab were pinching her inside. "There's nothing to tell. I'm sorry I kept you up," she said in a rush, anxious to change the subject. "I better get these last papers filed before school."

"You can always finish them tomorrow," Mama said, her eyes puzzled. "I forgot to tell you. Molly Lawler came in yesterday about her property taxes, and I asked her if you could use their old field off Poplar Lane for your film. She said no problem."

Now Rosie felt even worse. Here was Mama thinking about her again, helping to solve her problems, the same way she always did. "Thanks for doing that."

Mama ruffled her hair. "No trouble at all. I wonder if I missed my career calling as a set finder."

"It's called a location scout," Rosie said.

"Location scout—I like that," Mama replied. "I see an entirely new career in my future. I'm clearly meant for Hollywood." She assumed a pose, one hand on her hip, the other flung above her head.

Rosie couldn't help giggling.

A jingle of bells signaled an opening of the front door.

"Now, who could possibly have a complaint this early in the morning?" Mama sighed.

"I'll check," Rosie said, and rounded the corner into the lobby.

Sheriff Parker stood in the center of the room, his hands in his pockets, rocking back and forth on his heels. Rosie glowered at him. He was the last person she wanted to see before eight o'clock in the morning or before eight o'clock at night. Really, he was the last person she wanted to see ever.

"Good morning, Rosie," Sheriff Parker said.

"The office isn't open yet. I'm helping Mama out." Though Rosie was only helping out because Sheriff Parker had gotten her in trouble in the first place.

"It's good to see you doing something productive after the other week."

"I do a lot of productive things," Rosie said, trying not to glower at him. "In fact, I'm working on a new project with Mayor Grant, and I'm going to need some permits."

Sheriff Parker sighed and muttered something that sounded a lot like *not again*. "You'll have to go through all the official channels and fill out the paperwork. I expect it will take some time to process. We do have a system in place for these things, which everyone has to follow."

"Fine," Rosie said shortly. Sheriff Parker made everything less fun with his "official channels" and boring "systems."

Mama made her way into the room. "Why, Sheriff Parker, I didn't know you were here. What can we help you with this morning?"

Sheriff Parker's lips curled up in a weird expression like Mr. Waverman's donkey when she wanted an apple. It looked as if he were trying to smile but his face wasn't sure what to do.

"I was hoping for some coffee," Sheriff Parker said.

"We don't have any ready," Rosie said quickly.

Mama gave Rosie a surprised look. She gestured to the coffeepot on the table behind the receptionist desk. "Don't be silly. I made some when I got in this morning."

"I thought you drank all of it yourself," Rosie said, shrugging.

"No one can survive without coffee," Sheriff Parker said with another one of his weirdo smiles.

Rosie waited for Mama to make her usual coffee jokes—how she would trade her arm for a cup of coffee, how coffee was the only thing she'd bring to a desert island—but she only turned and busied herself pouring Sheriff Parker a cup. "One sugar, right?"

"You know me," Sheriff Parker said, reaching for the coffee cup.

"No she doesn't," Rosie mumbled so Mama couldn't hear.

Sheriff Parker fiddled with the stirring straw in his cup. "I was thinking about that budget meeting yesterday. Your point about taking the time to allocate costs to the proper department made real sense."

Mama waved a hand in the air as if it were nothing, but she looked pleased. "It's just good business. It helps us see where additional resources are needed within the town infrastructure." Her voice was oddly serious.

"Well, it was a good idea. I was never in these meetings when I lived in DC. It's interesting to see how all the departments work together. If you need help on the budget, let me know. It would be a nice break from answering questions about the state's law on finding stolen treasure. I got seven calls yesterday alone. I swear half this town is losing its mind over that train treasure." Sheriff Parker grinned at Mama.

This was the first time Rosie had ever heard Sheriff Parker sound friendly. Was Anna Lee right about him having a crush on Mama?

"Mama prefers to work on the budgets alone," Rosie said.

Mama cleared her throat. "I wouldn't say that. My job requires me to work with other people all the time."

Had Sheriff Parker's smile widened? Did he think Mama meant she wanted to work with him? Rosie narrowed her eyes.

"You told me you could get everything done a whole lot faster if everyone would stop sticking their nose in your business," Rosie said.

Mama gasped out a laugh. It was true she had complained about the planning commission last week, though maybe not quite in those words.

"I did not say that. She's kidding." Mama turned to

Rosie, her eyebrows somewhere up near her hairline. "Tell Sheriff Parker you're kidding."

Rosie shrugged and hoped he didn't think she was kidding. She knew she was pushing it, but this was a desperate situation. She couldn't have Sheriff Parker thinking he had a chance with Mama. He'd never stop hanging around.

Sheriff Parker only laughed. "Hey, I understand. Sometimes it's easier to do the job yourself, but keep my offer in mind. I know you've got a lot going on with the festival coming up. You probably need your own Miracle to get everything done."

Rosie glared at him. She didn't buy this nice-guy act for one second.

"The Miracles don't work that way, you know. Mama isn't going to wake up one morning to the entire festival planned and her desk cleared," Rosie jeered.

"I was only kidding," Sheriff Parker said in a patient voice, as if she were five years old instead of practically a teenager.

"The Miracles aren't a joke," Rosie said. "They're real."

"I didn't say they weren't," Sheriff Parker said, but there was something about the way he said it. Rosie bet he was one of those people who thought the Miracles were all some big coincidence, one of those skeptical, unimaginative people who wouldn't notice magic even if it was spitting in their face.

Mama placed a firm hand on Rosie's shoulder, digging in with her fingers. "I thought you had filing to do."

"It can wait," Rosie said, twisting away. "I'd rather stay up front."

Sheriff Parker clutched his coffee and took a step backward. "I should get going anyway. But I really am happy to help. I've got some time to spare. Things are a lot quieter here than what I'm used to. I'm not complaining though. It's one of the reasons I moved to Glimmer Creek in the first place." He stopped and reddened. "Anyway, see you around." He bumped into the door and stumbled over his feet before turning and heading outside.

As soon as the door closed behind him, Mama rounded on Rosie. "What was that all about? You were quite unfriendly, bordering on rude."

"I was trying to do you a favor and get rid of him," Rosie said. "You're the one who complained about Sheriff Parker for a whole year after he moved here."

Mama smoothed down her skirt and looked away, avoiding Rosie's gaze. "Sheriff Parker came from a big city, which is a whole lot different from Glimmer Creek. At first he didn't understand how we all know each other and pull together and try to avoid conflict if we can. But he's trying a lot harder these days. It took him a little while to get used to our ways."

Rosie snorted. "He's still not used to our ways. I can tell he doesn't even believe in the Miracles. A sheriff who doesn't believe in his own town shouldn't be a sheriff, in my opinion."

Mama swiveled her head to fix Rosie with one of her trademark tractor-beam stares. "There's no excuse for your acting rude to an adult. None." The corners of her mouth sagged like willow branches. "I'm disappointed in you."

Rosie swallowed, hating to disappoint Mama. "I'm sorry."

Mama sighed and walked back toward her office.

Rosie stared after her, torn between wanting to apologize again and knowing she was doing Mama a favor in the end by keeping Sheriff Parker away.

The door opened again with a tinkle of bells and a whoosh of air. Mr. Jack strolled in with his wife, Miss Jessie. His graying hair was carefully parted on one side, and he wore a pink shirt and one of his famous bow ties. This one had pink crabs scattered all over it. Miss Jessie wore a matching pink dress. Besides running the Bookworm, Rosie's favorite store in town, they gave her a real Hollywood movie script on her birthday every year and faithfully watched every single one of her films at least twice.

"Rosie, dear, we're here to see Caroline when she has a moment," Mr. Jack said. "The sidewalk in front of the Bookworm has a large crack in it that needs repair. Libby Willis tripped on it yesterday when she came to see me."

"Is Libby having love troubles again?" Rosie asked, delaying the walk back to get Mama.

Miss Jessie sighed. "She is, poor dear. She's convinced Tyler is growing tired of her."

"I hate to say it, but she's right," Mr. Jack said.

When he was younger, Mr. Jack had worked for the old trailer manufacturing company on the outskirts of town. One day, there was an explosion at the plant. Mr. Jack was near the front and shoved another worker away from the blast. Most of the explosion debris missed him except for a piece of metal, which ricocheted off his wedding ring. Though he broke two fingers, the ring deflected the metal away from his head and probably saved his life. After that Miracle, Mr. Jack turned into a genuine love expert. He'd matched up at least fourteen married couples in town. The sign on the Bookworm door read: BOOKS FOR SALE, MATCH-MAKING OPTIONAL.

"I really thought she and Tyler were going to make it. If I had to cast the perfect high school couple, they would make the callbacks—they were even the right height," Rosie said.

"Looking right together doesn't mean feeling right together," Ms. Jessie said, a regretful frown stealing over her face.

"She's right. It is too bad though," Mr. Jack said. "That Libby is a sweet girl. But you know what I always say."

"Without a spark, the love will fizzle," Rosie said, repeating back the words Mr. Jack had told her many times.

"Precisely." Mr. Jack nodded toward the door. "Now, we ran into Sheriff Parker on our way in here, and he and your mama are a different story. Mark my words, Rosie, there's a real spark between those two."

Rosie took a step backward. "There can't be. Mama doesn't like him at all."

Mr. Jack chuckled. "Maybe not yet, but she will."

"You've got it wrong this time." Rosie suddenly found it hard to breathe.

"I predicted three engagements last year alone. When I say there's a spark, there's a spark." Mr. Jack reached down to take Miss Jessie's free hand.

"I'll get Mama for you," Rosie said, hurrying away, not wanting to hear another word about Mr. Jack's sparks.

"Much obliged," Mr. Jack called.

Stopping midway down the hall, Rosie waved the papers in her hand back and forth to create a breeze on her flushed cheeks. She steadied herself against a filing cabinet. Mr. Jack was wrong, dead wrong. Mama didn't want a boyfriend. She'd always said it was her and Rosie against the world. Nothing could change that.

Rosie took a deep breath, then another. The problem was Mr. Jack didn't have all the information. All he saw was Sheriff Parker mooning around and Mama being nice to him the same way she was to everyone. But in the final cut of Mama's story, the leading man was definitely not Sheriff Parker. After all, Rosie was about to invite her father to Glimmer Creek. Mama might realize she already had a family and didn't need a leading man in her life just yet.

CHAPTER SEVEN

Rosie went straight home after school that day to break into Mama's e-mail. She had no choice. Between this morning's coffee fiasco, Mr. Jack's theory, and the festival getting closer with every day that passed, she had to do *something*. Deep down she knew Mama's answer if she asked to contact her father—Mama would say no. This was the surest way to reach him.

Mama's laptop was perched on a desk the color of maple syrup in their small study off the family room. Bookshelves, crammed full of old hardbacks that had belonged to her grandparents, flanked the closed study door. A leather chair, scratched up and sagging, filled one corner, and a worn rug in shades of faded burgundy and gold bunched along the floor. The house was still, but Rosie's pulse raced.

Pulling up Mama's e-mail account, Rosie put in the password Mama used for everything—rosie1. Mama's in-box popped onto the screen. Rosie typed *Michael Weath-*

erton into the search bar at the top. One message came up. It was dated three months ago.

Rosie clicked on it and read:

> Hi Caroline, I got your message last week. Sorry I've been out of touch. My old e-mail address was hacked, and my assistant changed it a few months ago. I'm booked for two indie films this winter, and life has been crazy. Anyway, here's the new e-mail. Talk soon. Michael.

Rosie sat back and reread the message four more times. She had so many questions. Why would Mama call him? Who had hacked his e-mail address? What indie movies was he working on? She stared at the screen, wishing she could ask him herself.

Shaking her head, Rosie laughed a little. There was no need to wish. Soon she could ask him whatever she wanted, when he came to Glimmer Creek.

Rosie opened up her own e-mail account and started to type. After a few false starts, she ended up with:

> Dear ~~Father~~ ~~Daddy~~ Michael,
> This is Rosie Flynn, ~~your~~ Caroline's daughter.
> I am writing to let you know I am directing a

documentary for the Festival of the Fish. The film is about Glimmer Creek's Miracles and what causes them, which I heard is a special interest of yours. I understand you are filming Revolutionary Threat ~~only two hours away~~ in Richmond (congratulations on the part). I am inviting you to attend the premiere of my film on October 21st in Glimmer Creek. I think you would really like it. ~~Please come~~.

~~Love~~ Sincerely,
Rosie

Rosie wanted to write about how she planned to work in movies just like him. She thought about reminding him how he'd sent her the camcorder and promised to come see her first movie. She longed to tell him this was his chance to meet his only daughter. But she didn't. She kept the letter short, not wanting to say the wrong thing and ruin her chances.

Hovering the cursor over the send key, Rosie blew out a long breath. Her hands were trembling. Mama wouldn't allow Rosie to call Michael or send him a letter. She always said it was best if she contacted him and told Rosie what he said. Now Rosie was doing the exact thing Mama refused to let her do. It had seemed like such a good idea last night, but at this instant it felt dishonest and sneaky. Looking at the e-mail made her insides ripple. Once she hit send, there was no way to take it back.

The front door opened with a faint scuffle. Rosie froze. She checked the clock on the computer. Mama was home early, way too early. Rosie inhaled a sharp puff of air. It was now or never. She closed her eyes, held her breath, and clicked send.

Mama called her name from the hall. Rosie exited out of her e-mail account, but Mama's e-mail remained on the computer screen. Rosie scrambled to close out of the account, but the computer froze. Mama called her name a second time, footsteps moving toward the study. Nothing moved on the screen. The little room spun in ever-quickening circles, leaving her dizzy and nauseous. She should never have broken into Mama's e-mail account; she should never have sent Michael an e-mail. She held down the power button. *One second, two seconds, three seconds*. The screen flickered. The study door opened just as the computer shut itself down. Rosie stood and exhaled.

"Hey, sugar, whatcha doing?" Mama asked, leaning against the doorframe.

Rosie moved her body in front of the computer. "Oh, nothing. I was just reading."

Mama gave her a quizzical look. "Were you using the computer?"

"No," Rosie said, and saw the light of the computer dim out of the corner of her eye. "I mean yes. I was reading on the computer."

"Is this for school?" Mama asked.

"No," Rosie said, her eye twitching.

"What for, then?" Mama asked, sharpening in on Rosie.

"It's a—a secret." Rosie said the first thing that came into her head.

Mama smiled, but her eyes narrowed. "Good thing I love secrets."

The bookshelves loomed over Rosie, drawing closer and closer. Everything she'd said sounded suspicious. All she *wanted* to do was announce that she'd e-mailed her father for the first time ever. But that would only make Mama upset, maybe even angry. Mama might even e-mail Michael and tell him not to come.

Rosie shifted on her heels, wishing she could fast-forward through the next thirty seconds. "I wanted to surprise you. I was researching documentaries because I'm working on a new film about the Miracles, and Mayor Grant said he would show it at the festival."

The lie slithered off her tongue and wiggled in the air between them.

"Mayor Grant is going to show *your* documentary at the festival in front of the entire town?" Mama asked.

"Yes."

"Well, why didn't you say so?" Mama said excitedly as she crossed the small study and wrapped her arms around Rosie, squeezing tight. "That's so exciting!"

Rosie pulled away and stared at the deep scratch across one corner of the desk and the velvety black wick of the candle beside the computer. She stared anywhere but at Mama's face.

"It's not a big deal," Rosie mumbled.

"This is a really big deal," Mama said, beaming at her. "What can I do to help? Do you need costumes, or someone to hold up the lighting, or script revisions, or a camera operator, or a cinematographer? I'm your girl, or grip, or whatever the right movie term is."

"I think I've got it covered," Rosie said.

Lying to Mama felt worse than the time she'd cracked her new camera lens in fifth grade. She usually told Mama everything, even when she got a D on her math quiz or when Alison Jones made fun of her haircut. Lying to Mama didn't come natural, and holding back the true reason for why she was filming the documentary felt like the biggest lie of all time.

"You're the perfect person for this film. You know the

Miracles as well as anyone in Glimmer Creek. I remember you made a whole list of them one summer," Mama said.

"You helped by telling me about them," Rosie said softly.

"That's true. Maybe you should dedicate the entire film to me. I'd like a large screen with just my name on it to start off the documentary," Mama teased.

"I don't think so." Rosie forced a smile.

"At least think about it," Mama said. "We'll need potato-chip sundaes tonight."

Potato-chip sundaes were Mama and Rosie's celebratory dessert. It was vanilla ice cream, caramel sauce, and crushed potato chips, and it was delicious. But Rosie didn't deserve a potato-chip sundae, not after what she'd done.

"Darlings, I've arrived, and I've brought truffles." Miss Lily's voice carried from the front door. She appeared in the study doorway in a sequined jacket and silver heels. "You are in for a true culinary treat."

"What have you got?" Mama asked, gingerly peering inside the paper bag.

"This package of white truffles was delivered yesterday. It's from an old suitor of mine who lives in France."

Mama raised her eyebrows. "Miss Lily, do you realize you are holding thousands of dollars' worth of mushrooms? Those truffles are worth a fortune."

"Thousands of dollars?" Miss Lily sniffed the truffles. "Good Lord, Pierre really should not have sent this through the postal service. This is what happens when you're exceedingly beautiful," Miss Lily said to Rosie. "Men send extravagant gifts. You'll see for yourself when you get older."

"Rosie is going to become an Oscar-winning director and send herself extravagant gifts." Mama double winked at Rosie.

A sharp knife of guilt stabbed Rosie in the rib cage. She swallowed hard and made herself wink back.

"Now, Miss Lily, let's see about cleaning these," Mama said. "I'm starving."

Rosie moved to follow them. Her feet felt heavy, as if weights were attached to the bottom of her shoes. On her way out of the room, she spied Mama's cell phone on one of the bookshelves. Rosie grabbed it, knowing Mama would be racing around the house searching for it in an hour, having forgotten where she'd left it again.

Except right as she lifted the phone, it lit up with an incoming text. Rosie glanced down and couldn't help reading: Enjoyed lunch today. I'm trying out that recipe tonight. Thanks for the suggestion.

The text was from Sheriff Parker.

Rosie read the words again. Her heart skipped several

beats. Mama and Sheriff Parker had eaten lunch together today?

Gripping the cell phone tighter, Rosie watched the screen blacken. She couldn't help remembering how Mama seemed too serious this morning when Sheriff Parker came by, and she'd defended him after he'd left. Meanwhile, Sheriff Parker had smiled and acted all friendly for the first time ever. The whole conversation was weird. Even weirder was what Mr. Jack had said about their—their spark.

Rosie's heart rate sped up, but she made herself breathe. *Stop panicking.* Loosening her grip, she carefully dropped the cell phone back on the shelf. She knew Mama better than anyone. After all, Sheriff Parker's text was friendly, but it wasn't *too friendly*. The more Rosie thought about it, the clearer it was. It was obviously a work lunch. Mama probably had lunch with lots of people Rosie didn't know about. There was no need to overreact.

Still, as Rosie left the room, she couldn't decide whether the queasy feeling in her stomach was because of the e-mail to her father or the text from Sheriff Parker. It was possible she wasn't the only Flynn girl keeping secrets, and she didn't like it one bit.

CHAPTER EIGHT

Rosie stirred her oatmeal and watched the beige blobs on her spoon plop back into the bowl. She'd checked her e-mail as soon as she got up and after her shower and before breakfast. It had been sixteen hours and twenty-two minutes since she'd sent the e-mail to her father, and he still hadn't replied. Of course, he was really busy filming, and she had to give him time. He'd write back.

Unless—Rosie sat straight up—what if Michael had changed his e-mail address again and never got her e-mail? That would explain why he hadn't written her back. Maybe she should find his number and call him instead—

"Rosie!"

"Huh?" Rosie looked up from her bowl, hearing Mama's voice for the first time.

"I've been asking you for the last thirty seconds if you wanted more orange juice," Mama said.

"I'm fine."

"Suit yourself." Mama bent down behind the counter and came back up holding a bag. Her smile was big and bright. "Guess what? I was walking past Clementine's yesterday and they had those striped hair ribbons you like. I bought you a few. Want me to tie one in now?"

"Oh, um, thanks."

Rosie cringed inside as Mama tied one of the pink and red ribbons in her hair. She didn't want to hurt Mama's feelings by telling her that no one wore *ribbons* in middle school. Even as Rosie felt Mama pulling on the bow at the back of her head, she knew she'd take it out and bury it in the bottom of her dresser after Mama left for work.

"There," Mama said, standing back. "You look cute."

"Thanks." Rosie went back to staring at her oatmeal. She didn't want to look cute.

Mama bustled around the kitchen, unloading the dishwasher and humming to herself. She'd even made two jokes before her first cup of coffee. For some reason, she was in an uncommonly good mood, which made it the perfect time to ask about Michael.

Rosie took a deep breath. "Mama?"

"Yes, sugar?"

"I had an idea."

"What is that?"

"I thought maybe, now that I'm twelve, maybe now is a

good time for me . . . " Rosie's voice halted. *Just say it.* She took another deep breath. "Maybe now is a good time for me to call my father."

"Oh." Mama put down the glass she was holding and stared at Rosie. "What brought this on?"

"Nothing particular," Rosie said. *Only that Michael is currently two hours away and I invited him to Glimmer Creek.* If Mama didn't want Rosie to call Michael, she definitely wouldn't want her to see him.

Mama's good mood seemed to evaporate right into the cinnamon-scented air. Her mouth pinched in along the edges, and she took a deep breath. "I know it's hard not having your father around, and I understand why you want to call him, but this—this isn't the right time." She tapped her fingers along the counter, avoiding Rosie's eyes. "When you get older, we can talk about contacting him. I promise."

Rosie bit her lip. She wanted to change the subject and wipe that expression off Mama's face, to bring back her humming and joking, to even let Mama tie another pink and red ribbon in her hair, but she couldn't. Not this time.

"I think it is the right time," Rosie said in a soft voice.

Mama closed her eyes briefly, then crossed the kitchen to the table and sat down beside Rosie. "Sugar, you are, without a doubt, the most amazing twelve-year-old in the world."

"You're not at all biased," Rosie said with a small smile.

"Not at all." Mama's smile flickered before extinguishing entirely. "But Michael, well, he isn't ready for a relationship yet. He has a lot of problems to work through that have nothing to do with you."

Rosie flinched. Mama's words were a thousand yellow jackets stinging her heart. She didn't want a father who needed to work through problems. She wanted a father who watched movies with her on Friday nights and made pancakes on Saturday mornings and showed up at her movie premiere. She wanted a real father.

"I know it feels terrible to hear this," Mama said, the little catch in her voice pulling the words deeper down into Rosie. "I feel terrible saying it, and I wish things were different. I really do."

"What if he's changed?" Rosie's face was hot.

"He hasn't," Mama said quietly.

"I still want to try to call him."

"I'm sorry, but no," Mama said. "You need to trust me."

"I do," Rosie said, swallowing. "But we could at least talk about this."

"We are talking about it, but that doesn't mean we're going to agree. I'm sorry, Rosie," Mama added again, but now it sounded like an afterthought.

"Isn't this my decision too?" Rosie's shoulders tensed against the back of the chair.

"Not this time," Mama said.

"If it's because you don't like him—"

"I like him fine. My feelings have nothing to do with this. Believe me. I'm doing what's best for you." Mama stood and moved over to the dishwasher as if their entire discussion were over.

But it wasn't over. Not even close.

Mama couldn't just change the subject. This was Rosie's *father*, and he was important to her. Mama might hate Michael for leaving her, but that wasn't a good enough reason to keep him and Rosie apart. Rosie was older now and could make her own decisions about Michael. How could Mama not see that?

Mama didn't know how hard it was not to have a father. She couldn't see the pit in Rosie's stomach when someone mentioned Father's Day or know how empty she felt when Alison Jones asked if she'd visit her father in Hollywood for spring break. Mama didn't understand any of those things.

Rosie's anger bubbled up to the surface and boiled over into her words. "Maybe the reason my father hasn't come to see me is because he doesn't want to see *you*."

Rosie sucked in a breath, shocked by what she'd said.

Mama froze for several seconds, finally turning away, but not before Rosie saw the tears shimmering in her eyes. Instantly, all of Rosie's fury drained away. How could she have said something so mean? She wished she could rewind the last five minutes.

Staring down at the table, Rosie's eyes burned. She wanted to say she was sorry and didn't mean a word of it. She wanted to say she didn't even care about calling Michael, though it wasn't true. But despite Rosie wanting to say something, the *right* something, she was unable to say anything at all. Her words were locked up deep inside.

"I should go to work," Mama said after several silent seconds.

"Mama—"

"It's okay, Rosie. We'll talk about it later." Mama left the room, quiet as a whisper.

Rosie sat alone at the table, her throat closed up. She knew they wouldn't talk about it later because they never talked about Michael Weatherton later. They barely talked about him at all. Staring down at the kitchen table, Rosie traced the scratches in the wood, noticing them for the first time. She sat quiet, unmoving, while Mama's car pulled out of the driveway.

All Rosie wanted was the chance to meet her father and for Mama to help her do it. Mama and Rosie were supposed to think the same way and to want the same things. Except right now, they weren't the same at all. They were broken right down the middle, and Rosie ached at the split.

Rosie's stomach was still twisted up into knots as she walked to school beside Cam and Henry. The sky was a flinty gray, and clouds covered the sun like a fresh bruise. A frosty breeze crept into her jacket, but Rosie couldn't tell if it was the early-morning air or the cold inside that left her chilled.

"Some species of cicadas come out of hibernation every seventeen years, but this isn't one of their life cycle years. It's such a shame because they look like a big swarm of cockroaches when they come out of the ground. That's something I'd like to see," Henry said.

"Henry, that's disgusting," Cam complained.

"You only think that because of our culture. We're taught to think of bugs as disgusting. But other societies see them as a delicacy. In Brazil, lots of people eat bugs," Henry said.

"You know, we could use bugs for our annual haunted house at Rosie's this year. It's already October and we've barely started planning. What if we have the neighborhood kids eat pretend bugs? We'll blindfold them and tell them spaghetti noodles are worms," Cam said, rubbing her hands together in anticipation.

"I don't know," Henry said, frowning. "We don't want to really scare them."

"That's the point of a haunted house. I'm definitely dressing up like a vampire again to freak out my little sisters. Come on, Rosie, I know you must have thought about some new scare tactics by now. You always have the best ideas for this." Cam turned to Rosie, drawing her into the conversation.

Rosie smiled a little. "Well, I was thinking we could have old horror movies playing on the TV in a dark room and make them watch the scariest parts. I could try to do some lighting special effects too so it looks like monsters are there, but I'll need to rent a strobe light."

"The lighting sounds complicated, but I love the monster idea," Cam said. "We should get that monster costume back out. Henry can wear it."

"I think I'll just be the guide again," Henry mumbled.

"You're boring," Cam said, tossing her stocking hat at Henry.

The hat slipped through Henry's fingers, and he nearly tripped off the curb trying to catch it. He scooped it up off the ground and tossed it back to Cam, who caught it one-handed.

"Why'd you have to throw it? You know I have poor hand-eye coordination," Henry said.

Cam gave Rosie a sideways look. Her lips were pressed together the way they did when she was trying not to laugh. Meanwhile, Henry turned his backpack around and pulled out an enormous book on bugs. He began pointing to a chapter on nutritional value while trying to walk in a straight line unsuccessfully. Cam kept tossing the hat up while asking Henry if they should serve real bug sandwiches instead.

Rosie couldn't help laughing. She noticed a patch of sunlight pushing its way through a hole in the clouds, and her stomach unclenched.

"Okay, I'm calling an official HenRoCam to order," Rosie said.

"Subject?" Cam asked.

Rosie stopped walking and took a deep breath. "Actually, I've got some huge news. I convinced Mayor Grant to let me film a documentary on the town Miracles, and he's going to show it at the Festival of the Fish on a big movie screen. It should run after the boat parade and before the fireworks, during the prime hours of the festival."

Henry slammed his book closed, giving her his full attention. "That's awesome! This is way bigger than your YouTube videos."

"I'll need your help with filming. I've got a list of scenes already in mind. I'll send you both the schedule." Rosie hesitated. "But that's not all. I found out my father is filming a movie in Richmond, and well, I e-mailed him yesterday and invited him to the premiere."

"Your father said he's coming to Glimmer Creek?" Cam gasped.

"I haven't heard back from him yet, but I bet he e-mails me later today. I'm not that worried about it. My whole plan is coming together like it was meant to be." Rosie gave them both a tentative smile and tried not to think about her empty in-box. Her dad was busy with filming last night. That was why he hadn't e-mailed her back, probably.

Cam stopped throwing her hat. Henry looked down at his hands. No one moved. It was as if someone hit pause on their entire conversation.

"What's wrong?" Rosie asked. A creeping sensation came over her like ants marching up her arm.

"Did you tell Miss Caroline about this?" Henry asked.

"I told her about the documentary part," Rosie mumbled.

Cam and Henry looked at each other before Cam said, "You need to tell her about inviting your dad, too."

"I don't think you should keep something like this from her," Henry said in a worried voice.

Rosie didn't need Henry and Cam to make her feel bad about lying to Mama. Even before this morning's disastrous breakfast, Rosie had woken up at two o'clock in the morning with the urge to run into Mama's room and confess everything like Terry Malloy did in the famous crime drama *On the Waterfront*. Although then she'd remembered how Terry got beat up and lost his girlfriend, so the confession hadn't worked out so well for him.

"You talk to her about everything," Cam continued. "You told her when Chase Corrigan watched our last YouTube video."

Rosie blushed. "So what? I like to tell her about my fans."

"That fan is the cutest guy in seventh grade," Cam said.

Henry shuddered. "Official HenRoCam request to change the subject."

"What I'm trying to say is if you told her about your dad's movie in Richmond, she'd understand why you want to invite him to Glimmer Creek," Cam said.

"She might even help you," Henry added.

Rosie shook her head, remembering Mama's refusal to even consider calling her father. "She won't. Trust me. I had to get in touch with him myself, and he's going to e-mail back."

"We just don't want to see you get hurt," Henry said, blowing out a breath.

How was meeting her father going to hurt her unless . . . unless Henry and Cam thought Michael wasn't going to show up. But he had to show up. If he didn't, she'd maybe never meet him. Rosie twisted the zipper on her jacket, suddenly unable to look at either of them.

A breeze rustled the leaves of a nearby bush, sending them bristling and crackling against each other. The sound of laughter drifted to them from the direction of Stratford Middle School while Rosie stared at the ground.

"Rosie, it will be okay," Cam said all of a sudden.

"Will it?" Rosie asked. Awful tears hovered at the back of her eyelids.

"If your dad doesn't reply to your e-mail, we'll contact the film set," Cam said.

"I can research the number for you," Henry chimed in.

"And I'll call it," Cam said. "I'm very persuasive."

Rosie exhaled. The tears stopped pricking her eyes. "I guess we could tell them his house in California got burglarized. That way we know he'll call back."

"I don't know about lying," Henry warned.

"We can probably say his daughter is trying to get in touch with him," Cam said.

"Or we could do that," Rosie said. "Once he gets my message, I know he'll come."

"Me too," Henry said emphatically.

Rosie looked to Cam, waiting for her to agree too.

Cam squeezed the hat in her hands. "I'm sure you're right."

"But?" Rosie could hear the question in Cam's voice.

"But you don't have to make the documentary to invite your father to the festival," Cam said. "It's going to take a lot of work."

"I *want* to make the documentary. Besides, he sent me a card saying he promised to come see my movie," Rosie said.

Cam cleared her throat. "It's just, the whole school goes to the festival, so they'll all see the documentary too. You don't want to . . . embarrass yourself, especially since it's about the Miracles."

"What does that mean?" Rosie's arms stiffened at her sides. "Do you think my films are embarrassing?"

"She doesn't think that," Henry rushed to say at the same time Cam said, "I didn't say that."

"You know I think your films are great," Cam said gently. "What I meant was not everyone at school believes in the Miracles."

"But we do," Rosie said.

Cam's eyes slid away. "Sometimes I wonder if there's a—well, if there's a reasonable explanation for them. There's no actual proof."

Rosie reared back, her knees buckling. What was Cam talking about? Her not believing in the Miracles was crazy!

"There's plenty of proof," Rosie said, her hands flying around her sides "How else do you explain Beth Moore? She was in a fire eleven years ago with her brother and should have died but for the Miracle of the firefighters getting her out right before the ceiling collapsed. Since then she's never cold and doesn't even own a coat. She dropped off cookies at the town hall yesterday, and they were still warm because she set them beside herself in the car."

"Maybe Mrs. Moore has a higher body temperature than other people," Cam said.

"But we've always believed in the Miracles," Rosie replied, her chest growing tighter and tighter. "Remember how many times we wished for a Miracle by throwing pennies into the Fishing Well, or standing on one foot at the exact spot where the creek ended? And then there was that time we spent a whole month turning around three times on the beach right as the sun set because your dad heard that might work."

"Yeah, and it didn't work. None of it did," Cam said, sounding irritated. "Besides, we did that stuff when we were little kids. It's different now."

"Not to me," Rosie whispered.

Cam tilted her head. "Look, the Miracles are sort of like the train treasure. It's fun to think about, but we all know they're probably fake."

"I disagree," Henry said matter-of-factly.

Rosie didn't understand. How could Cam think the Miracles were like the train treasure? They were nothing alike. The Miracles were real.

"All you have to do is look around. The Miracles don't make sense. My grandma could have used one last year when she fell and broke her hip. But she didn't get one. She was a really good person," Cam said.

Cam's grandma had gone into a coma after her fall last year and died a few days later. It was the only time Rosie had ever seen Cam cry.

"I didn't know you felt that way," Henry said.

Cam shot him a skeptical look. "Didn't you want a Miracle when Miss Betty got sick?"

"I hoped for one, sure," Henry said.

"And she didn't get one. Doesn't that make you a little doubtful?" Cam asked.

Henry's blue eyes crinkled. "Just because my mama didn't get a Miracle doesn't mean I gave up on them."

Rosie's heart was suddenly pounding, and words burst out of her like a faucet turned up too high. "There's only one Miracle a year. Not everyone can get one, not even people who deserve it like your grandma or Miss Betty. You know that's true."

"What I know is there's no explanation for who gets a Miracle or why. It doesn't make sense. Maybe the people we think are getting Miracles are only lucky, and that's all," Cam said.

"No way. It's more than luck," Rosie said. Her voice was shaking now. "I can tell you about every Miracle— all the details—and I bet that would convince you they're real."

"You don't have to get upset," Cam said, sighing. "See, I knew you would react this way. That's why I never said anything before."

"I'm not upset!" Rosie nearly shouted. But she was breathing hard, and her lungs had constricted. "In fact, I plan to figure out what causes the Miracles in my documentary."

Henry shook his head. "But there's no accounting for Miracles and—"

"*I'm* going to account for them, and *I'm* going to prove they're real. I've got fifteen days until the festival. You'll see." Rosie glared at Cam, waiting for her to disagree.

Cam only shrugged. "We should get to school. The bell is about to ring."

Henry nodded, and they started off down the sidewalk.

Rosie was a step behind, her mind already racing. Here was another reason why she had to make her documentary, to find out what caused the Miracles and prove they weren't only coincidence or good luck. She had to show Cam the Miracles were real. And once she did, Cam would have to believe . . . and Rosie would have her best friend back.

CHAPTER NINE

It took Rosie a few days to set up her documentary interview with Mrs. Grant. Cam had agreed to help with the film even with all her doubts. It was a good thing too because the filming wasn't going quite as smoothly as Rosie planned. She'd interviewed three Miracled people so far and couldn't find a single common reason for *why* they'd gotten Miracled. Rosie was sure it would only take more time, but the festival was eleven days away so she didn't have a lot of that.

Rosie zoomed in on Mrs. Grant's soft, wrinkled face and her unnaturally bright blue eyes with her camcorder lens. Mayor Grant had already left for the town meeting, and the house was quiet except for the occasional gong of the grandfather clock. The heavy satin curtains were drawn, and the brass lamps on either side of the pink flowered couch cast halos around the porcelain cat figurines that crowded every available surface. Somehow, despite the dimness of the room, Mrs. Grant's eyes beamed out of the camera lens like blue lasers. Everyone swore they got bluer the night her cataracts were miraculously cured.

"Henry, you've got the voice recorder ready?" Rosie asked.

Henry held it up and fumbled it through his fingers. The recorder slammed into the ground. "Oh man, I'm sorry." He scrambled along the cream carpet, stumbling forward.

Cam dropped to her knees and plucked the recorder off the floor. "Red light is still blinking. It's okay." She eyed Henry for several seconds before pulling him to his feet. "Will you excuse us for a minute," she said to Mrs. Grant, and dragged Henry and Rosie into the hallway.

One hand on her hip, Cam gestured to Henry. "Okay, what's wrong?"

For the first time that evening, Rosie took a good look at Henry. His face was pale, and there were dark smudges underneath his eyes. He looked like an extra in a zombie movie.

"Nothing," Henry said.

Cam narrowed her eyes.

"Fine, I'm a little tired," Henry said.

"Are you sure that's all?" Cam asked.

Henry stared at the top of Mrs. Grant's foyer table, not answering.

Cam opened her mouth, but Rosie cut her off. "He said he's okay, and we need to get started with the interview."

Cam hesitated before nodding once, still frowning at Henry. "I'll handle the recorder."

They headed back into the living room. Rosie hit the record button and sharpened the image of Mrs. Grant before asking her first question. "Ever since the Miracle, how good is your vision?"

Mrs. Grant smiled. "It's perfect, better than twenty-twenty. Why, I can see a speck of dust across the room, which is so useful when it comes to housekeeping."

"That is handy," Rosie said. It was not quite the exciting answer she'd hoped for though. "What else do you use your better-than-perfect vision for? Maybe give us an example of something that helps mankind."

"Well . . . " Mrs. Grant considered this. "I've helped animals. Does that count? There was this one time our cat, Princess, got out at night and I was able to see her hiding down the street in the bushes."

In moments like these, Rosie wished she were more like John Ford, the director of *Stagecoach* and countless other old Westerns, who was infamous for yelling at his actors until they did what he wanted.

"Ask her to go over her schedule the day before the Miracle," Henry whispered.

Rosie shot him a grateful look before turning back to Mrs. Grant. "Why don't we run through everything you did the day before your Miracle? Maybe that will help us figure out what caused it."

"Let me see . . ." Mrs. Grant looked up at the ceiling. "I'm sure I went to the grocery store. I do that most days, and I must have done some laundry. I fed Princess. I believe I had a Garden Club meeting."

"But did you notice a strange feeling or something? Anything that would explain why you got a Miracle?" Cam asked impatiently.

"I'm not sure. Y'all know there's no accounting for Miracles, and as far as I can recall, it was a normal day like any other."

Cam raised her eyebrows and looked sideways at Rosie as if to say, *See? I told you.* Rosie remembered how Cam said the Miracled people were "only lucky." Rosie gripped the camcorder tighter. She would prove otherwise.

"Think back really carefully. Take your time," Rosie said in a soothing tone.

Cam blew out a frustrated breath.

"Hmmm, let me think . . . " Mrs. Grant's voice trailed off and then she sat up. "Actually, something unusual did happen. Mayor Grant and I got a call shortly before midnight. It was a wrong number from Mrs. Birdsall. She lived a few streets away and was quite elderly at the time. She's since passed. You would have loved her. Sweet woman, real—"

"I'm sure she was great. And what happened next?" Rosie interrupted. Keeping Mrs. Grant on track was turning out to be tougher than long division.

"Well, Mrs. Birdsall hung up on me once she realized she had the wrong number, but I could tell something was wrong. I decided to check in on her. Good thing too because she'd taken a bad tumble down the stairs. Anyway, it was late and dark and my cataracts were terrible at the time so I could hardly see anything, but I still insisted on taking a shortcut. Wouldn't you know? I tripped right off the side of Mr. Gooch's yard and into the creek. I got to Mrs. Birdsall's house soaked clean through." Mrs. Grant's eyes took on a faraway look. "It's funny though. I did always wonder . . . "

"Yes?" Rosie asked, leaning forward.

Mrs. Grant shook her head. "It's silly. But I suppose I did wonder if the water had something to do with my cataracts getting cured. I remember wiping water out of my eyes, and I swear things looked clearer right then and there. I ignored it until I woke up the next morning and my cataracts were gone."

It took Rosie another hour to end the interview. Mrs.

Grant kept talking about her sudden inspiration for wanting to start a cat rescue organization named after Princess.

"That interview needs a lot of editing," Cam said as they stepped outside onto a darkened Magnolia Street.

"No kidding," Rosie huffed.

"I'm going home to research more about cataracts," Henry said. "I noticed a black dot in my vision yesterday. You don't think that's a symptom, do you?"

Cam bugged out her eyes and stuck her tongue out. "Can you see this?"

Henry ignored Cam and turned to Rosie. "What did you think about Mrs. Grant's story of falling in the creek? Could the water have caused her Miracle?"

"That's ridiculous," Cam said. "If the creek caused Miracles, everyone in town would have gotten one by now."

"Maybe it was a special time of night or a certain day or a specific part of the creek. It's worth looking into," Rosie said, but she couldn't hide the disappointment in her voice. She didn't remember anyone else falling in the water before their Miracle.

None of the interviews she'd done so far had proven a thing. Solving this mystery was starting to feel impossible, almost as impossible as getting her father to Glimmer Creek. She checked her e-mail every morning and after school every day and before bed every night, but Michael still hadn't responded. Five days and counting. She clutched her camcorder bag, nails digging into the strap. Maybe he would never e-mail back.

Cam glanced down at her watch and clapped a hand to her forehead. "Dang it! It's already seven thirty. We've missed half the town meeting."

"So?" Rosie asked.

"I told you I needed to be on time. I'm helping with the doughnut fund-raiser for Student Council. I'm supposed to talk about the different flavors," Cam said.

Rosie clenched her jaw. Cam had mentioned the doughnut fund-raiser no less than ten times since yesterday. The fund-raiser wasn't something just anyone could sign up for. You had to get invited to help by one of the eighth graders on the Student Council. Rosie didn't blame Cam for being excited. It *did* look pretty fun—selling doughnuts with a group of the cutest guys in school outside Hardaway Market. But Cam didn't have to talk about it every five minutes.

"I'm sure someone else can talk about the flavors," Rosie said.

"But Leila asked me to do it," Cam said, drumming her fingers against her leg.

"They always save announcements till the end. I bet we can still make it," Henry added.

Though they ran all the way there, Rosie, Cam, and Henry burst through the double doors of the Glimmer Creek Community Center right as Leila and four of her friends finished up their announcement. Cam's head drooped, and she heaved out a sigh.

"I'm sorry," Rosie whispered.

Cam shook her head and leaned against the wall, staring straight ahead. Rosie flinched at the disappointed look on Cam's face, though she couldn't help wondering why a fund-raiser announcement seemed more important to Cam than helping Rosie.

The community center was crammed full of people, same as every town meeting. Mama called it sardines in a can, and it felt that way now. The din of the room rose as Leila sat down. Cam, Henry, and Rosie stood against the back wall. Despite the crowd, Cam managed to put a few feet between herself and Rosie.

"Are there any more announcements?" Mayor Grant asked from the front podium.

Marvin Blandstone's hand shot into the air before he leapt to his feet. "I've got an important announcement. When you go outside this evening, I want you to notice the particular brightness of the moon. There's a reason for that. I've been reading on the interwebs all week and the moon is . . . *not real.*" Mr. Blandstone's face was turning purple, and he was waving his hands around in a frantic circle.

Cam cleared her throat and looked sideways at Rosie. Rosie rolled her eyes, and a corner of Cam's mouth tipped up in a smile. Talking without really talking, that was something Cam and Rosie had perfected. Rosie grinned back, her legs loosening, and she felt instantly better.

"I was shocked too," Mr. Blandstone continued. "But there's a high probability the moon is a hologram projected by an unknown source here on earth. I am no longer willing to sit by—"

"Thank you, Mr. Blandstone," Mayor Grant interrupted.

Mr. Willis stood up from the second row. He grabbed the bowler hat off his head. "Ladies and gentlemen, I want to talk to you about a new exhibit at the Museum of Extraordinary Artifacts. The mayor has been gracious enough to allow me to peruse Lonnie Garrett's journal, which was found down in the Fishing Well with his—his—"

"His dead body," Arthur Blue called out.

"Um, yes. Precisely," Mr. Willis said, looking squeamish. "The journal was found in Mr. Garrett's knapsack partially submerged in the water, but some of the pages are still legible. I plan to display it in the museum starting next Tuesday. Anyone is welcome to take a gander at this fascinating piece of Glimmer Creek history."

A chorus of whispered excitement broke out from the crowd.

"Settle down!" Mayor Grant banged the gavel. "In case you were getting your hopes up about the train treasure, the journal does not reveal its location."

A collective groan rose from the room.

Mayor Grant continued. "And I'm gonna warn y'all right now that we won't tolerate folks digging up dirt that don't belong to them. Sheriff Parker found five new holes this morning—one of them was smack-dab in the middle of Miss Melinda's prized roses and the other was in front of the town hall. Why, just last night Sheriff Parker arrested someone for defacing public property, and he'll do it again if the digging doesn't stop."

Shane Rodgers called out, "How many times can I get arrested for the same crime?"

Sheriff Parker stood. "As many times as you violate the law."

Henry poked Rosie. "We've got to go see that journal."

"Why?" Rosie asked. "Mayor Grant just said it doesn't say where the treasure is buried."

"But it might contain a clue about it," Henry said. "I've been researching Lonnie and—"

"Hold on. I thought we weren't searching for the treasure," Rosie interrupted.

"All I'm doing is researching, and researching never hurt anyone, right?" Henry asked.

"I guess not," Rosie said with an inward sigh. Rosie might not believe in the treasure, but she supposed she still had to help a little. After all, Cam was helping her with the documentary and she didn't believe in the Miracles anymore. At least, not until Rosie proved they were real.

Henry leaned in to her. "From what I've learned so far, Lonnie was just a regular guy before the robbery. He got into some trouble, and he wasn't the nicest, sure, but nothing like stealing. He had these two best friends, Hank and Ned Gooch. The three of them fished at White Stone Beach at midnight, poured maple syrup on the school toilet seats, and even threw firecrackers at people passing underneath the tree house they'd built. Can you imagine the injuries that could cause?" He shook his head. "If we go see the journal next Tuesday, it will only take a half hour."

Henry made a pleading motion with his hands. His face was tired, but his eyes gleamed like two lightning bugs.

"All right," Rosie said.

Henry beamed at her.

Next, Miss Matilda went on about harvesting oysters. Mr. Hardaway announced he had sold out of shovels at

Hardaway Market but was expecting more next week, and Mrs. Moore mentioned she was selling warm cookies to raise money for children's cancer research. The meeting ran long, as usual.

"If that's all . . . ," Mayor Grant finally said.

Rosie's fingers tingled, her heart drummed against her rib cage, and before she knew exactly what she was doing, she called out, "I have an announcement."

Every head in the room turned to look at Rosie. She rubbed her hands along her pants leg. *No need to be nervous.* Closing her eyes for a brief second, she pictured herself standing in front of a crowd like a heroine fighting for justice in a legal drama. A single spotlight would illuminate her face, the courtroom would hush, the music would swell, and—

Cam elbowed her.

Rosie's eyes popped open. "My, um, announcement is about a new project. I'm filming a documentary about the Miracles, and I plan to find out what causes them. I—I've already interviewed some of the Miracled, and I'd love to interview more of you. I'm also in the process of filming cutaways and live-action scenes, so you may see me around town working on that. Cutaways are when you interrupt the continuous filming to show something related to the main scene." Rosie turned around to see Cam miming for her to stop talking. "You get the point. I'm filming a documentary."

A few people nodded from their seats. A few others looked at their watches.

Miss Matilda stood up. "I'm not so sure about this documentary. Now, y'all know I love this town, but I don't like the idea of advertising ourselves to the rest of the world. Our Miracles are supposed to stay a secret. Most folks have never heard of Glimmer Creek, and I reckon that's a good thing. We live in a nice, quiet town. I don't want that to change."

How was Rosie's documentary going to change Glimmer Creek for the worse? If anything, publicity was good for the town. It could mean more visitors, more people. It could make the town bigger and better.

The townsfolk stopped looking at their watches and started looking at Rosie. Sweat dribbled down her sides. Backing up, she hit the wall behind her. She hadn't even thought there might be opposition to her documentary. She wasn't Stanley Kubrick, for goodness' sake.

Mr. Waverman stood up. "I already gave my interview, but I hadn't thought about what you said, Matilda. It's a good point. I can't have the paparazzi stalking me on my mail route."

"Oh, give me a break." Cam glared at Mr. Waverman and moved closer to Rosie.

Shane and Frank Rodgers leapt to their feet. "We don't mind getting famous," Shane said. "Frank and me would make great reality-TV stars."

Mr. Hardaway rose with a smirk. "I hardly think an amateur movie about a little town legend is going to send a bunch of media types to Glimmer Creek."

"The Miracles are not a legend, Fred. They're part of our life," Donna Davis said, planting her hands on her hips. "I found my great-grandma's diamond bracelet under my bed right when I needed it. It was missing for fifty years. I'd sold everything I had to keep my family afloat, but that bracelet was the Miracle that saved my home from foreclosure."

Since the bracelet, Mrs. Davis had won the scratch-off lottery twelve times and came across stray quarters any time she walked along the sidewalk. She seemed to find money everywhere after her Miracle. Mayor Grant had even wanted to turn the town's retirement fund over to her, but Mama talked him out of it.

"Simmer down, Donna," Mr. Hardaway said. "You know I'm a big supporter of the Miracles. I was the one selling Miracle T-shirts at the festival last year."

"Those T-shirts read: 'I came for a Miracle, and all I got was this lousy T-shirt.' They were an embarrassment," Mrs. Davis snapped.

"They were big sellers," Mr. Hardaway griped before sitting down.

The din of voices rose and rumbled through the room like thunder. The crowd drew closer to Rosie, every pair of eyes boring holes into her. She looked to the front, where Mama usually sat behind Mayor Grant. If only she were here instead of dealing with a burst pipe on Poplar Lane.

Sheriff Parker stood and locked eyes with Rosie. She cringed. He was probably about to arrest her for disturbing the peace with her announcement.

"Folks, this movie is not something to get worked up over. Let's all stop yelling at the kid," Sheriff Parker said.

Rosie blinked. Had Sheriff Parker just defended her in front of everyone?

"No one is yelling," Miss Matilda yelled.

"No one is being quiet either," Sheriff Parker said, glancing at Rosie again. "We need to calm down."

Rosie couldn't believe it. For once Sheriff Parker was trying to help her. Maybe he wasn't completely terrible.

Mr. Willis stood. "Sheriff, I'm plenty calm, but I do think we need to talk about preserving the character of Glimmer Creek. I'm not sure a documentary posted online is really part of our town culture."

Rosie made herself step forward again. She had to stop this. "I—I never said I was going to post it online, and I definitely won't if it's such a big deal to everyone."

This could work better. It meant Rosie's father must come to the festival. She couldn't even send him a link to the documentary. Although now if he didn't come, he might never see the film she was making *for him*.

"There you go. You can stop snowing on Rosie's parade. She won't put the movie up in a video chatroom. That solves the problem," Mayor Grant said.

"I don't agree," Miss Matilda began.

A hubbub broke out with half the room out of their chairs and no one able to understand what anyone else was saying. Cam and Henry stepped closer to Rosie, guarding her on either side. She swayed on her feet, wanting to say something to convince everyone the documentary was a good idea, a great idea even, but her lips were glued shut. If Mayor Grant wouldn't show her film, she'd have nothing to show her father. Her entire plan would be ruined.

"Shush!" Mayor Grant yelled.

The room went silent.

"Now, keep your britches on, all of you. I'm the mayor, and I say this movie is not going to harm Glimmer Creek one bit," Mayor Grant said. "The Miracles are part of our town pride and not something to hide. That's the final word on the matter. Meeting adjourned!"

Cam and Henry grinned at her. Rosie tried to grin

back, but her face had frozen in a grimace. She expelled a long stream of air. Her documentary wasn't canceled. She *would* have a movie premiere in eleven days. Thank goodness for Mayor Grant.

With the meeting over, the crowd began to stretch and shuffle their way down the aisles to the exit. Henry hurried off to talk to Mr. Willis, and Cam was on her tippy-toes, trying to see above the crowd.

Rosie collapsed back against the wall. "That was a close one."

"Uh-huh," Cam said.

"I thought the documentary was going to get canceled for sure," Rosie said.

Cam made a noncommittal sound under her breath. Then she brightened and waved a frantic hand over her head. "There's Leila. I better go over and apologize for missing the announcement. I hope she's not mad."

"Do you want me to come with you and explain how running over schedule is expected in filming?" Rosie asked.

"That's okay," Cam said, already wading into the crowd.

"At least let me explain how it was my fault you were late," Rosie said, following behind.

Cam stopped and turned, nearly knocking into Rosie. "It's better if I go alone. Leila won't understand about the movie thing, and she doesn't even know you."

Rosie hesitated. "You could introduce me."

"Now isn't the best time," Cam said quickly.

"Want me to wait for you outside?" Rosie asked in a small voice.

Cam squeezed Rosie's arm for a moment. "I'll probably walk with Leila. I'll see you tomorrow, okay?"

"Sure, okay," Rosie said, her throat tight.

The crowd swallowed Cam up as she hurried away. Rosie pressed her arms to her sides, suddenly cold. What did Cam mean when she said Leila wouldn't understand about the movie thing? And why didn't Cam want her to meet Leila?

Feeling sick, Rosie turned and pushed her way through the crowd until she spilled out onto the sidewalk. Outside, the streetlamps winked on one by one. She waited for Henry as people continued to trickle out of the community center. No one stopped to talk to her. In fact, it almost seemed as though everyone was avoiding her, just like Cam and her new friends. Clumps of people glanced at Rosie before quickly looking away and whispering to each other. They had to be talking about her and the documentary, and it obviously wasn't good.

The light faded, and purple shadows crouched beside the nearby bushes. As the minutes ticked by and Rosie stood alone, a dark realization set in. Her documentary wasn't even close to complete. She still needed to film tons of interviews and live-action segments, and she had a mystery to solve. But how was she going to film a documentary about Glimmer Creek's Miracles if half the town refused to help?

CHAPTER TEN

A few days later, Rosie borrowed a table from Sook Diner and arranged it in the middle of the sidewalk on Magnolia Street. Rosie had roped off sections of the sidewalk and made a FILMING IN PROGRESS sign. She was waiting on Frank and Shane Rodgers, and they were already five minutes late.

Today's scene was crucial. She'd spent the last three days trying to convince more Miracled people to let her interview them. A few had canceled after Miss Matilda's speech at the town meeting, and Rosie was scrambling to get enough footage for the documentary. She needed this live-action scene of Shane and Frank Rodgers to go well; with fewer interviews and eight days until the festival, she was running out of options and time.

"Rosie, right?"

Rosie looked up from her watch. Lucy Rambler had stopped behind the rope. She was in Rosie's Spanish class, but they'd never talked before. Lucy had only moved to

Glimmer Creek last summer. Never shy about raising her hand, she spoke in a perfect Spanish accent. She had chin-length hair with blue streaks and wore black boots with heavy silver buckles that could crush an entire anthill in one stomp.

"I'm Lucy," Lucy continued, a friendly smile on her face. "We go to the same school."

"I know," Rosie said, smiling back.

"Are you filming a scene for the documentary?" Lucy asked.

"Actually, I am," Rosie said, surprised.

"I was at the last town meeting. I think it's a cool idea. So you're trying to prove they're real or something?" Lucy asked.

Rosie raised her eyebrows. "They *are* real."

Lucy shrugged. "I didn't grow up here, so it's never been my thing."

Lucy didn't sound challenging, just skeptical. Rosie guessed a town where a Miracle happened every year might sound a little crazy to an outsider. Clearing her throat, she adjusted the strap of her camcorder case over her shoulder. There was obviously a convincing explanation if she could only uncover it.

"What type of camcorder do you use?" Lucy asked, gesturing to the camcorder case.

"I've got a Canon XA30," Rosie said.

"Are you using the 58mm UV haze filter to block the sunlight?" Lucy asked.

Rosie's eyes snapped wide open. This girl knew what a 58mm UV haze filter was?

"Sometimes. I think it sharpens the picture," Rosie said eagerly.

"I agree. I've got a camcorder too, but it's nothing like yours. The Canon XA30 is the real deal. I used it in film camp in New York City last summer."

"You went to film camp in New York City?" Rosie asked in an astonished voice.

"My aunt lives up there. It was awesome. We made a student film about a hard-boiled detective and dangerous lady client, all in the film noir style."

"Did you use low-key lighting and dark silhouettes?" Rosie took a step forward.

"Totally. We went complete *Maltese Falcon* with the cinematography."

Rosie sighed. "I would kill to go to that camp."

"I'll e-mail you the link," Lucy said. "Maybe you can go next summer."

Mama could never afford to send her to film camp in New York City, but maybe her father could. He might insist on it after he saw the documentary, assuming he came to the festival. Rosie's knees wobbled like pepper jelly, thinking about her empty in-box again.

"Did you know Ms. Pullman is starting a film club at school?" Lucy asked.

"No," Rosie said.

"I saw a flyer and checked into it. The first meeting is next Monday, and we're going to watch Hitchcock's *North by Northwest*. You should come." Lucy brushed a lock of blue hair out of her eyes. She'd drawn a tiny sun in red pen near her knuckles with a smiling face and long eyelashes.

"The crop duster scene is one of my favorites," Rosie said, straightening up.

"It's a classic," Lucy agreed. "Ms. Pullman said we're going to deconstruct that whole sequence after the film."

"I'll talk to Cam and Henry about going." Rosie said. "Oh wait, I forgot. Cam sometimes has a soccer game on Mondays, so we can't make it. Maybe after the season ends." A sharp pang of disappointment stabbed at Rosie. She could always watch *North by Northwest* at home, but analyzing it with a group sounded fun.

Right then Frank and Shane turned the corner, shoving each other back and forth on the sidewalk and talking in loud voices.

"My four thirty subjects are here. I should go," Rosie

said reluctantly. It was fun to talk to someone who cared about movies like she did.

"Sure." Lucy rapped a hand along her leg. "Good luck with filming. And hey, if you need any help with your documentary or another film, let me know. I'm pretty into writing scripts."

Rosie inclined her head and smiled. She was flattered that Lucy, who had gone to an actual film school, wanted to help *her*, though she couldn't imagine working on a film with anyone but Cam and Henry.

An hour later, Rosie flung open her front door and announced, "It's official. My documentary has turned into a disaster movie."

Mama poked her head out from the kitchen. "Who's playing the role of King Kong?"

"Take your pick. Shane Rodgers? Miss Matilda? Mr. Waverman?" Rosie shrugged off her backpack. "Everyone is trying to ruin my movie."

"I'm guessing the Rodgers brothers' scene didn't go so well today?"

"That's an understatement," Rosie said, kicking her backpack. "I was trying to film a live-action sequence where they read each other's minds, but I didn't get the chance because they got into a giant psychic fistfight right in the middle of Magnolia Street."

"Whoa. How did that happen?" Mama asked, stepping into the foyer.

"Well, Shane told Frank he looked like a Yankee in his new shirt, and Frank told Shane his shirt looked like it was covered in dog poop. They started off insulting each other in their heads, but soon they were yelling out loud and punching. It was a huge commotion, and I'm pretty sure someone called Sheriff Parker."

Mama crossed the foyer and laid her hand on Rosie's back, rubbing it in small circles. "They should have called Shane and Frank's mama. She's the only one who can talk sense into them. Those boys would never have needed a Miracle in the first place if they could keep their hands off each other."

The Rodgers brothers were famous for their dustups. Shane once drove Frank's truck into the creek, and Frank broke Shane's fishing rod over his head in retaliation. After that, neither of them spoke to the other for twenty-two years. It was a Miracle they showed up at Sook Diner one day at the exact same time, both intending to call the feud quits. Ever since, each brother seemed to know what the other was thinking without saying a word. But when Rosie asked Shane and Frank why they'd each decided to forgive the other on that particular day, neither of them had a reason. They were one more Miracle Rosie couldn't explain. In fact, all the Miracles were starting to seem more and more . . . random.

"Everything is going wrong. What if I can't get this movie made?" Rosie asked, her body slumping against the door.

"You'll make it. You've hit a few roadblocks. That's all," Mama said.

Rosie gazed down at her hands. "It's more than that. It feels as though this whole film is cursed, like that Howard Hughes movie *The Conqueror*, where the cast and crew died of cancer caused by radiation poisoning."

Mama snorted. "Sugar, I think you're being a little dramatic."

"I'm not," Rosie protested. "I've never had so many things go wrong on a film set. Three people canceled their interviews after the town meeting, and a bunch of others won't call me back. The festival is in eight days, and I'm no closer to proving what causes the Miracles than I was when I started. This is my worst movie ever."

"I don't believe that," Mama said. "That movie you made in fifth grade was much worse than this."

Rosie jerked her head up in surprise, and Mama's eyes twinkled down at her.

"I'm joking." Mama hugged Rosie's shoulders. "The documentary will turn out fantastic. You just have to keep going. What if I call Miss Matilda and talk her into helping you? She holds a lot of sway in this town. If she agrees to help, everyone else will follow."

"That might work." Rosie brightened a little.

"Do you want to show me your storyboard? We could brainstorm," Mama offered.

Rosie's chest expanded with air, and she reached for her backpack. Maybe Mama was right and her film career wasn't over yet. "I could use your help figuring out who else to interview. I've got some notes on different scenes and—"

The knock on the door startled them both.

Mama walked to the front of the house. As she opened the door, her shoulders immediately straightened. "Well, hey there."

Rosie craned her neck to see who was behind the door. It was Sheriff Parker.

"Come on in," Mama said.

Sheriff Parker stepped over the threshold.

Rosie held up her hands. "I know why you're here, but I had a permit. You signed it yourself. I wasn't doing a thing wrong filming on Magnolia Street. I didn't start the fight, and I can't help it if the Rodgers brothers won't stop arguing."

Sheriff Parker ran a hand over his hair and sighed. "In the future, I'd appreciate it if you could minimize the potential for public disturbances. The police department does have actual crimes to investigate instead of patrolling your movies."

Rosie forced herself not to roll her eyes, but only because Mama was standing right there. Obviously, she didn't want to cause a public disturbance; she only wanted to direct a film.

"But I'm not here about the fight." He turned to Mama. "We've got to close the parking lot for the Alder building tomorrow on account of the utility company needing to do some emergency line repair. I know it's last minute and folks get upset when we close things without telling them." Sheriff Parker's smile was rueful. "I wasn't sure how to inform people in advance, and you seem to know how to handle these things best."

Mama blushed. She actually *blushed*.

"I'm sorry I came by without calling," Sheriff Parker said.

"Why didn't you go see Mrs. Stevens, who's in charge of the electric department?" Rosie asked, crossing her arms.

Sheriff Parker shifted back on his heels. "Um, well, your mama is better at dealing with the public."

"We're about to eat supper and work on my storyboard,

right, Mama?" Reaching into her backpack, Rosie pulled out the folder where she kept all her documentary notes.

"Oh, I'm sure I can spare a few minutes since you came all the way over here," Mama said. "Rosie, will you go to the kitchen and check on the sauce?"

"Right now?" Rosie asked. Her hand holding the folder deflated to her side.

"Yes, right now," Mama said, still looking straight at Sheriff Parker. "We're having leftover spaghetti."

"I love leftover spaghetti," Sheriff Parker said.

"There's only enough for two people," Rosie retorted.

Mama gave her a look that could have cut through steel and gripped her arm. "Sheriff Parker, will you excuse us for a quick minute?" She pulled Rosie into the kitchen.

As soon as the kitchen door swung closed behind them, Rosie flipped up her palms. "I'm sorry, but you said we would work on my documentary and he—"

"What has gotten into you?" Mama interrupted, narrowing her eyes. "Sheriff Parker is here for work, and he needs my help. We talked about this last week. I expect you to be polite and quit acting so ugly. I'm serious, Rosie."

"Okay," Rosie said defensively, crossing her arms in front of her chest. "But are we going to work on my storyboard?"

Mama sighed. "Yes, of course we will, but I need to deal with this first." She turned and left the room.

Rosie could hear their voices murmuring as she stirred the red sauce simmering on the stove. Surely Sheriff Parker could solve a little road closure problem himself. Why did he need to come over to their house during suppertime and bother Mama when Rosie needed her help? She frowned down at the bubbles popping in the sauce, each one a mini volcanic explosion. After a moment, she tiptoed back to the edge of the kitchen and peered into the foyer.

Mama stood half a breath away from Sheriff Parker. Right then they weren't saying anything. And the way they were standing so close . . . well, it did not look like official town business. Rosie's stomach jumped like a shaky camera.

She took a step forward and cleared her throat. Sheriff Parker and Mama both looked over and took a small step back. There was a crackling in Rosie's ears like frying chicken. *Did* Mama like him?

Sheriff Parker looked left and right as if he didn't have a darn clue where to rest his eyes. He patted his pockets, pulling out a small notebook and pen. "So yes, I wanted to talk about closing the Alder parking lot. We're planning to redirect traffic to Dogwood Lane, but I was trying to decide if I should call some of the business owners tonight. I don't want to bother them in the evening."

"It might be worth a few quick calls," Mama said in a

brisk voice, glancing back at Rosie, who was still rooted to the patch of floor outside the kitchen.

Sheriff Parker backed into the doorknob. He bent down to get a better look at the faded gold lock. "This lock couldn't keep out a stiff breeze. If you wanted, I could send Nate Plodder over here to install a dead bolt. He does handyman work for our department and he's reasonable. I'd feel a whole lot better if you had a real lock on this door."

Mama smiled, and Rosie went cold. This was *their* home, no one else's. Mama and Rosie could handle real locks on their own. They didn't need Sheriff Parker's handyman friends. They could take care of everything together.

"We don't need a new lock," Rosie said, squeezing her elbows against her rib cage.

"A new lock would be nice." Mama gave Rosie a warning look.

Sheriff Parker straightened, and his head grazed the bottom of their old crystal chandelier. He was too tall for this house, for this foyer, for Mama.

A knock sounded on the front door again. Sheriff Parker opened it to reveal Henry with a worried look on his face. Rosie motioned him inside, past Mama and Sheriff Parker, who had started talking about traffic patterns.

"I saw the police car," Henry said, crossing the foyer to Rosie. "He's not here to arrest you for filming without a permit, is he?"

"No, he's here about something else," Rosie said.

She led Henry into the family room and collapsed onto one of their squishy cream couches, her legs weak and shaky. Mama was smiling up at Sheriff Parker now and laughing in the same way she always laughed with Rosie.

"Are you all right?" Henry asked.

"Fine," Rosie said, and lowered her voice. "At least I would be fine if Sheriff Parker would go away."

"He doesn't seem that bad today," Henry said, sitting down beside her.

Mama let out another peel of laughter from the foyer. Rosie cringed.

"I think he might like her . . . *romantically*," Rosie said, nodding to Sheriff Parker. She shivered, unable to even think about Mama liking him back.

Henry's eyes widened. "Sheriff Parker and Miss Caroline? Are you kidding?"

"I wish I were," Rosie grumbled.

"I'm sure he's only here about work," Henry said. "Sheriff Parker doesn't like anyone. I wouldn't worry about it."

"I guess," Rosie said quietly, turning her head and noticing Sheriff Parker weaseling his way closer to Mama.

"Hey, what happened to you today?" Henry asked.

"What do you mean?" Rosie said, tearing her gaze from the foyer.

"You were supposed to meet me at the museum so we could check out Lonnie Garrett's diary. Remember? I waited for a half hour."

Rosie clapped a hand to her head. "Henry, I'm sorry! I forgot. I was upset about filming and came straight home after the Rodgers brothers got into a fight."

"I figured," Henry said. "It's fine."

Henry picked at the stitches on the couch cushion, and Rosie knew it wasn't fine at all. Rosie slumped down, wishing she'd remembered to meet Henry. She pictured him standing by himself waiting for her and glancing at his watch every few minutes. What sort of thoughtless person forgot to meet their best friend? She couldn't get anything right today.

"We could go over there tomorrow?" Rosie offered, and Henry looked up and started to smile.

Rosie bit her lip. "No, wait. I'm interviewing Warner Carson tomorrow afternoon. Do you know he fell off the First National Bank roof sixty years ago while trying to fix a leak? He walked the next day and eventually became an Olympic high jumper. And the day after that, I'm trying to get an appointment with Dr. Rhodes. She survived a deadly dog attack when she was little and now she's a vet. I heard she can tell what's wrong with any animal. I hope she returns my calls. Her interview could be really cool. Anyway, this week is so busy. Maybe next week?"

Henry stood. "It's okay. I'll go by myself."

"Are you sure?" Rosie asked. A twinge of guilt made her look at him more closely.

Henry's smile wavered but stayed in place. "I'm sure. I know you've got a lot to do for the documentary."

"I really do," Rosie said, relieved Henry wasn't mad she'd forgotten their plans.

"I should go," Henry said, standing up and heading for the front door.

Sheriff Parker was still staring at Mama and pretending to write down answers to his unnecessary questions. And Mama . . . she was staring right back at him, not making a single move to send him on his way. Couldn't she see it was time for their spaghetti dinner and to work on the storyboard? Didn't she know this meeting had gone on much too long? Rosie closed her eyes, not wanting to see them talking or laughing together anymore.

They were only steps apart, but at that moment Rosie had never felt farther away from Mama.

CHAPTER ELEVEN

Rosie had woken up Saturday morning to the smell of sugar and strawberries. Mama had made her favorite breakfast: strawberry pecan pancakes.

They were now watching *The Parent Trap* (the original and far superior version) while eating pancakes over the coffee table. Mama and Rosie spent every Saturday morning together in just this way. They stayed in their pajamas until eleven o'clock, even if their house needed cleaning or Rosie had a school project or there was some event in town. Mama said it could wait until after their movie. Saturday-morning movies were sacred.

Everything was back to normal. Though they hadn't talked about Sheriff Parker and his visit the other day, he hadn't stopped by since. Rosie was beginning to think she'd overreacted and there was nothing romantic going on between Mama and Sheriff Parker. Thank goodness.

"You're making a big mistake. Just because you're identical twins and very cute, you should not switch places and try to fool your poor parents. There's no excuse," Mama called out. Mama liked to provide what she called "relevant commentary," while their movies were playing.

"Sugar, promise me you will never switch places with your identical twin sister," Mama said.

"As far as I know, I don't have an identical twin sister."

"Exactly. I'm glad we have our stories straight," Mama replied, double winking at Rosie.

Rosie double winked back and settled into her favorite couch cushion, the one perfectly molded to her back. She took another bite of pancakes, the tart strawberries melding with the rich maple syrup.

When the doorbell rang a few minutes later, Mama looked over at Rosie in surprise. "Who could that be? Everyone knows its Saturday-morning movie time."

"I'll get it," Rosie said, hopping out of her seat. "Press pause."

"You've seen this movie twenty times. You can repeat all the lines by heart."

"I still don't want to miss any of them," Rosie called back.

Cam waited on the front stoop, her hands in her pockets. "Sorry to interrupt the movie."

Rosie opened the door wider. "Come on in. Mama made pancakes if you're hungry."

Just then Betsy hurried down the sidewalk, clutching a paper bag from Sook Diner and a small shovel with a red handle. She was headed in the opposite direction of her house.

Rosie waved. "You're going the wrong way."

Betsy held up the shovel and kept up her brisk pace. "Mr. Blandstone forgot this outside Sook Diner, and I'm returning it. But if you see Miss Matilda, don't mention I found it right next to the new hole beside her dumpster."

"This town has treasure fever." Rosie laughed and turned back to Cam.

But Cam didn't crack a smile. "I wanted to talk to you about the reenactment."

Rosie knew all documentaries needed at least one good reenactment. She planned to re-create Tom Bolling's Miracle save from a near drowning. Rosie pictured his head sinking beneath the surface like a waterlogged leaf until a bright yellow raft appeared from out of nowhere to save his life. According to Mama, no one could ever explain where the raft came from.

"I've got Perry Cabell from down the block all set to play Tom. He's eight but pretty small for his age, so I think it will work," Rosie said, tapping her fingers against the door.

"I was wondering if we could switch the time."

"There's no way you've got soccer practice tonight," Rosie said.

"It's not that. It's . . . something else. Remember how I'm spending the night with Leila?" Cam asked, staring at the brick steps.

Rosie went still. She didn't remember, and Cam hadn't mentioned it all week.

"She invited some guys from the soccer team to come over and hang out earlier. I think we're having pizza and watching a movie, maybe kicking the ball around in Leila's backyard. Anyway, it starts at four." Cam looked up and finally met Rosie's eyes.

Rosie's face burned hot. "That sounds fun," she said in a weird, fake voice.

"I want to help you though," Cam said, taking her hands out of her pockets before shoving them back in. "Could we do the reenactment earlier?"

"Perry has peewee football, so we can't move the time."

"Oh," Cam whispered.

The silence between them was thicker than Brunswick stew. Rosie didn't know where to look or what to say. It was as if she were talking to someone she barely knew instead of her best friend.

Rosie pulled at the sleeve of her pajamas. "If you'd rather go to the party, you should go. It's fine."

"I'll skip the party," Cam said, her entire body stiff.

Cam stared at a point over Rosie's shoulder. Though Cam had said the right thing, Rosie knew she didn't mean it.

"I can tell you don't want to miss it," Rosie said.

"I didn't say that," Cam said, sounding angry.

Rosie pressed her nails into her palms, focusing on the pricks of pain in her hands instead of the pricks of tears behind her eyes. "You should go to Leila's. It's not like you believe in the Miracles anyway."

Cam sighed. "All I said was I wanted more proof."

"What do you think I'm trying to do with the documentary?" Rosie asked, her voice rising.

"Have you found out what causes the Miracles yet?" Cam asked.

Rosie remained silent. She wished she could edit herself out of this entire conversation.

"That's what I thought," Cam said. "I get why you want to make the documentary, for your dad. But face it: you're not going to prove the Miracles are real."

Rosie sucked in her cheeks. Cam sounded like such a know-it-all.

"I'm sorry I haven't figured it all out yet. Maybe your new friends at Leila's party know the answers," Rosie said sarcastically.

"I doubt that." Cam snorted. "I'm pretty sure none of them are thinking about the Miracles."

Because thinking about the Miracles is immature. That was what Cam really meant. She meant Rosie was immature. Maybe she was right.

Rosie's chin trembled. Cam was skipping the reenactment and had deserted Rosie at the town meeting last week. Rosie was losing her best friend to Leila and parties and the Lounge. Her chest ached as if something had cracked inside her. Unlike the characters in her films, she couldn't direct Cam into wanting to hang out with her, as much as she wished she could.

"You know what? I've got Henry to help me, and we don't need you for the reenactment," Rosie blurted out.

As soon as Rosie said the words, she wanted to take them back. She did need Cam, same as always. But Cam was already stepping backward off the steps, looking relieved.

"If you feel that way, I guess I will go to Leila's, then," Cam said.

Rosie wanted to tell Cam she didn't mean it. She wanted to beg Cam to stay, but that would only make her sound more pathetic. She went into the house and closed the door before Cam saw her watery eyes.

Rosie leaned against the window, her chest hitching

up and down. Cam would rather hang out with Leila than work on her babyish film project. It made sense. Cam was getting invited to parties with boys, and Rosie was still stuck watching movies with Mama and riding her bike to a homemade film set.

"Rosie, what's wrong?" Mama asked from the doorway of the family room.

Rosie swiped at her eyes. "That was Cam. She can't help with the reenactment. She has to go to a party."

Mama crossed the foyer and put her arms around Rosie. "Oh, sugar, I'm sorry."

Rosie leaned into Mama, trying not to cry. "She doesn't even like me anymore."

"Of course she likes you," Mama said, patting Rosie's back and pulling her closer.

"She's embarrassed by me. I can tell she thinks the documentary is stupid," Rosie said, sniffling.

"It's not stupid," Mama said. "And you're not embarrassing."

"You have to say that because you're my mother."

"Not true. I would definitely admit if you embarrassed me," Mama said, pulling back and smiling down at Rosie. Her deep brown eyes shone bright, as if she too were holding back tears. "Cam loves you. I can tell. You'll work through this."

Rosie exhaled and looked up at Mama. "You mean it?"

"I do."

The tension left Rosie's shoulders. "Thanks, Mama."

"Plus, there's nothing embarrassing about doing the things you're passionate about, especially when you're an incredibly talented filmmaker who also happens to be thoughtful and loyal and a good person," Mama added.

Rosie lowered her eyes. A sour taste flooded her mouth. Mama was wrong about a few things—Rosie wasn't thoughtful and loyal and good. She was lying to Mama every time she didn't tell her the real reason for the documentary and about the e-mail. Her secret plan to bring Michael to Glimmer Creek weighed her down like a rusted anchor at the bottom of the river.

Michael still hadn't e-mailed her back, and Rosie was starting to wonder if he ever would. She'd even tried to contact the film set but couldn't find a phone number and had left messages with the production company instead, all of which went unreturned. What if all of this—the lying, the documentary, the reenactments—was for nothing? A pit cratered Rosie's stomach, and she turned away, biting the inside of her cheek. All she wanted to do was tell Mama the truth about everything.

CHAPTER TWELVE

At four o'clock, the beach in front of the Bolling house was half-washed away by high tide. The dock tilted to one side like a tired old man leaning on his cane. In the distance, the top of at least ten snorkels poked out of the water. Rosie had heard people were diving in the smaller creeks in search of the train treasure. Not that anyone was having any luck.

"When can I jump in?" Perry asked for the tenth time, pacing the dock in his bright red bathing suit and seemingly unaffected by the fact that it was only fifty degrees out. "Mama said I have to wait until you say so, but I've been waiting for hours."

"It's been five minutes," Rosie said.

"My, he has a lot of energy," Mrs. Bolling said. White whorls of hair framed her pink cheeks. "My grandson, Tom, was just like him."

"I wish I could interview Tom for the documentary," Rosie said wistfully.

"It's too bad he's away at college on a swimming scholarship. Ever since his Miracle, that child can hold his breath underwater for fifteen minutes." Mrs. Bolling gazed out at the water, not saying anything for a long moment. "You know I was at the town meeting."

Rosie's head shot up. "You don't have to worry, ma'am. I'm making the documentary very tasteful."

Mrs. Bolling chuckled. "Oh, I'm not worried about that. Though I did get to thinking. Do you know Bob Thornquist moved here after his cousin Bill told him about our Miracles? He thought he might get one of his own if he lived in Glimmer Creek. Bob left after a few months. Never did fit in. We've had a few people try that over the years, mostly folks from Gloster. They never do manage to get a Miracle either."

"I already promised not to put the documentary online," Rosie reassured Mrs. Bolling. "So I don't think a bunch of people are going to see it and move here if that's what you're worried about."

"I don't understand how that all works," Mrs. Bolling said, lifting one shoulder. "I do know there's a heap of good things about this here town. Things we can't explain, but that we don't want to change."

Rosie drew her eyebrows together, unable to think of anything else to say. She thought Glimmer Creek was a great place to live too. Besides the Miracles, it had the water nearby, an awesome bookstore, and the best crab cakes in Eastern Virginia. Rosie's documentary wasn't going to change any of those things, so she wasn't sure why Mrs. Bolling was acting so concerned.

Rosie sagged with relief when she spotted Henry and Miss Betty waving from the top of the driveway. "Oh look, there's Henry. Now we can get started."

Henry and Miss Betty made their way down the slope, past a large weeping willow tree in the center of the yard and a bed of violets huddled in a curve of the concrete.

"Mama wanted to see the set today," Henry said.

Miss Betty patted her emerald-green turban and peered down at the water splashing against the beach in gentle waves. "Henry George Thompson, you are *not* getting in this water. It's obviously freezing, and you are prone to chills."

"Mama, I already told you I'm not getting in the water." Henry sighed.

"I am," Perry yelled from the dock.

Miss Betty's hand fluttered up to her chest.

"His mama knows all about it," Rosie said quickly. "She said the cold would be good for him."

"I'm sure Clara knows what she's doing, though I guess she's never heard of hypothermia," Miss Betty said.

"The water is warmer than the air," Henry said. "It's because bodies of water are slower to cool than the land." Miss Betty shot him a bullet-fast look, and Henry hastily continued. "Not that I'm going to find out."

Mrs. Bolling's lips tipped up in a soft smile. "It was a day a lot like this when Tom fell in the water. That fool boy was never supposed to be out here in the first place, but he was trying to catch a rockfish for his daddy's supper. You see, he'd been deployed overseas and was due back that night. Rockfish is his favorite." Mrs. Bolling shook her head. "If that Miracle hadn't happened, we would have lost our Tom. I like to think his granddaddy was watching over him that day. Tom was wearing his granddaddy's army dog tags when he fell in. Richard wore those all through World War II and came home safe. They're a lucky charm."

Rosie perked up. *A lucky charm*. Maybe that was the secret of the Miracles. You had to have a lucky charm. Although—Rosie slumped back down—no one else had mentioned a lucky charm in their interview.

"Well, lucky charm or not, the Miracle is what really saved your Tom. This town is blessed," Miss Betty said, nodding her head and sending her turban bobbing. "Now, y'all have fun here. I'm going home to lie down for a while."

Henry stepped closer to Miss Betty, turning his body toward her as if to block the breeze. A fissure split through

Rosie. It wasn't fair Miss Betty had gotten sick and Henry had to worry about losing his mama.

Rosie had always thought the Miracles were wonderful, but no magic had come to help Miss Betty yet. She had to go through months of awful treatments, and she still wasn't well. Maybe the Miracles weren't as perfect as Rosie had always believed.

"Your treatments are going well?" Mrs. Bolling asked.

"Only one more left," Miss Betty said.

"She's doing great," Henry said in a firm voice.

"That's wonderful news," Mrs. Bolling said. "If anyone can beat cancer, it's you. Your maiden name *is* Gooch, and Gooches are born determined."

"That's a fact," Miss Betty said, nodding seriously. "When my granddaddy was the First Baptist Church pastor, he'd send around the offering plate three times if he didn't get a good collection."

Miss Betty started up the hill with Mrs. Bolling, moving slowly, as if the effort to put one foot in front of the other cost her. Henry watched, his body tense until she reached the top. Rosie tried to imagine how she would feel if Mama had gotten sick like Miss Betty. Her stomach turned over. She couldn't even stand to have such a thought prowling around inside her head.

"Hi, Henry," Perry said, hopping over a broken board

and onto the beach in front of them. Seaweed and sticks littered the white sand. "I trapped a stinkbug yesterday like the ones I helped you catch for your science project last year. Do you want it?"

Henry shook his head, placing one foot gingerly on the dock now that Miss Betty was gone. "No, thanks. I'm not entering the science fair this year."

Rosie looked up from the camcorder. "You're not?"

"Not this year." Henry took another step on the dock and wobbled to one side.

"But you enter the science fair every year," Rosie said. "And you *win* the science fair every year. Well, except for that year Robert Kim talked about black holes."

"I just don't want to do it, okay?" Henry didn't turn around.

"Th-that doesn't make any sense," Rosie said, sputtering. "The science fair is like your Academy Awards."

"I've got a lot of other stuff going on right now," Henry said.

"Like what?" Rosie asked.

Henry went still. "I'm researching the train treasure," he finally mumbled.

"Instead of the science fair?" Rosie gaped at him.

Henry turned to look at her. "I know the treasure seems ridiculous, but sometimes you have to go with your gut. That's what I'm doing. It's like you with the Miracles and your father."

Except Rosie's gut was all jumbled up when she thought about the Miracles and her father. Neither was turning out the way she wanted. She stared down at the blades of grass poking her shins. A breeze wafted between them, smelling of wet earth and smoke, as the water lapped against the riprap with a soft splashing sound.

"Are we still waiting on Cam?" Henry asked.

"She's not coming. She went to a slumber party at Leila's." Rosie bent down and fiddled with the camera lens. "I told her it was okay."

"*Is* it okay?" Henry asked.

"It's fine." Rosie had thought about what Mama said earlier concerning Cam and believed it, mostly, but Cam's decision still smarted. It was one more ingredient in the mixed-up mess inside of her. "I don't mind if she wants to hang out with Leila and stop helping me with my films."

"Cam doesn't want to stop helping you," Henry protested.

"She seems to have other things to do these days," Rosie said, straightening and staring ahead.

"Didn't she help with filming Mrs. Grant this week?" Henry asked.

"Sort of."

"And with some of the interviews the week before that?"

"I guess."

"So because she couldn't come to this one scene, now you decided she doesn't want to help? Come on, that's crazy. Cam always helps. She's our best friend."

Well.

When Henry put it like that, Cam's absence didn't seem *so* awful. The last bit of doubt about Cam fluttered away like the brown and green leaves drifting down around them. Rosie tipped her face up to feel the sunshine, the warmth settling onto her face.

Henry and Mama were both right. Of course Cam would help Rosie with the documentary, and once it was done . . . Rosie imagined a high-angle shot looking down on a crowd of everyone in Glimmer Creek: the closing credits rolled and applause rose. People exclaimed over how she, Rosie Flynn, had solved the mystery of the Miracles. She could see Mama telling everyone her daughter was all grown up now. There was Henry clapping her on the shoulder and Cam bragging about her to Leila Sellers. One after another, the people of Glimmer Creek came forward to congratulate her. And there, right in the front, was her father clapping as if he would never stop. Rosie's hands tightened on her shirttail. He would e-mail back. She couldn't think otherwise.

Rosie bustled around the camera. "You know, just because you get straight As every year doesn't mean you're right about everything."

Henry's eyed widened. "Shoot, Rosie, I know that."

"I'm kidding," Rosie said, bumping him with her shoulder. "I'll call Cam tomorrow and let her know about the next interview."

Henry grabbed the yellow inflatable and headed down the dock. "I'm going to get in position."

"Is it time for me to jump in now?" Perry asked from the end of the dock.

"Almost." Rosie adjusted the camera lens. She was starting with a wide-angle shot to capture the vast expanse of water, the dock, and Perry. Once he fell in, she would zoom in on him splashing around and calling for help. The problem was she had only one chance to get it right. It wasn't as though she could dry Perry off and start over again, so she'd tried to give him all the direction he needed in advance. Victor Fleming, the director of *The Wizard of Oz*, had treated young actors like adults, and Rosie believed in the same philosophy.

"Okay, Perry, on my cue, pretend to fall in like we talked about. And . . . action!" Rosie yelled, pointing to Perry.

Perry teetered on the edge of the dock before plunging

into the water with a terrific splash. Rosie smiled. He had nailed it. She tightened the frame to a close shot of Perry's head and shoulders. Water was splashing everywhere as he flailed his arms around and yelled—"Help! Help!" This kid deserved an Oscar.

"Hey, hey there! Someone help him!"

Rosie whipped her head up when she heard the yelling from two docks over. Two men dropped the crab pots they were fussing with and dove into the water. *Oh no!* They thought Perry was really drowning.

Instead of stopping everything, Rosie sped up. All she needed to do was get her final shot before the men reached Perry. She was so close.

"Henry, drop the raft," Rosie shouted.

Henry gestured to the two men swimming toward them. "But—"

"Just do it!" Rosie said.

Henry dropped the raft into the water, nowhere close to Perry.

"For goodness' sake, push it closer to him," Rosie yelled in an exasperated voice.

Henry got down on his hands and knees, reaching for the yellow float. Rosie panned the camera over the water, keeping Henry out of the frame. She needed to capture the raft gliding toward Perry as if by magic. Henry kept reaching, his hands outstretched. Rosie held her breath. Almost there.

Splash! Henry toppled face-first into the water. Rosie banged her forehead against the camera lens. The raft looked the opposite of magical now that it was holding up a screaming Henry.

The men reached Perry and lifted him onto the dock as he struggled against them and tried to explain he was the freestyle champion of his age group. The docks on either side had filled with people pointing in their direction. After a couple of tries, Henry clambered onto the dock and lay flat on his back. Miss Betty was going to kill him for getting wet, right after she killed Rosie.

With a heavy sigh, Rosie cut off the recording, collapsing on the edge of the bulkhead. Her legs dangled over the side. Pressing her fingers into her temple, she rubbed them in circles. She'd be lucky if there was one second of usable footage.

By the time Rosie finished apologizing to the men who'd jumped into the water to save Perry and apologizing to Mrs. Bolling for causing a disturbance, her throat was raw, as if fire ants had stung it in a hundred places.

Rosie trudged home and went straight into the study. Sinking into the desk chair, she booted up Mama's computer and waited. She should e-mail the footage from today to Cam. That would really make her glad she'd missed the reenactment.

As she clicked on her e-mail icon, Rosie's breath caught in her throat. She had a new e-mail and had to read the name on the sender line three times before it sank in. It was from Michael Weatherton. The hum of the furnace, the banging of Mama's pots, and the murmur of television voices from the family room faded away.

> Dear Ms. Flynn,
> Michael Weatherton received your e-mail. Though extremely busy with his filming schedule and publicity obligations, he looks forward to attending your documentary screening on October 21st. He asked me to convey his gratitude for the invitation.
>
> Sincerely,
> Lawrence A. Walker
> Executive Assistant to Michael Weatherton

Rosie didn't move. Tingles rushed up her arms and legs. Her plan had actually worked. Her father was coming! Her father was coming in six days . . . to see a documentary that didn't exist.

Yet.

CHAPTER THIRTEEN

It was impossible to eat at a time like this. Rosie ignored the waffles Mama had left out on Monday morning. She still couldn't believe her father was coming to Glimmer Creek. It was less than a week before she finally met the person she'd wanted to meet her entire life, and she couldn't wait.

Although . . . Rosie wasn't sure why Michael hadn't e-mailed her himself. This was the very first time she'd contacted him, after all. He could have taken a few minutes to e-mail back. Still, he was coming to her premiere; that was the important thing. The bigger problem was figuring out a way to tell Mama. She imagined Mama's face in extreme close-up when she saw Michael and Rosie together at the festival. Would her forehead furrow with worry, would her mouth fall open with betrayal and shock, or would her eyes look sad? Rosie shivered and shook the images from her mind. Right now she needed to concentrate on finishing the documentary. She would figure Mama out later.

Rosie opened her spiral notebook to the storyboard of scenes. Skimming the list of cutaways and interviews and live-action features she intended to do, she froze. For one second she worried she might throw up. It was worse than she thought. She didn't have a single completed scene.

How was it possible for a one-girl film crew to be this far behind on production? Rosie had shot snippets of interviews with Mr. Waverman, Mr. Carson, and Mrs. Grant that *maybe* could work with a lot of cutting. Dr. Rhodes and Deputy Cordell had canceled their interviews, both claiming they weren't sure a documentary about the Miracles was good for the town. Mrs. Dellarose and Mrs. Vickers refused to return her calls. Her demonstration scene with the Rodgers brothers had ended in a fistfight, and her reenactment was a total disaster. She hadn't even started editing yet because there was nothing to edit.

If that wasn't bad enough, the entire point of the documentary was to prove what caused the Miracles, but she still didn't have a single clue how to do that. Cam's words about the Miracles—they were only based on luck—kept running through her head during every interview. What if she was right? Rosie's arms itched as if covered in poison ivy. Keeping all this bottled up inside was enough to make her explode.

The hands on the kitchen clock clicked to eight, and Rosie propped her chin in her hands, trying to think. It was almost time to leave for school. An entire day spent staring at a blackboard was the exact opposite of what she needed. She had to interview Mrs. Davis and Mrs. Moore, refilm the Rodgers brothers, and come up with another live-action sequence. She wanted more time, period, and there was no one to help. She and Cam had made up yesterday, but Cam had soccer practice every afternoon this week and a big game on Thursday. Meanwhile, Henry was still occupied with his impossible treasure hunt. Even Mama was busier than normal getting ready for the festival on Friday. Rosie had to get this documentary finished on her own.

Suddenly, an idea popped into Rosie's brain, and her eyes widened with its terribleness and its brilliance. What if she skipped the first few periods of school to work on the documentary? It wasn't as though she was missing an entire day, and she *was* working on something valuable to the community.

But no way Mama would understand or allow it, which meant Rosie had to call the school, impersonate Mama, and claim she had a doctor's appointment. It was almost too bad to even think about doing. If she got caught, she'd get grounded for the rest of her life. But if she didn't do it, she might not finish the documentary. And if she didn't finish the documentary . . . well, Rosie couldn't even consider that possibility. Not finishing wasn't an option. There was obviously no choice. She was getting this documentary done no matter what it took.

Later that afternoon, a wall of windows scattered sunlight over the crumbs on the linoleum floor of the cafeteria. The muffled shouts and laughter of the other students rose in waves around her. Glancing over at the double doors, Rosie half expected Sheriff Parker to burst in and arrest her for skipping school that morning.

Scanning the room, Rosie searched for Henry and Cam. Kara and Melanie were at one table, and Libby and Mary were at another—all fine lunch companions on any other day. They were what Mama called sometimes friends. Rosie sat with them at lunch sometimes and invited them to sleepovers sometimes and chose them for partners in class sometimes. They were perfectly nice. Still, a girl did not share secrets with sometimes friends. A girl shared secrets only with her best friends, and Rosie needed hers now. Though she'd gotten two more interviews done, she still wasn't sure how she was going to finish her documentary in four days unless she skipped a lot more school.

Principal Bradley stopped at a nearby table. "Daniel, you're just the gentleman I'm looking for."

Danny scrambled to his feet, abandoning the chocolate milk he was trying to drink through a straw in his nose. "Yes, sir?"

"Someone stole the answer key for Mrs. Burdon's third-period pre-algebra test. You're in Mrs. Burdon's third-period pre-algebra class. You wouldn't know anything about that, would you?" Principal Bradley asked.

"Me? No, sir," Danny said, but he was shifting back and forth on his feet like there were fire ants caught in his tennis shoes.

People whispered about Principal Bradley ever since he'd come back from the Vietnam War. He'd gotten himself captured, interrogated, and nearly died over there. Folks called his return home a Miracle. They also said he could now see a lie coming from a mile downriver. Poor Danny Kopinski stood only twelve inches away.

Principal Bradley adjusted his wire-rimmed glasses. "Follow me, Daniel. I do believe we need to search your locker now."

Danny hung his head and followed Principal Bradley down the aisle between the rows of blue plastic cafeteria chairs. "I'm sorry, sir. The answer key is underneath my math book. My daddy says I have a lying affliction."

"Well, we will call him to discuss that," Principal Bradley said.

A hand tapped Rosie's shoulder. She twirled around and brightened when she saw Cam standing beside her.

"I'm so glad you're here," Rosie said in a rush.

Cam wrinkled her forehead. "You weren't in second period. Is everything okay?"

"Not really." Rosie took a deep breath, ready to pour out everything.

But at that moment, Henry rushed up to them, his blond hair flopping into his eyes. "HenRoCam right now!" He motioned them to a nearby empty table and flung himself into a seat, out of breath.

"Subject?" Cam asked, raising her eyebrows at Rosie to ask what was going on.

Rosie shook her head. She had no idea.

"Are you okay?" Rosie asked.

"Better than okay. I figured out where the train treasure is. I mean I'm not positive, but I'm pretty sure. I'd give it a fifty percent possibility, maybe sixty," Henry said.

Rosie bit the inside of her cheek. Not this again.

"Are you sure it's not sixty-two percent?" Cam asked in a joking voice.

"It could be sixty-two," Henry said seriously.

"Leila's brother is on the varsity basketball team, and she said they've made it their team mission to find the treasure," Cam said. "They rescheduled two entire practices to dig in their parents' backyards."

"What does basketball have to do with treasure hunting?" Rosie asked.

"I guess it's not directly related, but Leila says they're really determined. They did win regionals last year," Cam said defensively.

"Well, Anna Lee's cousin's boyfriend is an archaeologist and he might come out next week to look for the treasure. Archaeologists know how to search for ancient artifacts, so I think he has a better chance of finding the treasure than Leila's brother," Rosie shot back.

"None of them matter because I already know where it is." Henry hesitated, looking left and right before lowering his voice. "It's buried in the old graveyard at First Presbyterian Church beneath that oak tree that's right in the middle."

"The treasure is in a graveyard?" Rosie's question was coated in a thick layer of disbelief.

"It's a long story," Henry said. "But I found out the graveyard is where Lonnie and his girlfriend used to meet at night."

"We can't go to every place in Glimmer Creek where Lonnie hung out," Rosie said.

"This is a *special* place. I've spent weeks researching

Lonnie's life and reading his journal and old newspaper articles about him. This is the place," Henry said urgently. "We can go over there tonight when no one will see us and dig around the tree. My daddy has two shovels—"

"Henry," Rosie cut him off. "We can't dig a bunch of holes in the middle of a church graveyard at night. We'd get in so much trouble. You heard Mayor Grant at the town meeting. We could get arrested."

"But—but there's no other way to get the treasure," Henry said.

"What if we tell Mayor Grant what you found?" Cam asked. "Let the town look into it."

"No way." Henry kneaded his temple. "We can't tell anyone else. We'd have to share the treasure, and we need that money."

The intensity in Henry's voice made Rosie sit up straight. His eyes glittered as they captured light from the fluorescent bulbs overhead. Why did Henry *need* money?

Cam blew out a breath. "Look, it's fun to imagine we're going to find a million-dollar treasure, but it's not going to happen."

"Is that what you think?" Henry turned to Rosie. Were those tears in his eyes?

Rosie shifted in her seat. "I—I . . . maybe."

Henry blinked, and three long seconds passed. He

then set his shoulders. "I'm digging for the train treasure tonight at eleven o'clock. If you're my friends, you'll meet me there." He surged to his feet and stomped out of the cafeteria.

Cam and Rosie stared after Henry.

"He wants us to sneak out on a school night and dig for buried treasure on church property. What is he thinking?" Cam asked. "He won't even cut through Mr. Gooch's cornfield because he's afraid of trespassing, and Mr. Gooch is his great-uncle."

Rosie frowned. "I'm worried about him. He isn't entering the science fair this year, and did you hear what he said about needing money? What's that all about?"

"I don't know." Cam blew out a breath. "He's not acting like himself. We need to figure out what's going on."

"We can break into his room and search for clues," Rosie suggested.

"Or we could talk to him first," Cam said.

"Sure, all right," Rosie said, nodding. "If we both confront him, he'll have to tell us what's wrong. We can do it tonight when we're at the graveyard."

"Are we really going to do that?" Cam made a pained face.

"I don't think we have a choice. We can't leave him there all by himself." Rosie couldn't shake a sense of unease at Henry's expression before he left the cafeteria. It seemed like something a lot worse than them not believing in the treasure was bothering him. Something a lot worse was worrying her, too. She turned to Cam. "I really need to talk to you about the documentary. I—"

"Cam!"

The voice came from the right. Leila Sellers waved from a nearby table. Another interruption. The knot in Rosie's gut twisted tighter.

"Come over," Leila called.

Cam waved back and stood, a huge smile lighting up her face. She pulled Rosie up. "Come on," she whispered, and led her to Leila's table.

"Scoot down, Bailey," Leila said. "Both of you, sit." She patted the two seats now available beside her.

Cam sank down into the seat beside Leila, and Rosie took the chair on Cam's other side. It felt as if everyone in the room were staring at them. This table was the prime table in the cafeteria, the one closest to the doors with the best view of the courtyard. Across from Rosie sat Macon, the school president. She owned a real suit jacket and wore it for her school-wide speeches. Macon sat beside Aimee, the most beautiful girl in the entire school, with shiny black hair and dark eyes.

Leila leaned around Cam to examine Rosie. "Hi."

"This is Rosie," Cam said.

Leila didn't introduce herself. She probably figured Rosie already knew who she was.

"You and Cam are neighbors, right?" Leila asked.

"Y-yes." Rosie nearly choked on her response. Was that how Cam had described her to Leila—as her neighbor instead of her lifelong best friend?

"We've got the first doughnut fund-raiser after school today. You'll be there?" Leila asked Cam.

"I wouldn't miss it," Cam said.

"We have to raise enough money to bring in real pizzas on Friday instead of that cardboard stuff the cafeteria makes," Macon said, wrinkling her nose.

"Then let's make sure Turner doesn't eat all the chocolate glazed this time," Aimee said, rolling her eyes.

"Are you coming?" Leila asked Rosie. "We're looking for customers."

Rosie jumped a little in her seat, caught off guard by the question. "Oh. I—I don't know. Maybe."

"Rosie has a lot of stuff going on in the afternoons. She probably can't make it this time," Cam said.

Rosie's arms locked up. Cam didn't seem to want her at the doughnut fund-raiser. Was it because she thought Rosie would embarrass her around her new friends?

Leila shrugged and turned back to Cam. "We were

talking about Saturday night, and we all decided Chase Corrigan definitely likes you."

Rosie's mouth fell open in shock. *Chase Corrigan?* Cam knew Rosie had had a crush on Chase since first grade.

"He was practically ready to kiss you," Aimee said.

Cam glanced at Rosie for an instant. "We were only talking."

"I want someone to talk that close to me," Aimee said, tossing impossibly glossy locks over her shoulder. "He shared his popcorn with you."

"He was being nice," Cam said.

"Chase Corrigan is really cute for a seventh grader," Macon added.

"You should go for it," Leila said, nudging Cam.

Cam's gaze brushed against Rosie's cheek again. "I don't think so."

Rosie fixed her gaze on the table and tried not to flinch at each new bit of information. She and Cam used to tell each other everything, but Rosie knew nothing about Leila's party or Chase. Instead, she was the one standing on the outside of Cam's new circle.

"Next time we need to watch another horror movie. Everyone liked it," Macon said.

"Well, everyone except for Mr. Moose," Aimee replied with a sly smile.

Leila burst out laughing. "Oh my God! When Turner threw him in the air—"

"And he got stuck on the fan—"

"And then James was spinning him around—"

Cam sputtered with laughter, along with the other three girls.

Rosie sat motionless in her seat, her face stuck in a fake, unnatural smile. No one bothered to explain the joke to her, not even Cam. They ignored her completely. It was as if her body had disappeared. She wished she could disappear for real.

After several more seconds of laughter, Cam finally remembered there was another person at the table and said, "Rosie can tell you what horror movie to watch next. She knows everything about movies."

"Really?" Leila said, not sounding that interested. "Which one do you think is the best?"

Rosie froze as all four girls turned to stare at her. Her mouth went dry. She had to say something clever, something to impress them. "Um . . . I like the classics best, and some of the old horror movies are terrifying. Personally, I think Hitchcock's *Psycho* was the most suspenseful film ever made. Or you could watch a lesser-known but equally scary movie called *The Innocents* about a nanny and her possessed children. It's more psychological horror. Another one of my favorites is *The Haunting*. It's good old-fashioned fear with no blood or gore. Just make sure you don't watch the terrible 1999 remake with Catherine Zeta-Jones and Liam Neeson."

The table went silent.

Leila cleared her throat. "I rented *The Haunting* remake last Saturday night. I liked it."

Rosie's cheeks blazed with heat. "Oh. Well. I was talking mostly about critics. Critics always say remakes aren't as good, but most critics are really frustrated and want to criticize everything, which is probably why they became critics in the first place. I'm not a big fan of critics or criticism or—" Rosie pressed her lips together to stop babbling. She sounded like a lunatic.

The girls stared at her, their mouths turned down. They didn't say a word, but Rosie could tell they were all thinking the same thing, even Cam. Rosie Flynn was an uncool disaster who shouldn't be sitting anywhere near them.

"What are we going to do about the Gloster team's high-pressure defensive line this Thursday?" Cam said to Leila, twisting away from Rosie.

"I've been thinking about that," Leila said. "If we move the ball from one side of the field to the other and draw their defenders out of position, we can create a gap in the midfield and move forward that way."

Aimee sighed. "All y'all talk about is soccer."

"We've got to talk strategy. We need a miracle to win this game," Leila said.

Macon smirked. "Awww, are you asking for a Glimmer Creek Miracle?"

"Please," Leila said in a dismissive tone and rolled her eyes. "I'm not five."

Rosie stood and backed away from the table. She'd gotten dropped into a tank of sharks with vicious teeth made up of unsaid words and French braids, and she had to get out.

The girls kept talking. Cam looked up, but when Rosie met her eyes, they shuttered closed with a flick of her lids, and Cam turned away.

Whipping her head in the opposite direction, Rosie turned on her toe and pushed her way through the tables. Tears hovered on the tips of her lashes. Had Cam become a sometimes friend, or were they no longer friends at all?

CHAPTER FOURTEEN

Later that day, Rosie was trying to edit her documentary without much luck. Water dripped from the faucet in a slow and insistent drip-drop rhythm. The late-afternoon sun sliced a single beam of sharp-edged light across the kitchen table. It did nothing to brighten up the room. She kept staring at the crooked slant of one kitchen cabinet, her mind spiraling back around to the moment Cam had turned her back on Rosie in the cafeteria. Afterward, Rosie had rushed off to the bathroom, where she'd slipped into a stall and stared hard at the glinting silver lock on the door until she was sure she wasn't going to cry.

Mama came home, bursting into the kitchen with two bags of groceries and talking in one long stream of words. "I picked up Sadie's she-crab soup for dinner. I've got rolls from Hardaway Market. I've got sugar cookies from Sook Diner. Who's the best mother in the entire world?"

"You are," Rosie said in a barely audible voice.

Mama crossed to the sink and tugged at the faucet.

"That's about as sincere as Anna Lee offering to come in early."

"Anna Lee offered to come in early?"

"It was less of an offer, more of a grudging agreement after telling me she's frustrated with the patriarchal stereo-type of women serving as secretaries. But once I reminded her that being a secretary is actually the main part of her job description, she finally agreed. She looked about as happy as you do right now." Mama slammed her hand down on the counter. "Shoot! The faucet is leaking again. There's water all over the counter."

"I could try to fix it," Rosie offered. "My hands are really strong from holding my camcorder."

"It's all right. I'll call the plumber. But if he over-charges me this time, I'm going to spray him with this fau-cet," Mama joked, but her forehead wrinkled like a piece of crumpled paper.

Rosie's gaze fell on her expensive camcorder across the room. She bet her father didn't worry about paying for broken faucets. He probably didn't even have to hire a plumber himself. He had an assistant who could take care of things he didn't want to bother with, like plumber appointments and e-mailing his daughter.

"Enough about the faucet." Mama dropped into the seat beside Rosie. "What's wrong?"

Rosie shrugged. "Nothing."

Mama tilted her head, examining Rosie's face. "I don't believe that."

Rosie couldn't bring herself to tell Mama about the cafeteria. It was too humiliating. Even thinking about it now, her face heated up as she remembered how idiotic she'd sounded and the way Cam hadn't stood up with her. Mama wouldn't understand the importance of a cafeteria table. It sounded stupid even though it wasn't, and talking about it only made it bigger and more real.

"Is this about Cam again?" Mama asked.

Rosie bowed her head. Mama remained in her seat, for once not saying anything.

"Everything is different," Rosie finally blurted out. "Cam is busy with soccer and her new friends, and Henry is always studying or doing research. No one wants to help me with my films, and I—I miss when it was the three of us playing outside by ourselves. Summer seems so far away already."

Mama's gaze softened. "I don't blame you. You had a lot of good times together. Cam and Henry are like family."

"Not anymore. It feels like our friendship is over." Rosie's head drooped.

Mama tipped up Rosie's chin. "Just because everything isn't exactly the same way it was doesn't mean your friendship is over. It means it's changing, and that's okay. That's life. Lots of things are going to change as you get older, and sometimes it's good and sometimes it's bad. Sometimes it's both. The only thing in life that doesn't change is change."

"Change stinks," Rosie said.

"It's not worth giving up your friends over though."

"I'm not giving anything up," Rosie protested. "They are!"

"If you decide not to fight for your friendship, you're giving up."

Rosie opened and closed her mouth. She wanted to yell that Mama didn't understand, couldn't understand, but no words emerged. Mama hadn't seen how Cam had cut her to bits in the cafeteria with a flick of her eyes. She didn't know how it was in seventh grade.

Mama stood, pulled a plastic container filled with Sadie Dellarose's she-crab soup from a grocery bag, and set it on the counter. Pouring a measure of cinnamon-colored liquid into one of their chipped bowls, she spoke again. "Cam and Henry have worked on all your movies, even this latest documentary. They've also listened to you and helped you for years. If they don't have time to do everything you want anymore, that doesn't mean they aren't good friends. It means you have to work a little harder to spend time with them, but you don't stop being someone's friend because things get hard. That's not the way I raised you." Mama carried the bowl over to Rosie with a spoon.

Rosie took a small sip. The warmth traveled down her throat and into her stomach, where it spread through her body. Her shoulders relaxed. She took a larger spoonful.

Rosie didn't know if Mama was right, but maybe, *maybe* she wasn't wrong.

After slurping down most of her soup, Rosie's mood had lightened considerably. Mrs. Dellarose had gotten Miracled as a kid. She'd come down with an awful stomach sickness and nearly died. She'd even given away all her toys to her little sister. When she miraculously recovered, she was left with a special knack for cooking. Everyone said her she-crab soup had a touch of magic in each bowl and made you feel like the worst thing in the world hadn't actually happened to you. It just worked for Rosie . . . or had it?

Rosie toyed with her spoon, staring down at the remains of her soup. "Mama, do you—well, do you believe in the Miracles? You can tell me. I'm not a little kid."

Mama went completely still. "That's a hard question."

"Because you don't believe," Rosie said, her heart sinking.

"No, that's not it at all. It's hard because I wasn't always sure the Miracles were real. Your Grandma Rose believed without a single doubt. But I wanted proof."

"Did you find it?"

"Nope," Mama said. "At least, not really. Sure, the Blue brothers have this uncanny ability to predict the weather and Mr. Waverman seems to know if the mail is bad or good, but someone could still explain those things away."

"I don't understand what you're saying," Rosie said in a small voice.

"I'm saying I made a choice to believe years ago. It took me a while to get there, but once I did, it made the Miracles more real than ever," Mama said, her eyes shining.

"But *why* did you make that choice?" Rosie asked.

"That's not something I can fully explain."

"I wish you could," Rosie said, resting her chin in her hands.

"Oh, Rosie, some things don't have an explanation." Mama hesitated. "All I can tell you is it's important to believe in something you're not able to see or touch. We can't explain love and goodness and faith, but they're the most important things. Without them, we wouldn't have any hope at all."

Rosie filled her lungs with air and slowly let it out. Mama's speech sounded good, but it didn't prove or explain anything.

Mama tapped the counter. "Speaking of the Miracles, I still haven't had time to set up interviews for you with

Donna Davis or Beth Moore. I've been so busy helping with the festival. But I can do it tonight. I know you're anxious to finish the documentary."

"It's okay," Rosie said. "I already interviewed both of them."

"Do you still want me to call Miss Matilda to smooth things over?"

"That's all right. Miss Matilda hasn't caused much trouble since the town meeting, so you don't need to call her." Though Rosie still couldn't figure out what Miss Matilda or anyone else was worried about in the first place.

"How about I speak to Bob Willis about you filming at the museum?" Mama asked.

"I already convinced him to let me do that tomorrow," Rosie replied.

"Oh," Mama said, her chin dipping. "Well, you don't seem to need me at all."

Rosie could tell Mama was disappointed. "That's not true. You could . . . You could help me with the final cut on Thursday night. I'll need to add in some music and edit my final scenes, and I might be up late."

"I'm there!" Mama said. "I'll bring the hot chocolate with raspberry syrup."

"A Flynn girl specialty," Rosie said.

"A Flynn girl specialty," Mama agreed.

Rosie stood and carried her bowl to the still-dripping faucet. She set the bowl down and stared at the sloping hardwood floor. When she spoke, her voice was quiet. "I do *want* to believe in the Miracles, but I just don't know anymore."

Mama stopped unpacking the groceries and straightened, staring Rosie right in the face. "It's okay to not know everything." She put an arm around Rosie and pulled her close to her side.

Rosie sighed. Everything was different these days. The questions were different. The Miracles were different. Cam and Henry were different. She stood on her tippy-toes and rested her chin on Mama's shoulder. Last year, she wasn't tall enough to do that. She even fit in Mama's hug differently these days.

Rosie snuck out of her house after Mama went to sleep and headed down Magnolia Street toward the First Presbyterian Church. It wasn't as though she could sleep anyway. Her mind was too crowded with worries about the documentary and Cam and the Miracles. Each worry was like a toothache she couldn't help nudging with her tongue—always there, always aching, and thinking about it over and over made it hurt worse.

Thick clouds covered up most of the moon, leaving

only a sliver of silver in the sky. The graveyard felt like its own lightless tomb at eleven o'clock. Rosie huddled into her jacket. The raised white headstones took on a ghostly appearance, and the wind whipped through the branches overhead, rattling the leaves. It looked like the set of a horror movie in which rotting mummies popped out of the ground, one mangled hand at a time.

Cam was walking up the sidewalk, her braids tucked into a stocking cap. A pit formed in Rosie's stomach. After talking to Mama, she wanted to try to fix everything with Cam, but she still didn't know what to say to her.

"I wanted to talk to you about lunch," Cam said immediately.

Rosie's face softened. Cam must have realized she'd ignored Rosie.

Cam continued. "I felt so bad when you made that mistake about *The Haunting*. I tried to change the subject to soccer to make it less awkward."

That wasn't the response Rosie expected or hoped for.

"Thanks, I guess," Rosie said, staring hard at the black metal fence.

"So, we're good, right?" Cam asked, touching Rosie's arm. "Because you seemed a little mad when you got up from the table."

Mad? Rosie wasn't mad; she was chopped up into tiny

pieces. She'd wished Cam hadn't turned her back on her. She'd hoped Cam would run after her when she got up from the table. But she wasn't sure how to say any of those things without sounding like a sad loser.

"It's okay," Rosie said in a flat voice. "I shouldn't have brought up that movie."

"Luckily, I don't think Leila cared that much. No one even mentioned it after you left," Cam said.

Rosie gave her a stiff smile. She wondered what would have happened if Leila had cared. Would Cam have stood up for her? Right now Rosie wasn't so sure.

"I can't believe we're doing this." Cam gestured to Henry's figure ahead. "Have you talked to him since lunch?"

Rosie shook her head.

"Me neither," Cam said. "I'm worried though. This whole thing"—she threw her arm out, encompassing the creepy graveyard—"isn't like him at all."

They started into the graveyard. The tall branches of the oak tree reached up past the church spire like bony skeleton arms. Henry stood to one side, shoveling dirt over his shoulder.

"You came!" Henry exclaimed, his hair glowing white. He leaned the shovel against the tree and gestured to the shallow hole in the ground. "I've already scoped out the topography and started on the side farthest from the road. The ground gets more water runoff, so the dirt is softer. It's a logical place to bury treasure, like how dung beetles search for softer soil to bury their dung balls. I even brought some of Mama's yarn so we can set up grids to show which areas we've excavated."

Cam clicked on her flashlight. The shallow light illuminated her frown. "Henry, we don't have time to set up grids. We need to dig as fast as we can before someone catches us in here."

Henry looked over at the yarn and nodded. "You're right. No grids. Only digging."

A creak sounded from the opposite side of the graveyard like a long-suffering sigh. They froze. Rosie gripped her elbows, trying to quiet the tremors in her muscles. Was it the sound of a graveyard caretaker or a dangerous stranger?

"Let me check it out." Cam started forward. "I'll be right back."

Rosie grabbed her arms and whispered, "Never say that."

"Why not?" Cam whispered.

"Don't you know classic horror movie rules? The person who says I'll be right back never comes back. They end up dead," Rosie hissed.

Cam dislodged Rosie's hands and rolled her eyes. She headed in the direction of the noise. Seconds later, she was back. "It was the wind blowing open the gate."

Henry was examining the hole and mumbling under his breath. "The treasure is here somewhere. I know it."

Cam and Rosie looked at each other. Henry sounded like he was in a trance.

"Henry, is there anything you want to tell us?" Rosie asked.

"Because you seem weird," Cam said bluntly.

Henry started shoveling again. "I don't know what you're talking about."

"Well, we are in a graveyard in the middle of the night," Cam said.

"That's because of the treasure," Henry said. "Can you guys grab a shovel because I could really use some help."

Rosie tried again. "It seems like something else is bothering you."

"The dirt must have built up over time, right? I'm sure that's why I haven't found the treasure yet. It's the only answer." Henry increased his shoveling pace.

Cam grabbed the shovel out of Henry's hand.

"What are you doing?" Henry said.

"Is everything okay at home with Miss Betty?" Cam asked in a gentler voice.

"I guess." Henry stared at the ground.

"I know it's hard with her being sick," Rosie said.

"I really need to keep digging." Henry reached for the shovel, but Cam held it out of reach. He sighed.

"Just talk to us," Rosie said.

Henry kicked at the pile of dirt he'd created. "Fine. It is hard, okay? Sometimes Mama can't get down the stairs in the morning. My dad has to help her. She still tries to cook dinner every night, but she doesn't always finish because she gets too tired so my dad and I order pizza all the time. It's funny—I don't even like pizza anymore."

"Pizza is overrated," Cam said.

"The doctor says the treatments are working though, right?" Rosie asked hopefully.

Henry dusted off his hands, avoiding their eyes. "That's what my parents tell me, but I wonder. Once I heard her crying when she thought I went to bed." His throat convulsed. "She said her entire body hurt. I've never heard her cry before."

Rosie bit her lip, afraid she was going to cry at the way Henry's voice was trembling.

"Do you think they would tell me if she wasn't going to get better?" Henry whispered. "Maybe they wouldn't want me to know because I'm twelve and if my mama died, that would—"

Cam gripped Henry's arm. "She's not going to die."

"They would tell you," Rosie said, taking his other arm.

"I'm not sure. Sometimes . . . " Henry's voice trailed off.

"Sometimes what?" Rosie asked.

Henry shook off their arms. "It's nothing."

But Rosie knew he was hiding something. "You can tell us anything. We're your best friends."

"We want you to talk to us," Cam said. "We want to help."

Henry grabbed the shovel and hefted it up to his shoulder. "I should get back to work. We don't have a lot of time, and I have to find that treasure." His voice rose on the last word.

"What's so important about the treasure?" Rosie asked.

"I—I can't explain it," Henry said.

Rosie wrinkled her nose. "But—"

Henry had already begun digging again before Rosie could finish her sentence. Cam shrugged at Rosie and grabbed the other shovel. Rosie wanted to make Henry tell her what was bothering him and why the treasure suddenly seemed more important than anything else in his life, but she didn't know how to ask the right questions.

After nearly a half hour, Rosie took over for Henry, then Henry took over for Cam, and so on until all three were sweating and exhausted. There were holes all around the tree, but the most they'd found was an old shoe and a few cigarette butts.

"Maybe we should come back tomorrow," Rosie said, plopping down on the grass to rest for a moment. Her shoulders ached.

Cam collapsed next to her, rubbing her back. "Maybe we should stop."

Henry continued to heave dirt out of the ground like one of the pirates from *Treasure Island*. His jaw clenched, and his eyes squinted down at the ground without blinking.

"Henry, it's not here," Cam said.

Henry didn't stop shoveling. "It's here somewhere. It has to be."

"We've dug around the entire tree," Rosie said, sighing. "I'm sorry, Henry. We tried."

"It's got to be hidden deeper," Henry said in a choked voice.

"We can still research other places Lonnie went when he was alive. Maybe the treasure is buried at one of those. I'll help you next week when the documentary is done," Rosie said.

"I might not have a week," Henry said.

A beam of light shot across the graveyard. Henry dove

to the ground, and Rosie and Cam smashed their backs against the tree and slid down until they lay flat on the dirt. Heavy footsteps crunched in the dried leaves scattered among the graves. This was no creaking gate; this was a real live person.

Rosie and Cam stared at each other, eyes wide and scared.

"Who's there?" A high voice came from their left. Rosie recognized it instantly.

"It's Deputy Cordell," Rosie whispered. "You know she only sleeps one hour a day since her Miracle, when she came out of that six-month coma."

"I don't care why she's awake. I only care about getting out of here," Cam whispered.

Deputy Cordell's flashlight beam arced from one side of the graveyard to the other. She headed up along the left side.

Rosie thought about the famous chase scene in *The Fugitive* where Harrison Ford has to jump into a dam. If he could jump fifty feet, they could run through a graveyard.

"Follow my lead," Rosie said, moving into a crouch.

Cam moved her feet underneath her but remained low to the ground. Henry did the same. Rosie motioned for them to rise slowly.

"On my cue, we run," Rosie whispered.

Rosie, Henry, and Cam locked eyes and nodded in unison.

Rosie gulped in a breath, pointed with one finger, and took off down the right side of the graveyard. Cam and Henry sprinted behind her.

Deputy Cordell immediately spotted them and was yelling in their direction as she wove through the headstones. Rosie's shin banged into a statute and she slowed momentarily, but Henry grabbed her arm and pulled her along beside him.

They bolted through the swinging graveyard gate, heading up Magnolia Street. Deputy Cordell was still shouting but falling farther behind. They darted to the back of Sook Diner and leaned against the wall beside the rusting green dumpster, all of them panting loudly.

"We lost her," Rosie said. Her arms and legs shook with adrenaline.

"That was a close one," Cam whispered.

Cam and Rosie looked at each other and exploded with laughter. Rosie held her sides, her stomach cramping up. "I can't believe we did that!"

"I can't believe Deputy Cordell can't run faster!" Cam said between heaving laughs.

"Maybe she'll think we were ghosts," Rosie said, cracking herself up.

"I bet she doesn't know what to think," Cam said.

Henry remained frozen, not laughing or talking.

Rosie turned to him, and her laughter died in her throat. "Is everything okay?"

"We didn't find the treasure," Henry said, his voice sounding thick and broken. The sockets around his eyes were dark and hollowed out. He looked as if he hadn't slept in weeks, not just days.

"It's all right," Rosie said, unable to come up with something better.

"No, it's not," Henry said, his chin trembling. And then, all at once, there were tears trickling down his face. "It's never going to be all right."

Cam stepped closer to Henry, and Rosie stepped closer to Cam. They knew what Henry meant. Nothing was all right when you had a sick mama at home. They waited with Henry until he stopped crying before walking him home to his too-quiet house.

CHAPTER FIFTEEN

Later that week, Rosie rode to the end of Poplar Lane and left her bike propped up against a tree. She crunched through the branches strewn along the overgrown path in front of her. A thick tree line blocked her view to the right and left. She quickened her pace, ignoring the brambles that tore at her shins and the low-hanging branches that smacked her cheeks.

The festival was only two days away. Rosie had skipped a few hours of school every day that week to work on the documentary, calling the school with different excuses every time. She'd managed to film the Rodgers brothers, who were speaking to each other again after Frank complimented Shane on his right hook. She'd convinced Mr. Willis to let her film artifacts in the museum, and the Blue brothers, Dr. Rhodes, and Mrs. Davis had all agreed to talk to her on film. She had arranged each interview herself and handled all the setup and lighting for the scenes. Now she was determined to get this last interview done. She'd told the entire town she was going to find out what caused the Miracles. They were all expecting it in her documentary. Rosie hoped today would give her some real answers.

Up ahead, a small wooden cabin rose up from behind a cluster of trees. Overgrown holly bushes with pointed leaves crowded around the cabin, looking as if they were on the verge of breaking through the first-floor windows. The grass was knee-high and rustled in the breeze. There were no other houses for at least a mile. Rosie's throat went bone-dry. The cabin looked like the abandoned shack in every horror movie where someone dies a horrible death.

A white curtain at one window fluttered and pulled straight, as if someone were watching her. The hair rose on the back of Rosie's neck. She had spent the entire bike ride trying not to think about the rumors that Hazel shot at people to get them off her property and owned a dog named Deadeyes, who was part wolf.

Rosie took a deep breath. She was letting her imagination get the better of her. It wouldn't hurt to knock on the door, right? No one was going to attack her for knocking on the door. Besides, hermits could be surprisingly helpful, like Obi-Wan Kenobi at the beginning of *Star Wars*. He was also living in the middle of nowhere, and *he* was secretly a Jedi.

Rosie climbed the steps to the leaning porch, and the

front door swung open. She backed up in surprise. Hazel
Maywell stood in the doorway, a long gray braid over one
shoulder. Her wizened figure held a cane, not a shotgun.
She was missing a few teeth, but her milky blue eyes were
sharp.

"Just what exactly are you doing on my doggone
porch?" Hazel snapped.

Rosie's hands shook, and she plunged them into her
pockets. Hazel Maywell looked an awful lot like a type-
cast version of a witch. All that was missing was a pointed
black hat.

"Mrs. Maywell, I—I've come about an important matter," Rosie stammered.

"Name's Hazel, and I don't much like important matters," Hazel said. "If you're here trying to find that doggone
treasure, I'll tell you the same thing I told all the others.
Get lost."

"I'm not here about the treasure. I promise."

Hazel frowned. "You best get lost anyways. Ain't you
heard the story about Will Burns and how I shot him?"

"Yes," Rosie said. "I mean, no. I don't know about any
shooting."

Hazel motioned to something behind her. "I'd hightail
it out of here if I was you. I'm fixing to let out Deadeyes.
Bet you heard about my dog, Deadeyes. He's mean, feral,

likely has rabies. He'll bite anything, 'specially trespassers."

"I'm not leaving until you talk to me," Rosie said, though every instinct in her body was screaming at her to run.

"I've got a gun," Hazel added.

"Maybe," Rosie said in a quavering voice. "But I happen to know Will Burns is a big fat liar. He once told everyone he broke his leg falling down the stairs and woke up to it miraculously healed. When he tried to charge people five dollars to touch his Miracle staircase, we all knew he'd made the whole thing up."

"You saying I don't have a gun?" Hazel demanded, glaring down at Rosie.

Rosie shrank back but didn't budge. "I'm saying I'm willing to risk it." She gave Hazel a tremulous smile. "And I did bring Mama's chocolate chip cookies, so maybe you'd prefer to have one of those instead of shooting me?"

Hazel eyed the small parcel under Rosie's arm. "I do like chocolate."

"Most folks do," Rosie replied.

Hazel opened the door another sliver and considered Rosie before stepping aside. "You got five minutes, and you leave the cookies."

Rosie exhaled. "Deal." She handed over the cookie parcel and followed Hazel inside, hoping a large half-wolf dog wasn't snarling behind the door. Werewolf movies were her least favorite monster-movie genre.

The interior of the cabin was one large room. A small kitchen filled one wall, and there was a large pot on the stove out of which steam rose in curling gray tendrils. The only animal was a white cat with brown and tan patches, who was sprawled across the sofa in front of the fireplace. Books were crammed into every available corner, along with stacks of yellowing newspapers, blankets, pots, and empty dirt-streaked jars. A rickety wooden table was plunked down in the middle of the room. Hazel motioned for her to sit.

Hazel took a bite of cookie and closed her eyes. "Do these have bacon in them?"

"It's Mama's secret ingredient," Rosie said.

Hazel took two more bites, polishing off the cookie. "Never would have thought of bacon and chocolate together, but these taste pretty good. Caroline Flynn knows her way around a stove."

"You know Mama?" Rosie asked.

"I know more than a few things," Hazel said. "Don't know what you're doing here though."

"Right. I'm glad you asked. I'm here because I'm filming a documentary about the Miracles, and I want to interview you for the film."

Hazel burst into a cackle.

"Does that mean you'll do it?" Rosie asked in a timid voice.

"Lawd no, I won't do it."

"Why not?" Rosie asked.

"For one thing, I don't like people."

"You wouldn't have to see anyone but me and—"

"For another thing, the Miracle was the worst thing that ever happened to me."

"B-but it saved your life," Rosie sputtered.

"It ruined my life," Hazel said, glaring back at her. "I was only three years old when I got myself lost in the woods around here trying to find my daddy, or so mama always told me. After two days gone, everyone figured I'd drowned or worse."

"And then you turned up safe and sound," Rosie said, repeating the story Mama had told her many times. "Did you happen to have a lucky charm with you at the time you got lost? Or did you make a wish in the Fishing Well or go in the creek the day before, over by Mrs. Grant's house or—"

"How should I know? I don't remember any of it."

"But you must remember something," Rosie said desperately. "I need to find what causes the Miracles, so if you can think of any reason why you got one, it would really help."

Hazel shrugged. "I got no idea."

Rosie clenched her teeth. "But it *was* a Miracle, right? It wasn't just good luck that you were found. Maybe if you think really hard, you'll come up with a reason."

"There ain't no reason 'cept bad luck. I spent the rest of my life with this curse of telling people how to find things that are lost."

"It doesn't sound like a curse to me," Rosie said.

Hazel shook her head, a wry twist to her mouth. "Girl, you got a lot to learn. Nothing is as good as it looks from the outside."

"Well, what if you—you showed me? You could find something for me." Rosie leaned forward in her seat in growing excitement. If Hazel found something she'd lost, it wouldn't solve the mystery of the Miracles, but it might prove to everyone that they were real. It might prove to Rosie that they were real.

"I don't find things anymore. Not ever."

"It couldn't hurt to find one small thing," Rosie said in a pleading voice.

"Yeah it could, and I won't do it. Haven't done it for forty-three years. Finding don't make people happy," Hazel said matter-of-factly. "And sometimes what's hidden don't want to be found."

Rosie sighed and shook her head. "I don't believe you."

"Oh no? One time Mack Johnson lost his dog, Patsy. That dog was his best friend. For weeks he begged me to help, so I told him what I knew about finding the dog's collar. He needed to go look under the largest tree in River Bend Park. When he got there, Patsy was underneath it. Dead."

Rosie shivered. "I can see how that would make you upset, but at least he found out what happened to her. Besides, you must have happier stories than that."

Hazel snorted.

"There's got to be at least one," Rosie said.

"Maybe," Hazel replied grudgingly. "Ivy Wallace asked for help after she lost a locket belonging to her best friend, Tara May. I told her to find that locket, she needed to stop finding so many boyfriends. Next thing I know, she'd dumped that no-good Ty Pritchard, who'd stolen the locket right out of her room. Her and Tara May opened up a flower shop together in Savannah. Heard they live down the street from each other." Hazel's eyes were far away, wrapped in wisps of clouds. A small smile touched her lips.

Rosie framed the shot in her mind. That. She needed *that* on camera. Maybe she couldn't convince Hazel to find something or explain the Miracles, but Rosie had to convince her to do the documentary.

"Hazel, if you'll let me record that story, I'll leave here and never bother you again," Rosie said.

"Already said no." Hazel crossed her skinny arms over her chest.

Hazel's interview was crucial to the documentary. Her Miracle was one of the most sensational, even more so because she refused to see anyone in town. Everyone in Glimmer Creek was part scared, part fascinated by her. Hazel's interview alone would make some people want to see the documentary. But if Hazel refused to do it . . .

Rosie imagined a field of people staring up at the big screen, waiting for her documentary to start, thinking they were finally going to learn the secret of the Miracles. Instead, she pictured the documentary with a few measly interviews and no other scenes. Everyone would stare at her with pity. People would cluck their tongues in embarrassment. The kids at Stratford Middle School would laugh. Leila would ask Cam if she was really friends with such a loser. Mama would gather her up and rush them home. And her father— Rosie's temple pounded—her father would probably get in his car and drive straight back to Richmond.

Rosie's hand shot out and clung to the frail skin on Hazel's arm. "Please. You don't understand how important this is. The entire town is coming to see this film. My *father* is coming to see this film. I have to get it right."

"Your father?" Hazel unthreaded her arm from Rosie's hand. "Your father don't live here." She raised an eyebrow at Rosie's startled expression. "Told you I know things."

"It's the first time I'm going to meet him," Rosie whispered, afraid if she said anything else she might burst into tears.

The room fell silent. The deep wrinkles on Hazel's forehead reminded Rosie of ripples on the water: long, deep, and wavy across a sunburned face. Dust motes floated up, caught on the air, and drifted back down.

Finally, Hazel spoke. "My father left when I was a baby. Don't remember him, though I do remember how my mama used to cry every night with missing him. I know what it's like. It's lonely not having a father."

A thin crack splintered down the center of Rosie's heart. Her skin felt all wrong: too tight, too raw, too red. She knew how to react when people talked about Father's Day, or if someone said their daddy never missed a dance recital or a school play. She'd turn her lips into a slight smile, relax her posture, and act interested but not too interested. Eventually, she'd change the subject and no one would know the truth. No one would know how she felt like the only person in the world without a father. No one would know about her hollowed-out stomach and the way her throat was coated in a thickness worse than the sludge below Miss Matilda's dock. But Hazel knew, and it was as if she could see right through Rosie's skin to the emptiness inside her.

"I—I have a father," Rosie said, not sounding convincing even to herself. She had tried to ignore the emptiness again and again. She never wanted to admit how much it hurt that her father didn't come to see her, didn't call her, didn't show up ever, but she couldn't deny it anymore. Not when Hazel was staring at her, and not when she was about to see him for the first time.

Hazel looked at Rosie before nodding once. "All right, I'll do it."

"You'll do what?" Rosie asked.

"I'll do your doggone movie, but I won't find anything, and this best be short. I got to feed Deadeyes soon." Hazel gestured to the sleepy cat behind her, who lifted her head, opened one eye, and promptly closed it again.

"Thank you," Rosie said quietly.

Rosie got out her camera and searched for the best interview backdrop, but she didn't feel the triumph she expected for landing Hazel's interview. She realized now the documentary wasn't the end of her story with her father. It was only the beginning. And she couldn't help asking herself if any good story could really begin twelve years too late.

CHAPTER SIXTEEN

The town library had a two-story atrium in the center with an entire wall of curved glass behind it, an endless ceiling, and a balcony on the second floor lined with books. Prisms of light flared out in all directions, highlighting the polished wood tables and gilded book spines. A few people ambled up and down the rows of books, stopping to peer at the shelves and speaking in hushed voices.

Mrs. Arbuckle, the librarian, sat behind a desk helping Jim and Curtis Cope, who were wearing matching fedora hats, backpacks, and hiking boots. "We only have one town map from the 1800s. I've placed it on the table over there beneath the glass. Do not try to touch it. It's quite delicate and I don't want to call security like I did yesterday with the Rodgers boys."

Jim leaned forward. "Did you happen to notice an X on the map? You know, X marks the spot of a treasure."

"Did you check the back for any hidden messages?"

Curtis asked. "Back in the olden days, people used lemon juice to write secret codes in invisible ink. I saw it in a movie."

Mrs. Arbuckle sniffed loudly. "Gentlemen, this is a town artifact, not a treasure map."

Rosie stifled a giggle. The train treasure hunters were everywhere.

Lucy hurried up to her. "Well, what do you think of the light now?"

Cam had a soccer game, and Henry couldn't come until later, so Rosie had recruited Lucy to help her set up the final live-action sequence. Though Rosie was nervous to call a girl she barely knew, she was glad she'd done it. Lucy had taken one look at the filming area and run home to grab the tall tripod light her dad used to work on his car at night. She'd dragged it back through the library despite Mrs. Arbuckle's grumbling, and set up the work light to illuminate a corner that didn't get as much of the afternoon sun.

Rosie bent down and looked through the camera lens. The extra light made a huge difference. She straightened and clasped Lucy by the arm.

"You were right," Rosie said.

Lucy shrugged. "I learned about three-point lighting at film camp."

"I'm glad you came today," Rosie said.

Lucy smiled at her. "Me too."

"Do you think we'll talk about lighting in film club?" Rosie asked.

"I thought you weren't doing film club," Lucy said.

Rosie shrugged. "I changed my mind."

Cam and Henry weren't joining film club, but that didn't mean Rosie shouldn't do it on her own. If she learned more things like three-point lighting, it would be worth it.

"We should get started. I still have to slot this scene into the documentary," Rosie said, and it was an important one. This was her last chance to prove the Miracles were real.

"How close are you to a final cut?" Lucy asked.

"I have some editing to do, but I can finish if I stay up late. I have to show it to Mayor Grant in the morning before the festival begins," Rosie said.

The very thought of the festival sent vibrations down Rosie's spine. Over the past two days, Rosie had used the excuse of editing to stay in her room and avoid talking too much to Mama. But when Rosie was alone and the only sound was the branches tapping against her window, her mind spun in a thousand different directions, each one scarier than the next. What if her father hated the documentary? What would happen when Mama found out the truth about what she'd done?

Mr. Jack and Miss Lily appeared from behind a row of books and waved her over.

"I'll be right back," Rosie said, crossing the room to where they stood. "Are you here to watch the final scene?"

Miss Lily adjusted the sleeves on her silky flowered kimono, and Mr. Jack scuffed his foot against the floor. Neither of them said anything. Rosie got an uneasy tickle in her chest.

"Well, darling, of course we want to support you," Miss Lily said.

"Of course," Mr. Jack agreed.

"And we're so proud of you," Miss Lily continued.

"Immensely proud," Mr. Jack agreed again.

"But we do have some . . . reservations," Miss Lily said.

Rosie swallowed. "What does that mean?"

"We've been thinking about what Miss Matilda said at the town meeting. Maybe she has a point about keeping our Miracles a secret," Mr. Jack replied.

"I don't understand." Rosie stiffened. "I'm not posting the documentary online."

"But you are trying to explain the Miracles," Mr. Jack said.

"I mean, I have a few theories about what causes them," Rosie said. She was still hoping if she went through all the footage tonight, the answer would suddenly become clear.

"Darling, have you ever considered that part of the magic *is* the mystery? Perhaps the Miracles should stay that way," Miss Lily said.

"Maybe this documentary isn't right for the town," Mr. Jack added.

Rosie opened and closed her mouth. She didn't know what to say to reassure them. There was nothing wrong with telling the story of the Miracles. But as she looked at their anxious faces, her stomach fluttered. They would never suggest canceling the documentary unless they really thought it could harm Glimmer Creek.

"Are you saying you want me to pull your interviews from the documentary?" Rosie asked in a shaky voice.

"No," Mr. Jack said. "We wouldn't ask you to do that."

Ms. Lily clasped her shoulder. "But we don't want you to make a mistake you can't take back."

Rosie's face froze in a grimace. They didn't know what they were asking. She couldn't cancel the documentary. Her father was coming tomorrow to see it. She would not disappoint him at their very first meeting.

"I'll keep that in mind," Rosie said, slowly backing away. She wanted to escape this entire conversation. "I have to get Dale in position now."

Dale stood on the far side of the library table, staring

down at his phone. He picked it up and shook it. "Dang it. I burned up another battery. I can't keep a phone working for longer than a month."

"I guess there are worse things. I heard you can turn on your toaster with the electricity in your hand," Rosie said.

Dale only shrugged.

"Besides, getting hit by lightning would have killed most people, and you didn't have a single burn. You're lucky," Rosie said.

"It was more than luck," Dale said simply. "It was a Miracle."

But was it?

Rosie clasped her hands together, entwining her fingers and pulling them back apart. "I guess—I guess you don't have an idea about why you got a Miracle, like maybe the creek water healed you or you were wearing a special amulet or made a wish in the Fishing Well?"

"Afraid I can't help you there. I don't have a clue," Dale said.

Rosie's shoulders slumped. She shouldn't have even bothered to ask.

Dale chuckled. "I never even thought about wanting one, to tell you the truth. I was just a regular guy looking for a cat in a thunderstorm when that lightning struck me. Nothing special about that."

"I didn't know you had a cat," Rosie said.

"I don't," Dale said. "It belonged to my grandma, and I didn't even like the darn thing."

"All ready?" Lucy called.

"All ready." Rosie stepped back to the camcorder and suddenly found herself jittery with nerves. She had to get this scene right. Peering into her lens, she adjusted the angle one last time. "Action."

Dale reached for the lightbulb Rosie had placed on the library table. He held the bulb gingerly between his thumb and finger. Holding out his other hand, he placed the bottom of the bulb on his outstretched palm. The light inside the bulb flickered. Rosie held her breath. All at once, the light blinked on full-force and glowed with a steady light. It was as bright as if Dale had screwed it into a lamp, but all the power was coming from Dale's own hand. A collective intake of breath from the few people around the library sent Rosie's heart cartwheeling in her chest.

Rosie zoomed in on the glowing white of the bulb until it filled the frame. Her insides fizzed as if she had Coca-Cola in her veins. Right then, she knew this scene would be the highlight of the documentary. The visuals alone made it film-worthy; the way Dale turned on an actual lightbulb with his hand . . . well, that looked utterly magical. It *looked* like a Miracle. No one could question that.

After clicking off the camera, answering questions from the onlookers, and putting away the now dim light-bulb, Rosie and Lucy sat at a table. They peered into the camera lens and watched Dale over and over.

"I love the extreme close-up of the light," Lucy said. "It's so powerful."

"It is," Rosie said, delighted. "I'm even thinking of doing a quick freeze-frame like the director Frank Capra did on George Bailey's face in *It's a Wonderful Life*. It's a great technique for getting the audience's attention."

"You'll definitely have their attention with this scene. Dale is like this guy I watched on YouTube who can hold live electrical wires with his bare hands. He's got millions of views. Apparently he doesn't sweat, so his skin can conduct electricity. Dale must have the same skin thing," Lucy said.

"I've never heard of that guy," Rosie said slowly.

"Really? He's super popular. You should research him. He can do the same thing Dale did. It was way better see-ing it in person though," Lucy said.

Rosie deflated and looked back down at the camcorder. She'd wanted this scene to make up for not finding the cause of the Miracles. She'd wanted to show actual magic, but all she'd done was prove Dale had the same talent as a random YouTube star and maybe a weird skin condition. It seemed there was a stupid scientific explanation for everything. Rosie didn't know what to believe anymore. The Miracles were either a random twist of fate . . . or they weren't Miracles at all.

Henry was lumbering up the steps as Lucy and Rosie stepped out from behind the library doors.

"Sorry I'm late. Did you already film Dale?" Henry asked.

"We just finished," Rosie said in a dejected voice. The documentary was sure to be terrible without proof the Miracles were real. What was she going to do?

"I think the scene turned out amazing," Lucy said. "But I should get going. I have to help my dad with dinner. Call if you need me, okay?" She hopped down the library steps, turning to wave once before disappearing down the street.

"I guess we should head over to Cam's game," Rosie said with a sigh. The camcorder strap weighed heavy on her shoulder.

"Sure." Henry's chin dipped low. He wavered for a second as if he might sink into the library steps.

Rosie peered down at his face. "Are you all right?"

"Just a little tired," Henry said, shrugging and not looking up.

Silence expanded to fill the small space around them. Outside, the light grayed as the day prepared for night. The breeze whipped through Rosie's jacket, and she shivered.

"Henry, what's the matter?" Rosie asked, lowering her camcorder to the ground and turning to fully face him.

Henry kicked the steps, still looking down. He shook his head. But Rosie was tired of not getting answers, and she wasn't letting his silence take over this time.

"We're not going anywhere until you tell me. If I have to follow you home tonight and bang on your door and howl at your window, I'll do it," Rosie said in a dramatic voice.

"Mama will call the police if you start howling," Henry said, cracking a tiny smile.

"Then I guess you better start talking."

Henry hesitated. "It's Mama."

"Has she—has she gotten sicker?" Rosie asked, a trickle of fear winding its way down her spine as she remembered Henry's worry from the other night: that his parents wouldn't tell him the truth about Miss Betty's illness.

Henry shook his head. "No, it's not that. But . . . my parents have been up at night talking about her medical bills. I—I overheard them because I can't really sleep anymore." He stared down at the clouds of dust that rose and fell with every kick of his tennis shoes. "I guess the insurance company isn't paying for everything, and there's this thing called balance billing that means they're responsible for a lot of the bills, and—" He stopped and swallowed. "They owe a lot of money. We might have to sell our house and move in with my aunt and uncle in Richmond until they can pay everything off."

"But Richmond is two hours away!" Rosie said. "You'll have to switch schools. We'll never see each other!"

"I know," Henry said. He plopped down on the steps and cradled his head in his hands. "I'll be all alone."

Rosie swallowed as she stared down at Henry's defeated form. He couldn't move away. He just couldn't.

She sat down beside him, the stone steps cutting into the back of her legs. "You won't be alone. I'm always here. Cam too."

Henry remained silent.

"Why didn't you tell us this at the graveyard?" Rosie asked.

"I was hoping it wouldn't happen, but my parents sounded more serious recently. They even called a real estate agent about selling our house. Mama was crying about having to leave Glimmer Creek."

"Is this why you aren't entering the science fair?"

"What's the point if I'm not going to be here to present? I thought if I found the train treasure, we could pay off the medical bills and we wouldn't have to move." Henry's voice was barely above a whisper.

His voice pricked Rosie's heart in a thousand places. She wanted to wrap Henry up tight in a blanket, the way Mama always did for her when she was sick, until he forgot all about moving and medical bills and cancer.

"I wish you'd told me sooner," Rosie said, guilt pinging inside as she thought about Henry worrying over this all by himself. "I should have asked more questions about how Miss Betty was doing and how you were doing."

"You couldn't have known about this," Henry said.

"But I know now, and we'll find another way to keep you here," Rosie said, rubbing her eyes and trying to think. "We can—we can hold a town-wide fund-raiser. I'll organize the whole thing. We'll sell cookies or—or flowers or copies of my best films. I can even make another documentary to raise awareness."

"I don't think my parents would go for that," Henry said. "Mama says it's impolite to talk about money. She won't want this spread all over town."

"Okay . . . then you can all move in with me and Mama. We have plenty of space," Rosie said.

"No, you don't. Your house has two bedrooms." Henry smiled sadly. "There's no way to fix this. I heard my parents say our only choice now is to rely on family."

"But I'm your family," Rosie said, putting her arm around Henry.

Henry leaned against her. The shadow of the library loomed over them. Glimmer Creek glinted in between the buildings on Magnolia Street. The moody gray of the water rippled along, always moving, always changing, regardless of what was going on around it.

Rosie couldn't come up with another thing to say. Unlike the movies, there were no perfect words on a script for this moment. Instead, she sat beside Henry while the street got dark and hoped everything would turn out okay.

CHAPTER SEVENTEEN

Rosie trudged home, barely seeing anything. After what Henry told her, they'd skipped the game. She exhaled the cold air in short, shallow puffs. When she thought of a Glimmer Creek without Henry, she could hardly breathe.

A dark-gray truck was parked in front of Rosie's house when she got home. She stopped and stared, not recognizing the car. Mama never had company on a weeknight.

Rosie opened the front door and called, "I'm home."

Mama hurried into the foyer from the family room. She was wearing a black dress Rosie had never seen before, shiny heels, and pink lipstick. Her dark hair was pulled back from her face, making her eyes sparkle like bits of brown sugar. She looked like Audrey Hepburn in *Breakfast at Tiffany's*.

This wasn't normal. None of this—the truck, the dress, the lipstick—was normal.

"What's going on?" Rosie asked, her gaze darting around the room.

Mama's hands fluttered along her sides as she looked down at her dress. "I thought you were going to Cam's game tonight with Henry."

"I changed my mind. I need to talk to you about something important," Rosie said. "But—are you going somewhere?"

Mama shifted her weight to one heel and gave Rosie a strained smile. "I . . . um . . . I thought you'd get home later . . . after."

"After what?" Rosie asked, not smiling back.

That's when she heard the couch springs creaking from the other room and a heavy shoe fall on the ground. Rosie stiffened. Suddenly, she knew. The truck belonged to Sheriff Parker, and he was here to pick Mama up . . . for a date.

"It's a funny story," Mama said, scuffing her heel along the faded striped rug. "I ran into Sheriff Parker today on my way home from work and he mentioned he'd never been to Sunsets Restaurant. Not once. Can you believe that? It's the best restaurant in Glimmer Creek. So I said, 'You have to try it. Sadie Dellarose is the best chef in the country, in my opinion.'"

Rosie wondered if Mama planned to breathe anytime soon.

"Sheriff Parker then said, 'I sure would like to try it, but I can't go to a place like that by myself.' And I said, 'You're right—you can't, because most of the tables are two-tops and two-top tables need two people at them. Plus, if you're alone, you may look like a sad, lonely weirdo, and no one likes to look like a sad, lonely weirdo.' So then he said, 'How about we go over there for supper tonight? I heard they're serving rockfish.' And I said okay. Mostly to help him avoid looking like a sad, lonely weirdo."

The room tilted on its side. "You're going on a—a date."

"I wouldn't call it a date, more of a social intervention."

"It's a date," Rosie said. She could feel her elbows pressing into her sides and her face heating up. Sheriff Parker was probably sitting on Rosie's side of the couch right now, flattening her back cushion.

Mama took a step toward Rosie and stopped. "It's supper, okay? It's not a big deal. A big deal would be if I were going out with someone like Cary Grant."

"He's dead," Rosie said.

"That's why it would be a big deal," Mama replied, trying out another smile before turning serious. "I'm sorry to spring this on you. It came up so last minute. I thought you were going to Cam's game and I'd get home before you."

"I can't believe this." Rosie's eye twitched. "Were you planning to even tell me?"

"Of course," Mama said. "Yes. As soon as you got home."

Rosie didn't know if she believed her. Mama had a last-minute date to a fancy restaurant that just so happened to occur when Rosie had already made plans? The whole story sounded suspicious.

"I don't suppose you've eaten dinner?" Mama asked tentatively. "I could throw something together real quick. How about a sandwich?" She made a move toward the kitchen.

"I'm not even hungry." Rosie actually felt sick to her stomach.

Mama stopped short and bit her lip. "What if I call Miss Lily to come over and keep you company?"

"I don't need a babysitter. I'm twelve," Rosie said. And Miss Lily was the last person she wanted to see after what she'd said at the library.

"I know you don't need a babysitter. I just thought it might be nice."

"Well, it's not," Rosie said, "unless you're planning on staying out until midnight."

"That's impossible in Glimmer Creek," Mama said, laughing lightly. "Even our all-night convenience store closes at nine o'clock."

"Did you forget you were supposed to help with my

documentary tonight?" Rosie's heart was shriveling up inside her chest. She needed more than help with the documentary. She needed to talk about Henry and how wrong everything was right now.

"I would never forget that. This is a quick date—I mean a quick supper." Mama coughed and smoothed down her dress. "I'll be home before you know it. I already made the raspberry syrup for our hot chocolate, and I'm ready for a late night of film work."

Rosie couldn't talk. There was a painful lump in her throat. She didn't want Mama to go.

Mama took a deep breath. "Did you say you had something you needed to tell me before we leave?"

Before Rosie could even respond, Mama glanced back toward the family room and Sheriff Parker. Rosie sagged against the door. She knew what that glance meant. Mama didn't really want to talk to her. She couldn't wait to get away from Rosie and back to Sheriff Parker.

"I'm going to my room," Rosie said. She didn't want to see Sheriff Parker coming out of their family room, acting like he belonged in their home and with her mama.

Mama's hand reached out for Rosie's shoulder as she swept past. "I can tell you're upset. Do you want to talk about it? David can wait."

David? She was calling him by his first name now?

Rosie jerked away from her. "What's there to talk about? You've got a date, and I have work to do. Seems to me everything is fine."

Rosie winced at the hurt look on Mama's face. She wished she could throw her arms around Mama and snuggle in close the way she always did. But how could she when Mama was the one leaving *her*?

"I'll be home in an hour," Mama finally said in a quiet voice.

"Take your time," Rosie said, heading up the stairs. "I don't care."

Rosie threw herself onto her bed. From downstairs, she heard the front door close and the new dead bolt turn. She lifted her head and looked out the window onto the street.

Sheriff Parker opened the door of his truck for Mama, and she smiled up at him. It was as if a cinematographer were backlighting her. Her face actually glowed. Sheriff Parker stared down at her in the same way Cary Grant stared at Katharine Hepburn at the end of *The Philadelphia Story*, as if he never wanted to stop staring.

It was awful.

Rosie buried her head in her pillow, her thoughts bouncing around like Ping-Pong balls inside her brain. Did this mean Sheriff Parker would stop by their house whenever he felt like it? Would Mama start bailing on their grilled-cheese nights, Saturday-morning movies, and Friday-night cinnamon-sugar popcorn feasts so she could spend time with Sheriff Parker instead of her? Was abandoning her tonight only the beginning?

Rosie lay still on her bed. She should work on the documentary right now, but she couldn't make herself get the camcorder out. Her life was a bigger mess than any disaster movie, and she had no one to talk to about it. She couldn't bother Henry; he had his own major problems. Cam was playing in a soccer game, and things were still strange between them anyway. And the one person she could always turn to—Mama—wasn't there.

Rosie hadn't moved when Sheriff Parker's truck pulled back up sixty-five minutes later. Car doors opened, and Mama's laugh floated up to the window, along with Sheriff Parker's rumbling voice.

Rosie stood by her bedroom door, waiting for Mama to come up and make everything okay again. She listened for Sheriff Parker's car engine but heard nothing. What was taking them so long?

Creeping down the stairs, Rosie stood on the bottom step and waited for the door to reopen.

She rubbed the top of the wood banister and watched speckles of dust float to the floor. Taking care not to step on the creaky board by the front door, Rosie tiptoed over to the window and peered out. Underneath the porch light, Mama stood close to Sheriff Parker. Unbelievably, she stepped even closer and tilted her head up. Time suspended for a long, still moment before Sheriff Parker leaned down to meet her with a kiss.

Rosie gasped and leapt back. Her eyes burned, and her chest felt as if an anchor were pressing it down to the river floor. She jerked open the front door. Mama and Sheriff Parker sprang apart. Rosie couldn't see anything except Mama's wide eyes beneath the light of the porch. Without saying a word, Rosie fled up the stairs, away from them both.

CHAPTER EIGHTEEN

Rosie woke to the sun peeking underneath her eyelids. The softness of sleep faded, and her neck tingled as she remembered. She bolted straight up. This was the day everything changed.

Rosie's heartbeat hammered inside her ears. Now that the festival had arrived, she didn't feel ready to meet her father. She couldn't even think of what to say to him or how to talk to him. And she still didn't know how to explain what she'd done to Mama. Her plan was a gigantic, *Titanic*-movie-sized mistake.

Fastening her eyes on Mama's laptop resting on her desk, Rosie shuddered. After staying up late, she'd finally finished the documentary—or at least, she'd made it the best she could. But it wasn't enough. She hadn't proved what caused the Miracles. The documentary was missing the real story she'd wanted to tell, the one she'd told everyone she *would* tell. Instead, it was mostly a bunch of random interviews with some people who might have gotten lucky once in their lives. Rosie wasn't a real director; she was a failure. After tonight, everyone was going to know it, including her father.

Mama pushed the door open with a slow creak. Rosie turned over, pretending to sleep. She wasn't ready to talk about what happened, same as last night when she'd refused to open her door after Mama knocked on it over and over. She'd only unlocked it after Mama gave up and went to her own room.

Rosie cringed, remembering. The image of Mama and Sheriff Parker *kissing* had run through her head all night like a never-ending horror film. It was a film with horrible lighting and terrible characters and a dreaded leading man who ruined everything.

"We have to talk," Mama said.

"There's nothing to say," Rosie mumbled into her pillow.

"That's not true. We could talk about the weather or your schoolwork or the newest Steven Spielberg movie or—" Mama stopped and swallowed. "Or we could talk about how you felt when you saw me with Sheriff Parker."

Rosie shuddered, unable to help herself. "I didn't *feel* anything."

"Then why wouldn't you talk to me last night?" Mama asked.

Rosie sat up and shrugged.

"That's not a response," Mama said.

"I don't want to talk about it." Rosie's jaw clenched around each word.

Mama's face softened. "I know this is uncharted territory for us. I haven't dated much."

"Ever," Rosie corrected. "You haven't dated ever."

Mama swallowed. "That's true. I've spent all my time focusing on us, and my job, and that's what I wanted. But I like Sheriff Parker. He makes me feel different, happy."

Didn't Rosie make her happy? Why wasn't she enough? They were two halves of the same perfect whole . . . except not anymore.

Rosie swallowed down a mouthful of bile. "I'm sorry, but I don't like him."

"You don't know him," Mama corrected.

"I know he's shut down three of my films and yelled at me in front of the entire town for no reason. I know he made things harder for you at work when he moved here. You complained about him all the time too."

"We worked through all that. He was new in town. He didn't understand how things worked," Mama said. "If you'll give him a chance—"

"I have to get ready for school."

Mama didn't move. She fixed Rosie with her tractor-beam stare, the one that made it impossible to look away. When Mama tractor-beamed, Rosie usually confessed everything she'd ever thought about doing. But not today, not now, and definitely *not* after last night.

The phone rang, cutting short their staring match.

"I'm going to answer that, but I'm coming right back. We don't—this isn't—" Mama blew out a breath. "We don't fight like this, and we're not going to start now. When I come back, we're going to talk." She hurried out of the room.

That was where Mama was wrong. Rosie couldn't talk about Sheriff Parker. Ever.

Swinging her legs out of bed and hopping to the floor, Rosie opened her closet door. She stared at the folded jeans and sweaters and the dresses hanging to one side. Should she wear the blue flowered dress or the pink sweater? Was it better to dress up to show how important this day was, or should she look more casual to appear relaxed about meeting her father?

Rosie squeezed her eyes shut. For a moment she let herself imagine Michael racing up to her in the middle of River Bend Park and swinging her around in a joyous hug. She could see the lighting (soft and muted) and hear the music (orchestral swell), except—Rosie exhaled—her imaginings looked like a dream sequence in a movie. In real life, there wasn't any music playing in the background, the lighting was usually too dark, and no father could sweep a daughter he'd never met into a hug. In fact, there might be no one at all. No Michael, no Mama, just Rosie alone.

Mama burst back into the room, slamming the door against the wall. "You are in so much trouble, young lady."

Rosie shrank away from Mama's red face. Electricity crackled off her. "W-what's wrong?"

"What's wrong is that was Principal Bradley on the phone," Mama said.

Rosie's stomach plummeted; she tried to stay cool. Better to play dumb, admit nothing. Maybe he was calling about the documentary or a school assignment. "What did he want?"

Mama barked out a short, sarcastic laugh. "He wanted to remind me that student attendance is mandatory and ask that in the future I not schedule all your out-of-school appointments for the same week. He mentioned you'd missed classes every morning this week for doctors' appointments and dentist appointments and eye appointments and something else I can't even remember right now because I'm about to explode with anger!" Mama slammed a hand on the bed, punctuating her point.

Sweat coated Rosie's forehead.

"Where were you this week?" Mama yelled.

"I was—I was working on my documentary," Rosie stuttered, too scared to even come up with an excuse. "I had problems with filming and I didn't think I could get it done in time unless I missed some school. I knew you wouldn't understand."

"You're right! I do not understand." Mama threw up her hands. "You lied to me, and you lied to the school! I've always trusted you. Apparently that was my mistake."

Shame burned in Rosie's chest. "I'm sorry," she whispered.

"You should be." Mama turned away from Rosie, as if she couldn't stand the sight of her.

"Did you tell Principal Bradley the truth?" Rosie asked.

"I was too shocked by the call," Mama said, turning around. "So you made me into a liar too."

Mama kneaded her temples, looking as if she were about to cry. "I'm so disappointed in you, Rosie."

Rosie felt sick. How could she have lied to the school? How could she have misled Mama? What sort of person did that? A terrible person, that's who.

Rosie had gotten in trouble before. Like the time she caused some damage on her film sets or didn't take the trash out for three days, but not like this. Mama had never looked at Rosie the way she was looking at her now—as if she were disgusted and hurt and sad all at the same time.

"I'm really sorry," Rosie repeated, tears streaming down her face in a hot river. "I'll tell Principal Bradley everything after tonight."

"What do you mean *after tonight?*" Mama said.

Rosie bit her lip, afraid to speak. "Tonight is the festival."

Mama was already shaking her head. "You're not going to the festival."

"But I have to give my documentary to Mayor Grant! Everyone is going to be there." *My father is going to be there.*

"You don't get it," Mama said. "You're grounded. There is no festival, no documentary, no nothing. This is serious, Rosie. I am not going to have you skipping school and lying to adults because you want to finish a movie."

"But, Mama, please. I can't miss this." Rosie's voice rose almost to a shout.

Mama pressed her lips together until they were white. "I said no, and that's final. I'll tell Mayor Grant the documentary isn't happening. Get dressed. I am taking you to school myself. At least that way I'll know you went."

Rosie knew when Mama's mind couldn't be changed. This was one of those couldn't times. She flung herself across the bed, punching her fists into the pillow. Why was this happening? This night was so important, and Mama didn't get it! She had no idea how awful this punishment really was—not that she cared. Rosie imagined Michael looking at his watch every few minutes and staring at everyone who walked by, wondering where his daughter was. He'd think she'd stood him up. He'd probably never want to see her again, and she would go her entire life without a father.

Rosie breathed in and out until the tears stopped. She sat up. Crying wasn't going to make anything better. Her only choice was to go to the festival, even if it meant sneaking out.

Rosie paced back and forth along the tile floor of the empty science lab. The overhead fluorescent lights glared down at the rows of tables. The floor was slick and hard, and the harsh smell of ammonia stung her nose. She glanced at the door. Where were they? She'd slipped a note in Henry's and Cam's lockers calling an emergency HenRoCam, and they were both one minute late.

Cam pushed open the door. "Can we make this quick? I'm meeting the crew in the Lounge before lunch."

Rosie bit her tongue hard enough to draw blood. *Make this quick?* This was the most important night of her life. "I'm sorry to bother you with my problems."

Cam sighed. "I didn't mean it that way."

Henry burst into the room. "Wait until you hear what

I found out! I know where the train treasure is. For real this time."

Rosie stared at him. "Are you kidding?"

Henry shook his head emphatically. "No. I can't believe it either. It's not going to be easy, but we can do it."

Rosie released a snort in frustration. "We do not have time for this. I'm having a major crisis with my life!"

"This is important too," Henry insisted.

Rosie bit back a scream. Henry only wanted to help his parents. She wanted to help too, but the treasure hunt was so farfetched.

"Henry, we talked about this. We'll find a way to keep you from moving, but it's got to be something real. Enough is enough with the train treasure."

"Wait, why is Henry moving?" Cam asked, looking from one to the other.

"The treasure is real," Henry said, stiffening.

Rosie crossed her arms. "No, it's not. This is like us digging in the graveyard for nothing. I know you're worried about Miss Betty, but this isn't going to work, and right now I really need your help. My documentary might get canceled."

"But what about the move?" Cam asked again.

"All you care about is that documentary," Henry said in a loud voice. "You don't even listen to me."

"I'm not going to listen to something that's completely pointless," Rosie said in a louder voice. "Especially not today, when I'm supposed to meet my father for the first time ever."

"Why are you both yelling?" Cam asked.

Henry stepped back, his chin quivering. "You know what? I don't need your help with the treasure or anything else. I'm going to find it myself." And with that, he stomped out the door.

Rosie stared after Henry, her heart jackhammering against her chest. How could Henry refuse to help her so he could search for a treasure he'd never find?

Cam peered out the window of the science lab door. "That was a little harsh."

"He needed to hear it," Rosie said shortly.

"Is he really moving?" Cam asked. Her brow wrinkled, and she knocked her fist against the table over and over.

"Maybe," Rosie said. She sighed. "He doesn't know yet."

"We should go after him," Cam said.

"We don't have time right now. I'm grounded, and this is the only chance I have to talk to you before tonight. I need your help sneaking out. I have to get my documentary to Mayor Grant and find my father at the festival, and Mama is going to be there the whole time." Rosie ran a hand through her hair and pulled a strand taut. Her pulse was racing.

Cam glanced down at her watch and flinched. She then looked at the door, and her shoulders dropped. It was so obvious she was worried about meeting Leila in the Lounge. She couldn't even give Rosie five minutes of her attention anymore.

Rosie clenched her fists. She'd had it with Cam choosing Leila and ignoring her. Cam knew how important tonight was to Rosie, but she was too caught up with her new popular friends to help.

"You know what? Go," Rosie said, blood pounding in her ears. "Go see Leila. She's the only thing you care about anyway."

"Whoa. What's your problem?" Cam asked, thrusting her arms onto her hips.

"You. You're my problem. You're *my* best friend, and you're supposed to help me. But you're too selfish." The awful words erupted from Rosie's mouth, but she didn't want to take them back. She only wanted to yell more, to spew out everything she was holding inside.

"No, I'm not," Cam said, her face darkening.

"You were a good friend, but you've changed. For the worse."

"Just because I want to do other things besides hang

out with you all the time doesn't mean I've changed for the worse."

This was the truth Rosie knew was coming. Cam didn't want her. She wanted Leila and parties with boys and doughnut fund-raisers.

"I don't care if you hang out with me," Rosie said, her voice shaking. "I don't need you."

"You're acting so immature. You just yelled at Henry for no reason. He's going through a hard time right now too. It isn't all about you," Cam snapped.

"What's that supposed to mean?" Rosie asked.

"It's always about you—*your* movies, *your* plans, *your* ideas—and you think Henry and I should go along with whatever you want. You're so bossy."

Rosie opened and closed her mouth before finding her words. "I am not!"

"You are so." Cam's eyes snapped and crackled at Rosie. "Why do you think Henry stomped out of here? He's sick of you telling him what to do, just like I am!"

Rosie's nails dug into her palms. Breathing hard, she glared at Cam. How had she ever thought Cam was her best friend? She was a traitor and a liar. Rosie wanted to tell Cam off right that instant and say the meanest thing she could possibly think of, but the words were clogged in her throat.

Instead, Rosie whipped around, rushing out of the room, away from her former best friend. Cam didn't try to stop her. Rosie's whole body was shaking. Henry wouldn't help. Cam wouldn't help. Mama wouldn't help. There was no one.

She had no one.

CHAPTER NINETEEN

Rosie managed to make it through the rest of the school day, though her head ached the entire time. When she got home, Mama was waiting for her on the front stoop with crossed arms. Rosie knew she had really messed up when Mama spoke less in the three hours they were home together than she usually spoke in two minutes. When Mama finally left for the festival, she didn't even call out good-bye.

After waiting a half hour, Rosie grabbed her camcorder and hurried outside. She sprinted down Magnolia Street and toward River Bend Park. The air was cool, with winter gnawing along the edges. Dusk had already set in, and the light turned amber like a jelly glass filled with sweet tea. Inside the park, silver-and-blue banners hung from the trees and twinkled in the darkness. Rosie could see boats decorated with lights in a rainbow of colors already lining up in Glimmer Creek for the nightly boat parade and fireworks.

Miss Matilda's grandsons had caught piles of stripers

and bluefish, and the smell of frying fish wafted out of the main blue-and-white tent. The Landon High jazz band was warming up on the raised dais of the stage. Nearby were giant inflatable slides and bounce houses in garish shades of orange and pink. Rows of games like beanbag toss and a dunking booth where you could win tickets and exchange them for prizes, like plastic swords and candy bars, lined the waterfront. The cheerful blinking lights of the rides made red-and-green patterns on the faces below.

White tents and homemade booths lined the sidewalk. Mr. Blandstone had decorated one booth with a large hand-lettered sign that read: TRAIN TREASURE HUNTERS CLUB—ALL MEMBERS WELCOME. Rosie could see the Rodgers brothers and Jim and Curtis Cope, along with Mrs. Green and Mr. Waverman. Mr. Blandstone was yelling about how aliens might have already gotten to the treasure.

As Rosie marched forward, her eyes darted left and right. She scanned every face around her, searching for Michael. Her heart was pounding in time with the drums on the stage, beating the same syllables over and over: *find him, find him.* Her father was here somewhere, waiting for her.

Rosie skirted the main paths to avoid running into Mama, half expecting her to pop up behind Rosie at any second and ruin her entire plan. Finally, she spotted Mayor Grant beside the stage. Crouching down, she crawled through the bushes and snuck behind the raised dais. She peeked around the corner. Mayor Grant was waving his hands and barking into a walkie-talkie.

Rosie whipped her head back behind the stage. Her heart beat so hard against her rib cage, she worried it might fly right out of her chest. She did not want to walk out to the center of the dance floor in plain view. Mama could show up at any moment, but this might be her one chance to talk to Mayor Grant alone. Rosie took a deep breath. She didn't have a choice.

Hurrying around the stage, Rosie sprinted up to him. "Hi, Mayor, I've got the documentary right here, all ready to go."

Mayor Grant frowned. "Caroline said the documentary wasn't happening. She said something about you getting in trouble."

Rosie's mind raced. She hadn't even considered how to explain away what Mama might have told him. "That's because . . . she thought it wasn't done. She was trying to give me an excuse. But I—I finished it last minute as a surprise for her. You're both going to love it."

"I don't know . . ." Mayor Grant averted his eyes. "I haven't had a chance to watch it yet, and Caroline said—"

"You could watch it right now," Rosie interrupted. "It's only twenty-three minutes long."

Mayor Grant looked back at the stage and glanced down at his watch. "I'm knee-deep in coordinating right now. I don't have time to watch anything."

"It's really good, I promise," Rosie said desperately.

"I can't show something I haven't seen," Mayor Grant said. "I'm sorry, Rosie, but I did tell you I needed to see it in advance."

Rosie had to convince him to screen the documentary. It might not be good, but it was better than nothing. She didn't want her father to think she'd lied about the premiere. This screening had to happen. The famous director Orson Welles didn't give up when he was trying to finish his film *Othello* and kept running out of money. He took on other jobs and financed the film himself. And after everything she'd done—lied to Mama, skipped school, snuck out—she couldn't fail now.

"Mayor, please. I worked so hard. Just . . . please. This means"—Rosie's voice broke—"everything to me."

Mayor Grant examined her face on the verge of tears and finally shook his head. "All right, honey. Now, don't go crying over spoiled milk. We'll show your movie before the main feature. Let's go find that technology fellow."

Exhaling, Rosie swayed on her feet when she realized how close she'd come to failing.

After explaining how to set up her film, Rosie went

back to searching for Michael. She kept to the edges of the park where the trees were the thickest, but still managed to check behind every ride and food stand. She scoured the sidewalks and rows of games. There was no sign of him. She wanted to scream out for everyone to be quiet, for the music to stop playing, for the rides to stop chiming, so she could call out Michael's name and find him before Mama found her.

"Henry Thompson, please report to the stage," the loudspeaker blared.

Rosie stopped walking, her eyes focused solely on the stage, her body becoming completely still. Henry? Her neck prickled with warning. *Henry?* Why did Henry have to report to the stage? A sudden and terrible feeling wormed its way around the pit of her stomach.

Pushing through the crowd, Rosie rushed forward. Her eyes blocked out everything else except the raised dais of the stage. Miss Betty and Henry's father, Mr. Joe, stood near Mayor Grant and Mrs. Grant. Miss Betty was pacing near the edge of the stage, wringing her hands. Cam ran up just as Rosie did. They looked at each other once before their eyes veered in opposite directions.

"What's wrong with Henry?" Rosie asked.

"I'm sure it's nothing, but we're having a little trouble finding him," Mrs. Grant said.

"What does that mean?" Cam demanded.

"He's missing," Miss Betty said, never ceasing her pacing. "He never came home from school today. I thought he must be here at the festival, but I can't find him anywhere. I ran into Principal Bradley a few minutes ago, and he said Henry missed his last two classes. Have you girls seen him?"

"Not since lunch," Cam said.

A cold chill zipped down Rosie's spine.

"Now, honey, he can't have gone far," Mr. Joe said in his slow, deep voice.

But despite Mr. Joe's assurance, queasiness grew in Rosie's stomach like she'd swallowed too much river water. The minutes ticked by without Henry appearing. It wasn't like him to wander off alone. Mayor Grant made another announcement over the loudspeaker, asking Henry to come to the stage immediately. He was nowhere in sight.

Miss Betty began to fan herself. "Oh, dear Lord, something has happened to my Henry. We must find Sheriff Parker immediately."

Rosie was woozy, unbalanced on her feet. The lights above the stage glared down, and the insistent dinging of a nearby game rang in her ears. The faces around her blurred as the truth sank in. Henry was gone.

Miss Betty was barking orders at Mr. Joe. Within

minutes, Sheriff Parker and Deputy Cordell showed up and started asking questions. Mayor Grant began talking about shutting down the festival early and asking if anyone knew where Caroline had gone.

Rosie told Deputy Cordell how Henry had wanted to search for the train treasure. The problem was she couldn't give Deputy Cordell any idea where Henry had gone to search because she hadn't listened to him. She was more concerned with sneaking out and getting her documentary to Mayor Grant. She had ignored Henry and for what? To find a father who didn't care enough to find her for twelve years? To screen a documentary everyone would forget in a day?

A missing child quickly sucked any fun from the Festival of the Fish. As news traveled through the crowd, whispers of concern overflowed into River Bend Park. People gathered in small groups near the stage, but Rosie didn't even bother to look for Michael or Mama. She could worry about all that later, *after* she found her best friend. Clutching her elbows, she rubbed her arms and worked to bring the feeling back into her fingers. If something terrible happened to Henry, she would never forgive herself.

Hazel hobbled up to Rosie. Her gray braid hung down her back. She wore a long black dress over a pair of black pants with a black cloak thrown over it and a black scarf tied around her neck. It looked as if she had put on every piece of clothing in her closet.

"What are you doing here?" Rosie asked.

"Thought I'd take a gander at your movie," Hazel said. "Guess that ain't happening now, with that boy going missing like he did."

"He's my best friend," Rosie said.

"That so? He tried to ask me about finding something yesterday," Hazel said.

Rosie's heart soared into her throat. "You talked to Henry yesterday? Did he tell you he was looking for the train treasure? Did you tell him where it was?"

Hazel backed away from Rosie's rapid-fire questions. "Didn't tell him nothing. Just like everyone else. Told you I don't find things anymore."

"But you could if you wanted to," Rosie said, stepping toward her. "If you tell me where to find the train treasure, then maybe I can find Henry. Please, Hazel! This may be life or death."

Hazel's eyes bored into Rosie's face. "Guess I could make one exception. Not 'cause I like you, mind you. Don't much like anyone. But I'm already here."

"Thank you," Rosie said breathlessly.

"Don't thank me till you hear what I got to say." A soft breath escaped Hazel, and her eyes went blank. Several beats of time passed before Hazel finally said, "You got to dig under the leaves of Lonnie's safe house."

Rosie scrunched up her nose. "That's it? I don't understand. I don't know where Lonnie hid out after the train robbery. Can't you give me some more details?"

Hazel shrugged. "Nope. All's I can do is tell you how to find things that are lost. Don't know how to make sense of what comes into my head."

"But what you said doesn't mean anything."

"That's what I got," Hazel said, flinging one end of her bedraggled cloak over her shoulder. Without even saying good-bye, she turned and hobbled down the sidewalk.

"Wait," Rosie called. "Are you sure you didn't see anything else? Like a street sign or a map?"

Hazel ignored her, and the crowd soon swallowed up her small, hunched form.

Dark clouds hijacked the sky and blotted out the stars. The air was hostile with cold. Rosie didn't know where to go or what to do next. A weight pressed down onto her chest.

Rosie wanted to chase after Hazel, but it wouldn't do any good. Hazel couldn't decipher her own clues on how to find things. She only knew what she'd told Rosie. And what she'd told Rosie didn't help at all.

CHAPTER TWENTY

Rosie stumbled through the crowd, avoiding eye contact with anyone. The more she walked, the more alone she felt. She wanted Henry. She wanted home. Most of all, she wanted Mama.

Miss Lily, Mr. Jack, and Miss Jessie materialized in front of her, matching expressions of concern on their faces. "Rosie, are you all right? We heard about Henry," Mr. Jack said.

Miss Lily put an arm around her, giving her a half hug. "You don't look good, darling."

"Have you seen Mama?" Rosie asked.

"There was a problem with one of the generators, and Caroline had to get on the phone with someone at the company. I'm not sure where she went," Miss Jessie said.

Miss Matilda clomped up to them, yelling at Mayor Grant. "Why'd you have to tell Miss Betty not to panic? Everyone knows if you tell someone not to panic, all they'll do is panic."

"I am doing my best to prevent hysteria," Mayor Grant huffed. "You're supposed to avoid that like the plaque."

"You mean the plague," Mr. Jack said.

"I mean plaque," Mayor Grant said. "No one wants plaque on their teeth. Smells worse than week-old crabs."

Mr. Jack bent close to Rosie. "Can we help you look for Caroline?"

"Do you want to come back to my house?" Miss Lily asked.

"Give the girl some space," Miss Matilda barked.

Shaking her head, Rosie tried not to release the tears crowded right behind her eyes. If Mama were here, she'd know how to answer these questions. She'd know to take Rosie somewhere quiet.

They were all staring at her, waiting for an answer, but Rosie wished everyone would disappear. She closed her eyes and saw Henry locked in a basement, his face pale and lit up by a spotlight as a menacing silhouette loomed above him. It was every rated-R horror movie Mama wouldn't let her see come to life.

Rosie's airway narrowed, and she swayed on her feet. Her brain was a movie screen fading to black. All at once there she was. Mama ran straight toward her, pushing her way through the crowd and throwing her arms around Rosie. Rosie sagged against her, burying her face into

Mama's shoulder, which smelled of honeysuckle and coffee. She took a deep breath, and air filled her lungs.

"I've been looking everywhere for you," Mama said.

"Oh, Mama, Henry is gone," Rosie said, tears trickling down her cheeks.

"We'll find him," Mama said, patting Rosie's back. "I know we will. There are only so many places a kid can go in Glimmer Creek, and there's even fewer places when that kid is afraid of water, allergic to grass, and possesses a healthy fear of the dark."

"But what if we don't?" Rosie asked.

"Don't think like that," Mama said.

Rosie squeezed her eyes shut. The people around them melted away. It was quiet in the circle of Mama's arms. Rosie nestled in, never wanting to leave.

"I'm sorry," Rosie whispered into Mama's shoulder.

"I know you are," Mama whispered back. "And I'm sorry too. I shouldn't have gone to dinner last night without talking to you first."

"I wish I hadn't gotten so worked up about it," Rosie said.

"It's understandable," Mama said, squeezing her tight. "But there's nothing for you to worry about. I don't think Sheriff Parker and I are going out again."

Rosie looked up in surprise. "Why?"

Mama's eyes dimmed. "It isn't the right time for us to start dating. There's too much going on with you and work getting busy and, well, everything. We only went to dinner that one time, and we're more like friends anyway."

This was what Rosie had wanted all along—for Mama to not date Sheriff Parker—but there was no rush of happiness at the news. Instead, she pictured how Mama's face had glowed when she talked about him and the way Mama had smiled when he opened her car door. Rosie frowned. She wasn't sure what she wanted anymore except to go home.

Rosie rested her head back on Mama's shoulder and let out a huge breath. "Can we get out of here?"

"Absolutely," Mama said with a tremulous smile.

River Bend Park was quieting down as they started toward the exit. Mrs. Grant had her arm around Miss Betty over by the stage. Mr. Jack and Mr. Willis were gathering a growing group and talking about a search party. Miss Matilda and Anna Lee passed out cups of coffee to all the volunteers. Everyone in Glimmer Creek was pitching in to find Henry. Rosie hoped it was enough.

She stopped short when Sheriff Parker strode past. He was looking down at a small notepad in his hand, not seeing them or anything else. Rosie pulled away from Mama. "Please, Sheriff? Have you found Henry yet?" Her voice wobbled on the name.

Sheriff Parker stopped and thrust the notepad back in his pocket. "Not yet, but we will."

"I already told Deputy Cordell about Henry looking for the train treasure today, but then I talked to Hazel Maywell here at the festival and found out something else. She said the treasure was under the leaves of Lonnie's safe house, so if you can find wherever Lonnie hid out after the robbery, maybe you'll find Henry. He's got to be in the woods somewhere," Rosie said anxiously.

Sheriff Parker made a note on his notepad. "We'll take that into consideration."

Rosie brushed away the tears in her eyes, suddenly furious with herself. "You should also know that I saw Henry at school today. I was distracted with doing something stupid, and we had a fight. And Henry—he was—he was really mad at me. I was acting terrible. He may not have been thinking straight because of me."

Mama put an arm around Rosie's shoulder. "You didn't cause this."

Rosie couldn't speak. That wasn't true. If she had listened to her friend the way she was supposed to, he wouldn't have gotten lost.

"I'm glad you told me about this," Sheriff Parker said. "It's useful to know his state of mind. Sometimes that can lead to a clue about where he went."

"I know you're talking to people, but is that really enough? Could you send out search dogs or offer a reward? I know from multiple movie sources that you have the best chance of finding a missing person in the first twenty-four hours," Rosie said, her voice cracking.

Sheriff Parker crouched down until he was on the same level as Rosie's eyes. "Did you know I was head of the Missing Persons Division in Washington, DC, before I moved here?"

Rosie shook her head, trying not to cry again.

"I have a lot of experience with finding people, and I'll do everything I can to find Henry. I know it's hard to trust someone you don't know very well, but I'm asking you to trust me now to find your friend."

As she stared into Sheriff Parker's eyes, Rosie's shoulders dropped. Nothing could make her feel better. Nothing was going to fill the pit in her stomach when she thought about Henry alone and scared. But somehow, knowing Sheriff Parker was in charge of bringing Henry home helped a little.

"Okay," Rosie said in a calmer voice.

"Okay," Sheriff Parker echoed. He straightened and nodded at Mama. "I'll call you later to check in."

"No need. I know you'll be busy," Mama said.

"Not too busy for a quick call," Sheriff Parker replied.

"That's all right. I'll be busy too." Mama looked only at Rosie.

Sheriff Parker put his hands in his pockets. "Sure."

"Thanks, Sheriff," Rosie said.

"You're welcome, Rosie." Sheriff Parker walked away, glancing back three times before finally facing forward for good. He looked an awful lot like Humphrey Bogart in *Casablanca*, staring all lovesick at Ingrid Bergman right as she left him for her husband.

"We need sustenance," Mama said. "We need muffins and cookies and maybe a slice of cake. We need root beer and candy, and we absolutely need ice cream."

"I'm not hungry," Rosie said.

Mama steered her toward Willow Lane and home. "Not hungry isn't a phrase I ever want to hear my daughter utter. In times of crises, gorging ourselves on baked goods is obviously the best thing we can do."

"That makes no sense," Rosie said. "We'll both feel sick."

"So what? We can feel a little sick tonight."

Rosie kicked at the dirt along the sidewalk. Was she wrong or was Magnolia Street eerily silent despite the people back in the park? It was as if a shadow loomed over all of Glimmer Creek.

"Mama, I'm scared," Rosie said.

"It will all work out. There's nothing to be—" Mama stopped and swallowed up the rest of her words. Her eyes were wet. "I know, sugar. I'm scared too."

Back at home, Mama settled Rosie on the couch and headed straight back to the kitchen, digging up snacks and banging around, unaware of the turmoil in Rosie's head. The lilac walls looked gray and dull, and the empty room only magnified the empty space in Rosie's chest. She pulled a blanket up to her chin.

Suddenly Rosie sat up. *Michael!* She hadn't thought of him for the last hour in all the worry and confusion about Henry. He was probably looking for her everywhere. He must have e-mailed to ask where she was.

Rosie hurried over to Mama's laptop in the study and logged into her e-mail account. Sure enough, an e-mail from Michael Weatherton waited in her in-box. Clicking on the message, she read:

Dear Ms. Flynn,

Michael Weatherton regrets to inform you that he is unable to attend the documentary screening and festival this evening. He apologizes for the late notice; however, it is unavoidable due to filming commitments. He wishes you the best of luck with your film endeavors and will be in touch soon.

Sincerely,

Lawrence A. Walker

Executive Assistant to Michael Weatherton

Rosie read it three times. Her breathing hitched. The letters on the screen wavered and blinked at her, but they didn't change. Her father wasn't coming.

All at once, a memory seared into Rosie's mind. She was waiting at the dining room window, staring down the street. Her hair hung at her ears in two perfect braids. Rosie didn't know her exact age, but she did remember her rising excitement every time she heard the sound of an engine rumbling down Willow Lane. Her father was making a special visit to Glimmer Creek to meet her. Mama had even gotten her a new dress. It was pink lace and scratched at her sides, but she didn't complain. She wanted to look her absolute best. She had watched the street for hours, refusing to eat dinner, sure he was about to appear at any moment. It wasn't until Mama had tucked her into bed and turned off the lights that she'd realized he wasn't coming.

Rosie saw her younger self so clearly, and the image wasn't in soft focus with a hazy light surrounding her. There wasn't a backdrop of beautiful music. The scene was not romantic or over-the-top tragic or tension-filled. It was simply sad. Her pillow was soggy with tears, her stomach still itched from the remnants of the dress, and she fell asleep only when Mama curled around her as the big spoon in her bed.

How could she have forgotten?

It wasn't that Michael lived on the other side of the country or was busy with movies. It wasn't because Mama wouldn't let her see him. Those were all excuses. No, the truth was Rosie hadn't met Michael because he didn't want to meet her. And Michael wouldn't be in touch soon, no matter what the e-mail said. He had his own life that didn't include her. He'd made his choice a long time ago, and a documentary wasn't going to bring him to Glimmer Creek. Nothing was.

CHAPTER TWENTY-ONE

A knock sounded on the front door. Rosie peeked around the curtain covering the window and saw the Blue brothers framed against the starless sky. She opened the door, her arms heavy.

"We brought you sandwiches," Arthur Blue said, holding up a paper bag. "Miss Matilda sent us. She thought you might need some supper."

"That's really nice of you," Rosie said, reaching for the bag and wanting to cry all over again at the thoughtfulness.

"You're lucky. Miss Matilda refused to give me any coffee after I asked whether the coffee beans were organic." Charlie leaned on his cane.

"We heard about organic on the news," Bill added.

"We like to keep up with the times," Arthur said. "We got ourselves an electronic mailbox last week."

"We're sharing it," Charlie said.

Rosie couldn't help smiling a little despite the past few

hours. "Do you want to come in?" She moved out of the doorway, and the Blue brothers hobbled inside the foyer.

"Have they found your friend?" Charlie asked.

"Not yet," Rosie said.

"That Henry is a smart boy," Arthur said.

"Real smart," Bill echoed. "He'll find his way home before the nor'easter storm hits tonight."

"Nor'easter?" Rosie asked, clutching the bag so tightly that she ripped a hole in the top. "I didn't hear about a nor'easter hitting Glimmer Creek." A nor'easter meant driving rain and treacherous winds and flooding. It meant dangerous weather.

"The Weather Channel said it's going to miss us," Bill said.

"The Weather Channel is wrong," Arthur said serenely.

"But don't worry. Henry can take care of himself," Charlie said. "A lot like us during the hurricane. He's what you call resourceful."

"But h-he's not," Rosie said in a quivering voice. "He's not brave. He's cautious and gets lost all the time, and he wouldn't go into a storm because of a dare like you."

Charlie smiled at that. "It's funny how stories get told as time goes on."

"What do you mean?" Rosie asked.

"He means our Miracle story—the one about how we

went out on our boat because of a dare. That's the way everyone tells it," Arthur said.

"I like it that way," Bill said. "Makes us sound debonair."

"Makes us sound fearless," Arthur added.

"But it's not true," Charlie said. "We didn't go out on the *Blue Dolphin* on a dare."

Arthur and Bill shook their heads, their matching blue eyes glinting.

"We went out on the water that day because Daddy had lost his favorite fishing rod, the one that belonged to our granddaddy," Charlie said.

"But Granddaddy passed away, and that rod was the only thing Daddy had left from him," Arthur said.

"We heard him tell Mama how he'd left the rod on the sandbar near Oyster Point, where he was fishing," Bill said. "He wouldn't risk heading back out with the storm blowing in."

"But we did," Charlie said. "We weren't wishing for any Miracle. All we were thinking about was saving our daddy's fishing rod."

"Never told anyone. We didn't want Daddy to feel bad," Arthur said.

"I still think it's a crying shame we didn't get that rod too," Bill said. "The hurricane knocked us off course."

Rosie stared at them, at soft, wrinkled faces and wispy white hair. Suddenly, something clicked inside of her like that final moment in a film when the whole story comes together. She thought of Mrs. Grant helping her elderly neighbor right before her cataracts were cured and Dale Irvine trying to find his grandma's cat in a thunderstorm when he was hit by lightning. Mr. Carson fell off the roof trying to fix a leak for the town, and Mrs. Moore was shielding her brother from a fire when she was rescued. Even little Tom Bolling was saved from drowning after he tried to catch a fish for his father's first supper home.

Miracles weren't because of lucky charms or healing water or wishes. Miracles didn't happen by chance, and they weren't a coincidence or plain old good luck. They were *real*. People took a risk to help someone and got a Miracle in return.

A lightness expanded inside Rosie. There was such goodness in this world. There was such goodness right here in Glimmer Creek, and Rosie wanted to be a part of it. She wanted to be the kind of person who believed in magic, who was brave, who took a risk for someone else. She wanted to be the kind of person who believed in Miracles.

Rosie shot straight up. She wouldn't waste another second on anger or jealousy. Those things never did anyone a bit of good. They certainly never caused a Miracle. All she had thought about the past few weeks was herself instead of what was really important, like Mama and Henry and Cam. Rosie needed to make things right with everyone she loved. Starting now! As her favorite director, Michael Curtiz, used to say, "The only things you regret are the things you don't do."

The kitchen door swung open, and Mama appeared holding a mug with steam rising out of it. "Hello, gentlemen. Did I hear you brought supper? How lovely. I made an extra pot of coffee if you're interested. It's in the kitchen."

The Blue brothers perked up and started toward the kitchen.

Rosie bounded over to Mama and clasped her in a tight hug. "I love you."

Mama laughed. "Well, I love you too. What brought this on?"

"I just realized something important about, well, everything," Rosie said urgently. "And I have to go right now."

"But I've made you hot chocolate with raspberry syrup, and the Blue brothers brought supper," Mama protested.

"I need to see Cam," Rosie said, already at the door.

"I don't want you out right now. I should come with you, unless . . . " Mama's voice trailed off. She set the mug on the foyer table and considered Rosie. "Do you need to do this alone?"

Rosie nodded. "I'm only going to Cam's house."

"Home in a half hour, okay?" Mama said.

Rosie was already throwing open the door to find Cam coming up the front walk. She halted in surprise. "What are you doing here?"

"Coming to see you," Cam said.

"That's funny. I was on my way to your house," Rosie said. She looked at Cam, with her understanding eyes and sturdy shoulders, which had seen Rosie through a million different adventures, and found it wasn't hard at all to tell her the truth. "I'm sorry."

"No, I'm sorry," Cam said.

"It's my fault for yelling at you today."

"You wouldn't have gotten mad if I'd listened to you."

"I still shouldn't have said you changed for the worse," Rosie said.

"And I don't think you're bossy," Cam said.

"Well . . . I can be a little bossy," Rosie said. "But can you forgive me anyway?"

Cam's face cracked into a smile, and that was all the encouragement Rosie needed. She threw her arms around Cam. The breeze softened, the porch light brightened, and everything seemed better all at once.

Cam pulled back. "I know I haven't been around as

much since school started. Soccer and the team took up a lot more time than I expected."

"That's okay. You should play soccer. You're great at it, and I understand you don't want to work on my movies anymore." It was a tough thing to admit, but she wanted Cam to know they were friends no matter what.

"That's not true. I like helping you, except when you get me in trouble," Cam said ruefully. "But there's less time now. There's more homework, more practices—"

"More friends," Rosie offered.

"The eighth graders on the soccer team were really nice when we first started school," Cam said, sounding defensive. "They're the ones who introduced me around."

"I don't blame you for wanting to meet new friends."

The wind whistled through the tree branches, and Cam tapped her toe against the porch floorboard. It was quiet for a moment.

Cam cleared her throat. "If I'm being honest, I guess maybe I . . . I guess maybe I *tried* to get to know Leila and Aimee and Macon. Everyone in school likes them, and I wanted them to like me. I wanted to hang out in the Lounge and work on the doughnut fund-raiser and go to Leila's parties. You probably think it's stupid to care about stuff like that."

"No, I don't. Everybody cares about stuff like that." Rosie exhaled. "That's part of what's hard. When I'm around you and Leila, I feel really left out . . . and jealous. But that's my problem, not yours." There. She'd said it.

Cam nodded slowly. "I get it. I feel that way around her too, and then sometimes she starts talking and I nod my head even if I don't agree with her. I think I'm flattered she wants to hang out with me." She covered her face. "That's so embarrassing to even say."

"No, it's not. She's the most popular girl in eighth grade."

"Yeah, but she's not my best friend. You are," Cam said.

Rosie smiled. Warmth seeped into her chest. "You're my best friend too, but it's okay for you to have other good friends. And I don't have to always be included in everything you're doing."

"But I want you there! When I was at Leila's party, I was by myself on the couch while everyone else talked to the boys. I pretended to watch the movie because I didn't know where else to look. It was so awkward. I think Chase only sat down next to me because he felt sorry for me. I really wished you were there. I always have more fun when you're around."

Rosie couldn't believe it. She'd figured Leila's party

was the most fun thing since they'd gone to see *The Wizard of Oz* on the big movie screen in Gloster.

"I guess we can't always do everything together anymore," Rosie said.

"I guess not," Cam replied. "But sometimes I miss how it used to be—just you, me, and Henry."

"Me too," Rosie said sadly.

But neither was smiling anymore because one of them wasn't there.

"If only I had listened to Henry about the treasure instead of thinking about my documentary again," Rosie said.

"If only I had gone after him at lunch instead of going to see Leila," Cam added.

"Hey there!"

Cam and Rosie looked up. Betsy was coming up the walk, holding something bulky in her arms.

"Is Henry here?" Betsy asked.

"You haven't heard?" Cam said. "Henry is missing."

Betsy's mouth fell open. "Oh no. He forgot this." She held out the bulky thing in her arms, and Rosie immediately saw that it was an orange life jacket.

Rosie swallowed. "Where did you find that?"

Betsy shrugged. "I was on my way to the festival and

noticed it out in Henry's driveway. I knew right away he'd forgotten it. I figured I might find him here since you three are always together, but if he's missing . . . " Her voice trailed off.

The hair rose on Rosie's arms. If Henry was missing and he forgot a life jacket, there was only one place he could be—on the water somewhere. Rosie thought back to the times Henry talked about the treasure and froze.

"Henry told me Lonnie used to fish at White Stone Beach," Rosie said in a rush. "What if he thinks the treasure is there?"

Cam went still. "White Stone Beach is on that little island in the middle of the Chesapeake Bay. You can only get there by boat. You don't think he'd actually go there by himself, do you?"

"He might." Rosie thought of Henry's determined face when he stormed away from her, and then she remembered Hazel's clue. "I talked to Hazel Maywell tonight. I know you don't believe in the Miracles, but we have to listen to her. She's our one hope, and she said the train treasure was under the leaves of Lonnie's safe house. Are there any trees on the island?"

Betsy nodded. "I used to climb them when my daddy took me fishing there."

The sky rumbled overhead. "A nor'easter is headed

our way. If he's on the water—" Rosie couldn't finish her sentence.

Rosie met Cam's eyes, which were wide and frightened. Rosie grabbed Cam's hand and set her shoulders. It wasn't too late. She knew it wasn't. Between Hazel and Betsy, they'd gotten clues to where Henry was . . . Now it was up to them to find him.

CHAPTER TWENTY-TWO

Cam discovered Mr. Joe's rusted-out jonboat missing from the dock. Rosie rushed back inside and told Mama everything. After contacting the police station, Mama left to go tell Miss Betty what they'd learned. Cam and Rosie hopped on their bikes. Rosie left a note this time explaining how she'd gone to help Henry. She hoped Mama understood she had no choice.

They pedaled to the end of Magnolia Street, down Poplar Lane, and over Birch Street, past the shops and churches. Dead cornstalks loomed over either side of the road like sand-colored monsters. The wind had picked up and clawed at their hair. Rosie shivered. The pit in her stomach was the same one she always got when the music to the movie *Jaws* began, right before the giant shark bit someone's legs off.

They turned in to the Windwheel Marina parking lot. Rosie threw her bike behind a nest of bushes. A blinking red-and-blue police light cast beams in every direction from the boat on which Sheriff Parker and Deputy Cordell were untying the knots tethering it to the dock.

Deputy Cordell groaned as soon as she saw them.

Sheriff Parker looked up. "Rosie, what are you doing here?"

"We have to come with you," Rosie said.

Deputy Cordell rolled her eyes. "Sheriff, we don't have time for this. There's a storm blowing in."

Rosie ignored Deputy Cordell and fixed her eyes on Sheriff Parker. "Please let us come. We could help. We know Henry the best, and maybe—maybe we can tell you which direction he may have taken or where he would put down his anchor."

"Absolutely not," Deputy Cordell said. "We cannot let a couple of civilians—children civilians at that—accompany us on official police business."

Rosie squeaked out a protest. There was no way she was staying at the marina.

"If you don't let us come, we'll steal a boat and follow you," Cam said, lifting her chin high and staring them both down.

"Are you threatening a police officer, young lady?" Deputy Cordell asked.

"I'm telling you the truth," Cam said, crossing her arms.

Sheriff Parker sighed. "Do your parents know you're here?"

"Mine do," Cam bluffed.

Rosie kept silent. She'd had enough lying for one lifetime. She just hoped Sheriff Parker agreed to take them anyway.

Sheriff Parker pulled out his phone. "I'm calling both your parents to let them know where you are." He then gestured to the boat. "Get in."

"This is highly unusual, Sheriff," Deputy Cordell protested.

"I agree," Sheriff Parker said. "But I can't risk any more kids out here alone tonight."

Sheriff Parker couldn't reach Mama or Cam's parents, but he left a message with both before starting out onto the water. The river was choppy and rough, battling against the wind. The police boat hurdled along, coasting up a wave and slamming back down into the water with a resounding boom every couple of feet.

A flock of birds soared overhead, black against the night sky. A clap of thunder blotted out their cries. Cam reached for Rosie's hand and held on tight. Rosie knew they were thinking the same thing. Was there any chance of finding Henry in all of this?

They emptied out of the Rappahannock River and

into the Chesapeake Bay. As soon as they hit the waters of the bay, the choppiness grew worse. The wind picked up. The boat crashed against the waves, and Rosie feared it would break apart into a thousand pieces.

A few straggly trees were silhouetted up ahead on White Stone Beach. Water crashed against the strip of rocky beach. The island itself was smaller than a football field, and half of it was buried under the rising water. In the distance, a yellow lightning bolt shattered the sky. The wind howled in Rosie's ears.

Sheriff Parker said nothing and edged the boat closer to the beach. He clicked on the boat's spotlight and swept it over the island. Rosie squinted and searched, desperate to catch a glimpse of Henry. After several long moments, her stomach sank. Despite the light, there was nothing to see. The beach was empty.

The thunder increased in volume and frequency. All at once, the sky unleashed a torrent of rain. Rosie was soaked in seconds. The drops drove into her skin as if needles were jabbing her exposed face and hands.

"We've got to turn back," Deputy Cordell shouted, her hair flapping in her eyes. "It's not safe."

Sheriff Parker turned from the steering wheel. His eyes met Rosie's. "She's right."

"But what if he never made it here?" Rosie asked. "What if he's still out on the water somewhere?"

"He doesn't know how to use a compass," Cam said.

"We have to look for him," Rosie pleaded.

"We don't have the right equipment." Sheriff Parker sounded defeated. "I'm sorry. There's nothing more we can do. We've already called the coast guard for help. They'll be out here soon. I'm sure Henry's taken shelter somewhere along the shoreline."

Rosie slumped on the side of the boat. She huddled closer to Cam, feeling her arms tremble at the same time. The rain continued to drive down into her face, but she barely noticed. She didn't believe Henry was sheltering on the shoreline. He was out there somewhere on the water, and he needed their help now.

Sheriff Parker pulled away from the beach and turned the boat toward the shoreline. The boat careened back and forth, up and down, making Rosie's teeth rattle.

Rosie closed her eyes, trying not to cry. They needed a Miracle. Henry was trying to save his family tonight. He was doing something good the same way he was always doing something good for his parents, for Cam, for her. Now she could only hope a Miracle would save him back.

Go to the left.

The words popped into Rosie's mind from out of

nowhere. No sooner had she thought it than Sheriff Parker made a sudden and sharp turn to the left. Rosie's eyes flew open.

Deputy Cordell turned to him. "Sheriff, where are you going? Marina is that way." She pointed to the right.

Sheriff Parker clutched the wheel, staring straight ahead. "I've got a feeling."

Rosie's heart jolted up to her throat as she leapt to her feet. Every part of her body tugged to the left side of the boat. She peered over the edge and would have jumped into the water herself if Sheriff Parker weren't heading in exactly the direction of the strange pull. Something was happening. Something big. Something outside of their control.

"Go faster," Rosie shouted.

"This is crazy," Deputy Cordell yelled.

As if to punctuate her point, thunder boomed around them and lightning electrified the sky, closer than ever.

"Girls, get in the cabin," Deputy Cordell demanded.

But Cam was now standing beside Rosie near the front of the boat, her feet sure despite the unsteadiness beneath them. She looked at Rosie, and hope radiated from her face. Cam could feel it too. Was it her imagination, or had the wind died down a bit? Had the rain slowed slightly? Was the boat cutting through the waves, steady and sure, almost as if it had a mind of its own? There was magic seeping off the water and swirling in the air. The Miracle was on its way.

Rosie held her breath and stared straight ahead at the black expanse of water and the whitecaps churning on the surface. And then somehow, unbelievably, over the wind whooshing and the thunder crashing, she heard it. Henry's voice! It was faint and nearly indistinguishable, but it was definitely him.

"Help!"

"I hear him!" Rosie said. "His voice is coming from over there." She pointed straight ahead and yelled above the storm. "Hold on, Henry. We're coming!"

"We're almost there!" Cam shouted.

Sheriff Parker shifted the boat in the direction of Rosie's finger.

A lightning bolt lit up the water only car lengths away. The wind rose higher. Rosie didn't dare breathe. Her body was immobilized with fear. Henry was in the water. A Miracle might be on its way, but so was danger.

"There!" Cam yelled. "I see him!"

Henry's head rose out of the waves, then slipped back below the water with a sickening splash. He was gone, swallowed up whole, almost as if he'd never existed at all.

Sheriff Parker pulled the boat to a sudden stop, sending everyone careening forward. Rosie's knees hit the deck hard, but she lifted her head as Sheriff Parker dove straight down into the darkness where Henry had disappeared. Rosie clambered to her feet, gripping Cam's arm, staring at the place where Henry had gone under as the seconds ticked past. The waves rolled and splashed over the side of the boat, and the rain was a thick, gray curtain.

Rosie squeezed her eyes shut. For a single moment, it was as if the entire world stopped midframe. The screaming of the storm silenced. The motion of the waves halted. The rain froze in the air.

I believe. I believe. I believe.

Sheriff Parker broke the surface with a sputtering, gasping Henry. He hauled him toward the boat, swimming with one arm and holding Henry with the other. Rosie rushed to the side, tripping over ropes and life vests, with Cam directly behind her. Deputy Cordell reached down and heaved Henry up and over.

Henry landed on the floor of the boat with a *thud*. Water dripped into his eyes and down his cheeks. He was pale and soaked, but he was alive. Without stopping to take a breath, Cam and Rosie threw their arms around him and held on as if they would never let go.

CHAPTER TWENTY-THREE

People bustled in and out of the waiting room of the police station. Miss Millie, the department secretary, sat behind the lobby desk, fielding phone calls and asking Cam, Henry, and Rosie if they wanted anything every few minutes. They huddled in a row of chairs under a mountain of blankets. Miss Millie had already brought them hot tea. Rosie held the mug and let the warmth flow into her hands.

Sheriff Parker leaned over the reception desk at the front of the lobby. His uniform dripped water onto the table, and he pushed wet hair out of his eyes. "Your parents should be here any minute."

Rosie studied Sheriff Parker's steady blue eyes and lined forehead. He wasn't exciting or flashy like a leading man in a classic old movie, but he was brave. He was the type of person who drove a boat through lightning to save a kid, took Mama to a fancy dinner to make her happy, and fixed the lock on their door because it needed fixing. He was a good person, and Mama deserved someone like that.

Rosie hadn't given Sheriff Parker a chance. She should have listened to Mama when she said he was trying harder and noticed the nice things he did. But she hadn't wanted to see those things because she didn't want Mama to have any reasons to like him. She'd wanted Mama all to herself, the same as always. She'd been jealous, and that wasn't fair to Mama or Sheriff Parker.

Rosie shrugged off her blanket and walked to the front of the lobby.

Sheriff Parker was shuffling some papers on the reception desk and looked up when Rosie approached. "Everything okay?"

"I wanted to thank you for what you did."

"That's my job."

Rosie met his gaze. "I don't think your job means you have to drive a boat through a nor'easter and dive into the river at night, in the cold, to rescue my best friend."

Sheriff Parker ducked his head. "I'm glad he's okay."

"You should ask Mama out on another date," Rosie said.

Sheriff Parker waved a hand. "I don't think your mama is too interested in me right now. It's all right."

"She likes you. I can tell. You should call her or something." Rosie's cheeks burned. "I wouldn't mind."

Sheriff Parker examined the lid of his coffee cup as if it held the secrets of the whole universe on it. "Well, thank you for . . . that."

"You know, your situation follows the rules of a classic romcom, just like *Sleepless in Seattle* with Meg Ryan and Tom Hanks," Rosie said. "Meg's a reporter who falls in love with Tom after hearing him on a radio show. She writes a letter asking him to meet her on the top of the Empire State Building. They have so many obstacles, but they find each other in the end."

"I have no idea what a romcom is," Sheriff Parker said.

"It stands for romantic comedy, and the rules are simple. One, the hero's goal is to win the love of another character, which you were trying to do with Mama. Two, there's always a big date, which was your dinner at Sunsets. Three, there are insurmountable obstacles separating the hero and his love, which was me."

"What was you?" Sheriff Parker asked.

Rosie really didn't want to get into how she'd acted like a brat and tried to convince Mama to dump him. "You know what? That part isn't important. The important part is rule number four: there's always a happy ending."

Sheriff Parker shook his head, smiling. "I don't know about all that, but if anyone deserves a happy ending, it's Caroline."

Rosie smiled back at him. "Seems like we can agree on some parts of filmmaking."

Sheriff Parker walked down the hallway to the offices in the rear of the station, and Rosie sank into her seat between Cam and Henry, pulling the blanket over her shoulders.

"Sheriff Parker deserves a medal for saving my life," Henry said.

Cam punched him in the shoulder. "Yeah, well, your life wouldn't have needed saving if you hadn't tried to take a boat to White Stone Beach on your own. That was so stupid."

It turned out Henry had never made it to White Stone Beach. He'd left right after school in Mr. Joe's boat. When he got out into the Chesapeake Bay, his engine stopped; he was stranded when the nor'easter arrived, and his boat capsized in the huge waves.

Henry shook his head. "I don't know what came over me. I was just so desperate to help my parents. I thought I could fix everything."

Rosie shook her head. How could she have possibly thought her problems were more important than Henry's? They weren't. Everyone's problems were important.

"It's my fault too. I could have talked you out of it if only I had listened to you at school. I'm sorry," Rosie said.

"Me too," Cam said.

"It's all right," Henry replied, his face still pale but also peaceful.

"But you didn't find the treasure," Rosie said. "What if you have to move?"

Cam clenched her fists. "Not happening."

"It might happen. I hope not. I really hope not." Henry tugged his blanket tighter around him. "If it does, I'll have to deal with it."

Hunched beneath the blanket, Henry looked thin and small. But what no one could see on the outside was how strong he was inside. He'd taken a boat out in the middle of a huge storm to save his family. He'd stood up to his best friends to follow his gut. He'd do anything to help the people he loved. Rosie put her mug down on the table. It was time for her to be brave as well.

"I have to talk to Mama about my father," Rosie said.

Cam clapped a hand over her forehead. "Sheesh, Rosie. I forgot all about him. Did you find him at the festival?"

"No," Rosie whispered.

"He's probably at the Glimmer Creek Inn waiting for you," Henry said, half standing. "We could go over there right now."

"He's not at the inn. He never came," Rosie said, staring down at her hands. She ached inside as if a fishhook were lodged within her heart.

After a few moments, Henry cleared his throat. "Most male beetles abandon their nests and leave the female beetle to care for their offspring alone. Having a single parent isn't unusual."

Cam set her face in a grimace. "I'd like to show Michael Weatherton the unusual force of one of my goal kicks into his shin."

Rosie couldn't help laughing. "It's all right. I mean, it's not, not really, but I'll live."

Henry nudged her arm, and Cam scooted closer. Rosie sighed. There wasn't anything that could make her father missing the festival okay, but having her best friends beside her helped.

"It's too bad you didn't find the treasure. Finding a million bucks would do a lot to cheer me up right now," Rosie joked. "Maybe we should go back to White Stone Beach."

"When it's not raining," Cam said.

"I'm not sure there's much of a point," Henry said ruefully. "All I know is Lonnie went fishing there sometimes. I don't have any real clues. It was just the next place on my list."

Rosie and Cam looked at each other and smiled. They hadn't told him yet about Hazel.

"What is it?" Henry asked.

"We have a clue," Rosie said. "A real one if we can

make sense of it. I talked to Hazel about the treasure tonight. I figured if I found it, maybe I would find you, too. She said we needed to dig under the leaves of Lonnie's safe house to find the treasure."

"It's a pretty random clue," Cam said, laughing.

Henry sat up, the blanket slipping off his shoulders. "Maybe not."

Rosie looked at him, her eyes widening. "Are you saying you know where Lonnie hid out after the robbery?"

Henry was already shaking his head. "I don't know that, but what if she wasn't talking about where Lonnie hid out *after* the robbery? What if she was talking about the one place Lonnie felt at home, the only place he felt safe?"

"Okay, I guess that fits, but where is it?" Cam asked.

"After his parents died, Lonnie had only his two best friends. They were like his brothers, and they built this tree house in the woods behind the Gooch place, where they spent all their time. If Lonnie managed to make it all the way back to Glimmer Creek after the robbery, after he was *shot*, maybe the only thing he wanted was to get back to the tree house."

"His safe house under the leaves," Rosie whispered.

The three of them stared at each other, and matching grins broke out across their faces.

"You know, we could film our treasure hunt for another documentary," Rosie said. "If we find the treasure, we might actually get distribution."

"Why don't we focus on coming up with a plan for locating the old tree house first," Cam said.

Henry held out his hands. "We could always do both. Official HenRoCam on Monday?"

"I can meet after film club," Rosie said.

"Soccer ends at four," Cam said.

"Great," Henry said, and clasped them both by the arms.

It wasn't going to be the same as elementary school. They couldn't always do everything together forever, but there would still be official HenRoCams, there would still be adventures, and there would still be friendship, and that was more than enough.

Miss Betty and Mr. Joe rushed into the lobby. Henry hopped out of his chair and was across the room in two steps before the arms of his parents swallowed him whole. Miss Betty's shoulders shook as she murmured his name.

Rosie wished she had her video camera to capture this moment. She could watch it over and over again: the meaning of real love.

Miss Betty crouched down until she was at Henry's eye level. "Why on earth would you put yourself in that much danger?"

"I wanted to find the train treasure. I overheard you talking at night about your medical bills, and I thought we could use the treasure to pay them off and then we wouldn't have to move," Henry said.

Mr. Joe hugged Henry to his side. "We're not moving."

"We're not?" Henry looked over at Cam and Rosie. A grin wavered on his face.

"Mayor Grant gave us the name of his cousin who's a lawyer. We talked to him this afternoon. He handles health care disputes all the time and says we have a good case for appealing our bills. I'm sorry you were worrying about that, son. From now on, you let your mama and me do the worrying, okay?" Mr. Joe said.

Miss Betty hugged Henry tight to her again, then pulled back and swatted him on the shoulder. "This excuse will only work once, young man. If you ever put yourself at risk like that again, you are grounded for the rest of your natural-born life. As it is, we've got to get you over to Dr. Ford tonight for a full check-up."

"I have developed a pretty bad cough," Henry said seriously.

Miss Betty looked around the room, her eyes settling on Rosie and Cam. "I can't thank you enough for saving Henry."

Rosie gestured to Sheriff Parker, who had walked back

into the lobby. "Thank Sheriff Parker. He did most of the work, and the Miracle did the rest."

"Wait until I tell the ladies at Beauty and Bows my son was Miracled," Miss Betty said, squeezing Henry's shoulders.

"It may not have been an actual Miracle," Sheriff Parker said. "We don't know for sure."

"How else do you explain finding Henry in the middle of the river at night?" Cam asked.

When she caught Rosie's surprised look, she rolled her eyes. "Come on, how could I *not* believe in the Miracles after tonight?"

Sheriff Parker blew out a breath, shoving his hands into his pockets. "I . . . I can't explain it."

Rosie knew the truth. She'd felt the magic on the boat. Henry had gotten a Miracle.

Pulling the blanket up around her, Rosie's elbow knocked into her still-full mug of tea on the side table. The mug tumbled toward the ground, heading straight for destruction. In a move right out of a classic martial arts film, Henry dove forward and caught the mug in his hand. The tea sloshed against the sides but didn't spill. Not a single drop!

Henry straightened up and stared down at his hands as if he couldn't believe it. This was the same boy who was unable catch a hat, much less a full mug of tea.

"Wow. Good reflexes," Sheriff Parker said.

Cam and Rosie exchanged shocked glances. It was more than good reflexes. It was more than amazing reflexes. No one could have caught that mug.

No one who wasn't Miracled.

CHAPTER TWENTY-FOUR

M ama stood behind their kitchen counter, her hands fluttering in every direction. She had shown up at the police station five minutes after Henry's parents, shuffled Rosie out the door, and whisked her straight home.

Now Mama gathered up a plate of food and set it in front of Rosie. "All the essentials are here: brownies, cookies, lemon squares. Miss Betty insisted I take it home after I went over to tell her about the missing boat. I swear half the town dropped something off at her house tonight. Is there an unwritten rule that if a child goes missing, you must drop off baked goods?"

"I think this is enough for the entire seventh grade." Rosie plopped down on a counter stool.

Mama poured a glass of milk, her movements never stopping. "Are you hungry? You must be hungry. I've heard people who face grave danger are hungry after their experiences. David told me how the storm was hitting but you insisted on going out on the boat anyway to get Henry. He said you were brave and—" She broke off and covered her face with her hands, suddenly still. A sob escaped from beneath her fingers. Her chest heaved with deep breaths.

"Mama?" Rosie asked.

Mama removed her hands. Her face was red and splotchy, her eyes filled with tears. "Oh, sugar, when I think about what could have happened to you . . . Why didn't you tell me first?"

Rosie squirmed in her seat. "Because I knew you'd say no." She met Mama's eyes straight-on, tractor beam and all. "And, Mama, I had to go. All I could think about was getting to Henry before something terrible happened."

"You should have told me." Mama's forehead wrinkled. "I can't help feeling like you're keeping things from me. First skipping school, then sneaking out. Now this. You've been acting so secretive."

Rosie put down the brownie and frowned at her plate. "There's something else I need to tell you."

"I knew you were upset about the whole David thing, but it's more than that, isn't it?"

Rosie's mouth went dry, her appetite suddenly gone. It was time to tell Mama the truth.

"I—I invited Michael to the festival to see my documentary."

"You invited your father?" Mama's voice rose on the last word.

Rosie swallowed hard. "Yes."

"But—but how?" Mama asked, looking wildly around the room, as if she expected Michael to materialize on the spot. "How did you get in touch with him?"

"I searched for his name on your e-mail account. I found out he was working on a film in Richmond, so I came up with this idea to film the documentary and convinced Mayor Grant to show it at the festival. I figured if I invited Michael to see my work on the big screen, he might actually come."

"You came up with this entire idea of filming a documentary to have an excuse to invite your father, who you've never met, to Glimmer Creek?" Mama asked.

Rosie winced. When Mama put it like that, it sounded a bit crazy. "Well . . . yes."

Mama looked away, her face unreadable. "And what happened?"

"Michael said he was coming, but he e-mailed and canceled while we were at the festival," Rosie said.

Saying the words to Mama made it final. Michael hadn't shown up, and he probably was never planning to.

Mama took Rosie's hands. "You should have told me about this."

"I know."

Mama opened her mouth, closed it again, then sat silently for a moment before continuing. "Michael was—is—a good man in a lot of ways. I loved him, and he loved me too, and for a time that was enough. But he never wanted to settle down. He never wanted to be a husband." She hesitated.

"He never wanted to be a father," Rosie said, saying what Mama couldn't.

"I suppose that's . . . that's right."

Rosie bit her lip to stop it from trembling. It wasn't a surprise, not really. She'd known this all along deep inside, but hearing the words tore at her heart just the same. "But—but why?"

"Michael wished for an exciting career, to travel all over the world. That doesn't make him a bad person. It's just the unfortunate truth."

"I guess it's hard to travel all over the world with a little kid," Rosie said, staring down at their joined hands and trying not to cry.

"Oh, Rosie. I'm so sorry." Mama squeezed Rosie's hands so tightly, almost as if she wanted to squeeze away the words she was saying.

It was the most Mama had ever said about Michael, and it made a horrible kind of sense. Michael was an actor, chasing down roles. He wanted adventures. He didn't want to be stuck in Glimmer Creek.

"D-did you ever want to travel the world and have an exciting career?" Rosie asked, needing to hear the answer and afraid to hear it too.

Mama tipped up Rosie's chin and stared into her eyes. "Sugar, I have something so much better. I have you. You are my greatest adventure. There is nothing—*nothing*—I would change about our life. Okay, maybe I'd get the faucet fixed, but that's it." She smiled down at Rosie.

Rosie stared back up at her. This was Mama, who kept her safe and warm and loved. She wasn't going to leave Rosie, not even if she started dating Sheriff Parker, not even if they didn't agree on everything. Mama and Rosie had always made two halves of a perfect whole, but maybe they didn't need to be only two halves anymore. Maybe they could make room for someone else.

Mama put her arm around Rosie, and Rosie leaned into her.

"I'm really sorry," Rosie said.

"For what?" Mama asked.

"For skipping school, lying about Michael, and e-mailing him without telling you." Rosie pulled back. "Only—I wanted to meet him so badly, and I know you think I'm too young."

"I was worried Michael would hurt you, and I don't want you to get hurt. Ever."

The lump in Rosie's throat expanded, making it hard to talk. "But it does hurt that my father doesn't want to see me, and there's nothing you can do to stop that."

Mama bowed her head, her own lip trembling. Her brown eyes were wet when she looked up. "I know that. I do. We could . . . " She swallowed. "We could drive to Richmond tomorrow. I can't promise we'll see Michael and I have no idea how he'll react, but we can try."

"I don't want to see him yet." The words tumbled out of her mouth before Rosie stopped to consider them. "Maybe someday, but not now."

Rosie didn't trust herself to speak. Letting go of Michael Weatherton shouldn't have been a hard thing to do. Not when he'd never been there in the first place. But letting go of the dream of a father wasn't easy either. Still, she was glad she knew the truth about Michael. There was a good side to most everything, and finding out the truth was a gift. She didn't want to spend time wishing for a father who wasn't coming home. There were too many other things to hope for. There were too many other hopes she could make real. It was time to find a new dream.

"If you change your mind, you can tell me," Mama said. "I'll be right here. Always."

"I know," Rosie said softly.

And that knowing felt a lot like its own Miracle.

When Rosie walked into the kitchen the next morning, Mama popped up from the kitchen table. The house smelled like lemons, and she spied a round, creamy cake studded with blueberries on the counter.

"Finally," Mama said, sighing dramatically. "I've been up for hours waiting on you. What movie are we going to watch this morning? Is it my turn to pick or yours? I think we need something light after yesterday, unless you want something serious, and then I guess I could watch it. Also, I woke up early and baked your favorite: lemon blueberry cake. I know we don't normally have cake for breakfast, but I figured you deserve it after last night." She said this all without taking a single breath.

Rosie peered at the clock over the table. "It's barely nine o'clock. I would have slept longer, but there was this loud commotion coming from downstairs. Did you drop those pots on purpose to wake me up?"

"Maybe," Mama said, smiling. "Okay, yes. But in my defense, I was bored."

"You do know I'm not here to entertain you," Rosie said.

"Yes, you are. Why else do you think I had a child?"

Mama said, slinging an arm around Rosie. "Henry and Cam have already called, and I invited them over for our Saturday-morning movie. Of course, they had a couple of requests."

Rosie rolled her eyes. "Let me guess. Henry doesn't want anything scary, and Cam said nothing boring."

Mama laughed. "That's about right."

"How about *Roman Holiday*?" Rosie said.

"Ah yes! One of our favorites."

They had seen that movie more times than Rosie could count. Come to think of it, when Gregory Peck got into the fight on the riverboat while protecting Audrey Hepburn, he looked an awful lot like Sheriff Parker before he dove into the water to save Henry.

"You know," Rosie said casually, "I've always thought Audrey and Gregory should have ended up together in the end of the movie. If I were the director, I would have filmed it differently. Scripts get rewritten all the time in Hollywood."

"I'm not sure you should rewrite a classic," Mama said.

"Why not?" Rosie asked. "Even the classics can be improved upon."

Mama's phone jangled on the counter. She checked out the caller ID and made a face. "This will only take a minute," she said before scooping it up and walking to the family room.

Outside, a dark-gray truck pulled up to the curb, and Sheriff Parker got out with a bunch of yellow roses in his hand. He lingered beside the truck, staring up at their house. He then turned around and opened his car door as if to leave, before closing it again. He looked back at their house. Rosie tried not to laugh. It was nice to see someone making him nervous for a change.

Mama appeared back in the kitchen moments later. "That was Mayor Grant. He convinced Gloster to let him keep the movie screen for another day. He wants to show your documentary tonight. Isn't that great news?"

Rosie's pulse jumped. "I don't know what to say."

"You should say yes," Mama said. "You've worked hard enough on it, though don't think you're free from a serious punishment for skipping school and sneaking out."

Her very first film premiere could take place tonight. Everyone in Glimmer Creek would see it, and she had time to add in what she'd found out from the Blue brothers—the cause of the Miracles. It would make her film great, and she would prove to everyone she had what it takes to become a professional director. Still, Rosie hesitated.

Miss Lily had said the mystery of the Miracles was part of what made them special. She worried that solving that mystery could somehow change their town and its people. It wasn't only Miss Lily who thought so. Mr. Jack, Miss

Matilda, Mrs. Bolling, and many others felt the same way. Rosie didn't know if her documentary could really alter anything about Glimmer Creek, but some things weren't worth risking. She didn't want to change the way everyone had helped look for Henry last night at the festival, or how the entire town turned up for the too-long town meetings. And Rosie couldn't think of a time when she walked down Magnolia Street and didn't run into at least five people who would ask how her Mama was doing and what movie she was working on.

Rosie had a responsibility to Glimmer Creek. After all, she *had* discovered the secret of the Miracles, or some of the secret, because nothing could really explain magic. But she knew the Miracles came from a choice to help, to save, to love. In this world, in this whole wide world, there really was no greater Miracle than that.

"You know, I found out something about the Miracles last night," Rosie said, lowering her voice to a whisper. "They only happen when you're trying to help someone else."

Mama leaned over the counter, face puzzled. "But the Blue brothers—"

"Were trying to find their daddy's fishing rod on the night of the hurricane."

"Miss Lily?"

"Wanted to make her family proud."

"Donna Davis, and Mr. Jack, and Beth Moore . . ."

Rosie lifted one corner of her mouth. "They were all trying to save someone."

Mama sat back. Her eyes glistened. "Rosie, that's . . . that's amazing. I've never thought of it that way before."

"I'm not sure anyone has," Rosie said.

"Is this all in the documentary?"

"Not yet," Rosie said.

"It will cause quite a sensation if you add that in. Your documentary would be a hit," Mama said.

"The thing is," Rosie said, "if people knew the secret, maybe they'd act different. Maybe they'd do things to try to get a Miracle, and I'm not sure that's how it works. Part of the magic is the mystery. I wouldn't want to ever do anything to make that go away."

Mama's gaze softened. "That's a good point, sugar. So, what are you going to do about the documentary?"

Mama's eyes shifted to one side, and Rosie got the feeling Mama knew what she was going to say before the words left her lips. Mamas were like that sometimes.

"I'm not going to add in the secret, and even though the documentary taught me a lot about Glimmer Creek and filmmaking, I can't show it tonight or ever," Rosie said, and exhaled. A calm she hadn't felt in weeks settled over her. "What if analyzing the Miracles makes them less powerful or less believable? I won't take that risk. Besides, I'll make other films, better films, and I'll get those on the big screen someday."

"I have no doubt about that," Mama said, reaching out to squeeze her hand. "I'll call Mayor Grant and tell him there's no need to hold on to the movie screen tonight."

"Wait!" Rosie said. "Maybe he'll still want to show the feature film he'd planned for the festival. I think everyone in town would like that. I'll call him and talk to him myself." And she planned to do so right after Sheriff Parker got up the nerve to ring their doorbell. It was lucky he'd come over this morning. *Roman Holiday* was a good place for her to start his movie education, and they had plenty of lemon blueberry cake to share.

"Has anyone told you how smart you are?" Mama said, and double winked at Rosie. "You must take after your mama."

Rosie double winked back. "I sure hope so."

When the doorbell finally rang, Mama was the only one surprised. Rosie let her answer it alone and waited for them in the kitchen.

Beyond the window, the morning sun draped the water in gold. A breeze sent lacy whitecaps skittering across Glimmer Creek, and falling leaves traced lazy crisscross patterns against the blue sky. Houses lined up on either side of her in crooked rows, connected like beads on an invisible thread, each one separate but also part of something bigger. It was the view she saw every day. It was home. Rosie's heart swelled at the sight.

It's true what they say—there's no accounting for Miracles. But there is accounting for love and there is accounting for goodness. And in Glimmer Creek, they wouldn't have it any other way.

Cinnamon-Sugar Popcorn
a snack that's sure to sweeten any day

ingredients:

- 1 tablespoon granulated sugar
- 1/4 teaspoon cinnamon
- 1/2 teaspoon salt
- 1 tablespoon vegetable oil
- 1/2 cup popcorn kernels
- 2 tablespoons melted butter

directions:

- Combine sugar, cinnamon, and salt in small bowl.

- Heat oil in large pot over medium-high heat. Drop two test kernels into pan and cover. Once test kernels pop, pour 1/2 cup of popcorn kernels into pan and cover. Shake occasionally to prevent burning. Turn off the heat when popping slows.

- Transfer popcorn to large bowl. Pour melted butter over popcorn and toss to combine. Shake sugar, cinnamon, and salt mixture over popcorn and stir while popcorn is still warm.

Chocolate-Cherry Muffins

a muffin capable of curing all manner of maladies

ingredients:

> 2 cups flour
>
> 3/4 cup granulated sugar
>
> 1/4 teaspoon salt
>
> 1 tablespoon baking powder
>
> 1 cup milk
>
> 1/4 cup vegetable oil
>
> 1 egg
>
> 1 teaspoon vanilla extract
>
> 3/4 cup chopped dried tart cherries
>
> 3/4 cup semisweet chocolate chips

directions:

- Preheat oven to 450 degrees. Spray a 12-cup muffin pan with cooking spray or use muffin liners.

- In mixing bowl, whisk together flour, sugar, salt, and baking powder. Set aside.

- In separate mixing bowl, whisk together milk, oil, egg, and vanilla until well blended.

- Toss cherries and chocolate chips with dry ingredients. Gently fold wet ingredients into dry ingredients until just combined. Do not overmix.

- Divide batter between muffin cups. Bake for 5 minutes at 450 degrees. Lower heat to 400 degrees and bake for 12 more minutes or until toothpick comes out clean.

Potato-Chip Sundaes
a dessert best saved for special celebrations

ingredients:

>1/4 cup water
>
>1 cup granulated sugar
>
>3/4 cup heavy cream
>
>3 tablespoons butter
>
>1 teaspoon vanilla extract
>
>1/2 teaspoon salt
>
>Potato chips
>
>Vanilla ice cream
>
>Whipped cream (optional)
>
>Maraschino cherry (optional)

directions:

- Add the water and sugar to a medium saucepan. Stir constantly over medium heat until sugar dissolves and begins to bubble.

- Turn the heat to medium high and bring to a boil. Do not stir the sugar as it boils. Let mixture continue boiling until it turns a light-brown color. This takes about 5 minutes.

- Remove from heat. Pour cream into saucepan while whisking. Then whisk in butter, vanilla, and salt. Set caramel sauce aside to cool.

- To assemble, place three scoops of vanilla ice cream in a bowl. Top with potato chips broken into smaller pieces. Drizzle with caramel sauce. Whipped cream and cherry are optional but encouraged.

Pecan Pancakes with Strawberries

a perfect treat to serve with Saturday-morning movies

ingredients:

> 2 cups flour
>
> 1/4 cup brown sugar
>
> 1/4 teaspoon salt
>
> 2 teaspoons baking powder
>
> 1/4 teaspoon cinnamon
>
> 1/2 cup chopped pecans
>
> 1 3/4 cups milk
>
> 2 eggs
>
> 1 teaspoon vanilla
>
> 1/4 cup melted butter + butter for cooking and
>   serving
>
> sliced strawberries
>
> maple syrup

directions:

- In mixing bowl, combine flour, brown sugar, salt, baking powder, cinnamon, and chopped pecans.

- In separate mixing bowl, whisk together milk, eggs,

vanilla, and melted butter. Blend with dry ingredients until just combined.

- Heat butter in a large skillet over medium heat. Scoop batter by 1/4 cups onto hot skillet. Bake until both sides are golden.

- Serve hot with butter, sliced strawberries, and maple syrup.

Bacon-Chocolate-Chip Cookies

a cookie with amazing powers of persuasion (they even work on hermits)

ingredients:

2 1/4 cups flour

1/2 teaspoon baking soda

1/2 teaspoon baking powder

1 teaspoon salt

1 cup butter, softened

3/4 cup granulated sugar

3/4 cup brown sugar

1 teaspoon vanilla extract

2 eggs

1/2 cup chopped bacon—about 7 pieces, cooked and cooled

1 1/4 cup milk-chocolate chips

directions:

- Preheat oven to 375 degrees.
- In mixing bowl, whisk flour, baking soda, baking powder, and salt.

- In separate mixing bowl, beat butter until smooth. Add sugars and vanilla and beat until combined. Add eggs, one at a time, and beat until combined.

- Beat in flour mixture gradually until well combined.

- Stir in bacon and chocolate chips.

- Drop dough onto parchment-lined cookie sheet.

- Bake for 9–11 minutes until cookies are golden around the edges but still soft.

Hot Chocolate with Raspberry Syrup
a drink guaranteed to comfort during stormy weather

ingredients:

>   2/3 cup water
>
>   2/3 cup + 1/2 cup granulated sugar
>
>   1 1/2 cups raspberries
>
>   1/3 cup unsweetened cocoa powder
>
>   1/2 cup milk + 4 cups milk
>
>   1 teaspoon vanilla extract

directions:

• Bring 2/3 cup water and 2/3 cup sugar to a boil in a small saucepan, stirring until sugar is dissolved. Remove from heat and stir in raspberries. Mash mixture using a fork. Allow to seep for one hour. Then drain mixture through a fine mesh strainer, discard solids, and refrigerate raspberry syrup until needed.

• Combine cocoa, 1/2 cup sugar, and 1/2 cup milk in a medium saucepan. Stir constantly over medium heat until mixture boils. Cook for another two minutes.

- Stir in 4 cups milk and heat, but do not boil.
- Remove from the heat and stir in vanilla and 3/4 cup of raspberry syrup.

Lemon Blueberry Cake
a cake to share with friends, both new and old

ingredients:

for the cake:

2 3/4 cups flour

1 1/2 teaspoons baking powder

1/4 teaspoon baking soda

1/4 teaspoon salt

1 cup butter, softened

2 cups granulated sugar

4 eggs

2 tablespoons lemon juice

1 tablespoon lemon zest

1 teaspoon vanilla extract

1 cup sour cream

2 cups blueberries tossed with 1 tablespoon flour

for the glaze:

1 cup confectioners' sugar

3 tablespoons milk

1 tablespoon lemon juice

directions:

- Preheat oven to 350 degrees. Butter a Bundt pan.

- In a mixing bowl, whisk together flour, baking powder, baking soda, and salt. Set aside.

- In a separate mixing bowl, beat butter until creamy. Beat in sugar. Beat in eggs, one at a time. Add lemon juice, lemon zest, vanilla, and beat until combined.

- Beat in flour mixture gradually, then beat in sour cream.

- Fold in blueberries gently.

- Spoon into prepared Bundt pan.

- Bake at 350 degrees for 55 minutes or until toothpick comes out clean. Cool in pan before removing.

- In mixing bowl, whisk the confectioners' sugar with the milk and lemon juice until smooth. Drizzle the glaze over the top of the cake until it drips down the sides.

ACKNOWLEDGMENTS

Thank you to my agent, Katie Grimm. You saw what this book needed to be long before I did and never gave up on me. I am beyond grateful for your brilliance, your fierce dedication, and your friendship.

All the thank yous in the world to my editor, Krista Vitola. Your guidance and passion for this story made it so much better. You are an utter joy to work with. To Justin Chanda, Catherine Laudone, Krista Vossen, Katrina Groover, Martha Hanson, Penina Lopez, Christina Pecorale, Victor Iannone, Emily Hutton, Chrissy Noh, and the rest of the team at Simon & Schuster Books for Young Readers, I'm thankful for all your hard work and still pinching myself that I get to work with you.

To Jen Bricking for your beautiful art that captures the story perfectly. To Juliana Brandt, PitchWars, Cara Bellucci, Alechia Dow, and my fellow Roarers for making me a better writer and cheering me along. To my pals on Briardale for sparking my imagination, to my girlfriends from Wake Forest for listening to it all, to my friends in Richmond for giving me a home, and to the beautiful Northern Neck for endless inspiration.

To Ashby, Lori, Alston, Claire, Parker, Jeff, Lucas, Scarlett, Miles, Pope, Erin, Gus, and Benny for brightening my life in a thousand ways. To Barry and Ginna for always treating me as their own daughter. To Uncle Glenn for giving me a regular dose of laughter. To Grandma, whose grace and love have lifted me in times when I needed it most. To Pop Pop, who shows me the true meaning of goodness simply by being himself. And to Dad for telling me stories, encouraging my hopes, and giving me a most magical childhood.

To Sarah, my sister, my confidante, my dearest friend, this book would never have happened without you. As with most things, I told you about this dream first, and your belief in me never wavered. That has meant more than you could ever know.

To Gray, Colter, Bo, and West, I adore you boys with every bit of my heart. You have brought more wonder and joy into my life than I thought possible.

Finally, to my husband, Roby, I could go on for pages about how you make me laugh at the exact right time, refuse to let me quit, and create space in our life for me to do this. Yet in the end it all comes down to one thing—finding you was my real-life Miracle, and I'm grateful every day.

Turn the page
for a sneak peek at

The Sisters of Luna Island

Rules of Aromagic:
Gather flowers before a rainstorm.
Enchant spices beneath a sliver of moon.
Blend charms with the clearest intent.
But beware the price of changing fate.

1

Cinnamon will attract prosperity and wealth.

The knock came at midnight. Sharp and staccato, it cracked open the silence of the house. Marigold Lafleur nestled further under the blankets but her eyes popped open all the same, her heart keeping pace with the rap-tap-tapping on the door.

Someone was here.

The stillness of sleep gave way to the softest of sounds; covers rustling, arms stretching, heads lifting. Lou groaned from the room next door and Birdie exhaled a tiny breath. Mama's footsteps pattered past. All the while, Marigold wondered who dared to turn up on their stoop.

No one came to Lilac Cottage in daylight. In truth, no one came much at all ever since the accident. Whoever was at the door needed something, and they needed it badly.

Marigold slid off the edge of her mattress. From her open window, the moonlight was a ribbon of silver rippling over her dresser tucked under the eaves and the single bed, which just fit inside the narrow walls. Tiptoeing across the room, Marigold shrugged on a robe. She crept down the hall, careful to avoid the creaky floorboard on the other side of her bedroom door.

Staying pressed against the wall, Marigold snuck halfway down the stairs and spied Tara Ricketts in the front doorway. Her brown hair was messy and tangled and her face was streaked with tears. Behind her, the night stretched out like the ocean behind it, dark and full of secrets.

"He'll never straighten up. It doesn't matter what I do. He can't hold a job to save his sorry life. We're broke. We might lose the house." Tara was sobbing so hard, her face had disintegrated into the wrinkles and folds of a crushed flower petal.

Mama shook her head in sympathy. "You could leave Luna Island."

"I've got nowhere to go," Tara said.

Mama took a deep, slow breath and squinted. It was a telltale sign. She was smelling Tara's fears. "I'm guessing you're most worried about that baby daughter of yours."

Tara nodded. "I want her to get off this Island someday."

"I know how that goes," Mama said. "I might have something to help, but it comes at a price."

Marigold shrank back, her stomach dropping like a stone

in water. Mama was tampering in someone else's life. Again.

"I'll pay, whatever it is. My mama gave me money. You can have it all." Tara's voice creaked out, high-pitched and clogged with tears.

"The cost I'm referring to isn't related to money. There's a price for changing the future, and I can't predict what it will be," Mama said.

Mama called them vexes—the consequences for altering fate. She could fix one part of Tara's life but a vex might make something awful happen to another part. It was the unpredictability and the danger of aromagic.

"I don't care. This is all I have left," Tara said in a defiant tone.

"You better come on back then," Mama said.

Marigold's mouth flooded with a sour taste. Sure, they needed the money, but what Mama did to get it—Marigold couldn't excuse it, not after last spring. She pushed the memory of a pale, still face back into a corner of her mind.

Mama looked up and met Marigold's eyes. "I wouldn't count on winning the role of a spy anytime soon."

Stupid. Marigold should have known Mama would catch her. Mama couldn't remember to open the mail or lock their back door, but she always knew when someone was watching.

"Since you're up, why don't you come on down?" Dark

circles ringed Mama's eyes but a hopeful half-smile tugged at her lips.

Marigold froze at Mama's request, torn between running down the stairs or back to her room. "I—I can't."

"Of course you can. You could help with the candles," Mama said.

Marigold's nose flooded with the scent of wildflowers and herbs. She pictured Mama smiling at her above the burner, and the tingling of her fingertips as she concentrated on the flame. It was powerful and exhilarating and exciting and . . . wrong. Marigold pressed her heels into the steps and reminded herself once again she wanted nothing to do with aromagic anymore.

Birdie appeared at the top of the stairs, hands on her hips. Her pajamas hung in a creaseless line on her tall, thin frame, and her auburn hair swept up in a perfect ponytail even though she had just been asleep. "Marigold needs her rest. It's the first day of school tomorrow."

"As far as I can see, she's already awake," Mama said.

"She's awake 'cause of all the commotion." Lou pushed past Birdie and clomped down the stairs on long legs corded with muscle. "Half the island could hear you carrying on down here."

"I'm sorry," Tara said. Her eyes darted to Mama, then up to Birdie, then over to Lou.

Birdie didn't even look at Tara, her eyes burning into Mama as she strode down the stairs and stopped right behind Lou. "Marigold needs to get back to bed like any other normal seventh grader. Not that there's anything normal about this family."

Mama closed her eyes a second too long at Birdie's jab. Marigold tried to think of something to say to dissolve the tension blanketing the room. Yet Mama was already shuffling Tara down the narrow hallway covered in peeling flowered wallpaper and past the crooked stairs stretching up in a maple-patterned jigsaw puzzle. Marigold watched them go, relief and disappointment battling inside her.

"I'm sorry for getting up, but we haven't had a visitor in a while," Marigold said as soon as Mama was out of earshot.

"It's all right. You go on to bed, M," Birdie said. "I'll keep watch over Mrs. Ricketts. I don't know what Mama is thinking, leaving some woman we barely know alone in our house in the middle of the night."

"Stop worrying for once. We all need sleep, and Tara Ricketts isn't going to hurt anything. She's too much of a mess," Lou said, exasperated.

"Exactly. She's in no shape to make a reasonable decision. Someone needs to keep an eye on her," Birdie said, frowning at Lou's dismissive tone.

Lou rolled her eyes. "Fine, I'll come with you. I'm not

going to stick you alone with Mama's latest bad decision."

"If you're both going to the kitchen, I'm going too," Marigold said. Now that her sisters were awake and actually doing something, she didn't want to miss any of the action.

Birdie held up her hand in an attempt to stop Marigold from moving. "But school starts—"

"I'll go to bed right after," Marigold interrupted and clasped her hands together in a plea. "I know it's late but at least we're all up late together. It's an adventure." If this were a movie and Marigold was the star, she'd sweep into the kitchen with her white nightgown swirling behind her to save Tara and her no-good husband.

Marigold deflated as Birdie chewed on her lip, clearly not seeing the "adventure." Sometimes it seemed as though Birdie helped Marigold only so she could boss her around a minute later.

Lou cuffed Birdie on the arm. "Oh let her stay. No one can fall asleep now, although . . ." She tapped her lip, pretending to think. "We could wrap this up early by locking Mama in the basement and telling Mrs. Ricketts the magic shop is closed tonight."

"Yeah right. Mama would kill us," Birdie scoffed.

They all knew not to mess with Mama's aromagic. The only time Marigold could remember Mama yelling at her was when Marigold spilled all their rosewater while attempting a friendship charm without permission.

"Don't worry. We'll let her out by morning," Lou said, winking at Marigold.

"I'll even throw down a pillow." Marigold grinned. "And maybe a blanket."

"Well sure, we don't want her to get cold," Lou said.

Birdie sighed. "You two are hilarious. Can we get this over with?"

"You're no fun," Lou said, sticking her tongue out at Birdie.

"So you're always telling me. All right, M, you can come," Birdie relented.

Marigold linked her arm through Birdie's and nestled close to her side. "I'd never really lock Mama in the basement."

Lou linked herself to Birdie's other side. "I definitely would, but only if you weren't home."

Birdie looked at Lou, her mouth twitching. She began giggling. Lou and Marigold joined in, arms still linked as they pulled each other down the hall.

By the time they reached the kitchen, Mama was already gone. Tara slumped at the kitchen table, her head in her hands. The kitchen was tattered and peeling with splintered cabinets and chipped paint on the wall, but it had gleaming wooden countertops that Birdie polished with lemon oil every night and green herbs lined up along the window in terra cotta pots.

Birdie grabbed the dinged-up kettle from the stove and bustled over to the sink, filling it with water for tea. Lou leaned against the countertop, picking at her fingernails. Behind her, the back porch light glowed and jagged fingers of gold light reached into the shadows. There was a banging downstairs, and the rich scent of cinnamon rose through the floorboards. Lou and Birdie stopped all movement.

"Prosperity charm," Lou whispered. "Got to be."

Marigold shivered. Faint echoes of lilac-tinged smoke followed the pungent cinnamon as it curled up from the basement below; the tendrils wound their way around Tara's calves and seeped into her skin. Tara shifted in her seat, uncomfortable but not knowing why.

Prosperity charms were notoriously difficult to control. The outcomes were unpredictable at best and horrible at worst. Money meant greed, and changing fate because of one's greed never led to anything good.

"If you want money, you should borrow it," Marigold urged Tara. "A lot of big stuff can go wrong if you use Mama's charm for money."

"I didn't ask for money," Tara said, her eyes bloodshot and bleary. "I'm trying to help Ray. He needs a job. That's all I want."

But at Tara's words, an acrid scent burned through Marigold's nostrils. She froze and breathed out, trying to dispel the smell and stay calm all at the same time. Yet the burning scent only grew stronger until the stench filled her brain. Not now. But her nose wouldn't listen.

"Gambling," Marigold blurted out.

Birdie sighed. "Not again."

"Gambling?" Lou asked and peered closer at Tara. "Yep, I can see it."

"What are y'all talking about?" Tara asked in a high, panicked voice.

"It's nothing," Birdie reassured Tara while frowning at Marigold.

"I'm sorry. I tried to stop," Marigold said miserably to her sisters. She'd thought she was getting better with the slips. "I'm an utter failure!"

"More like dramatic failure," Lou said, her mouth quirking up at the corners.

"I do everything wrong," Marigold cried, flinging herself into a chair.

"That's not true," Birdie said, her eyes softening in Marigold's direction. "But you need to try harder. We'll work on it. The goal is normal, right?"

"Right," Marigold said, hanging her head. Normal was good grades and sleepovers and Daddy back on Luna Island.

Normal was not blurting out the secrets you smelled.

"What did you mean by 'gambling'?" Tara asked, her face flushed and looking more worried by the second.

Silence thickened in the room. The kettle screamed into the quiet, and Birdie hurried to take it off the stove. "Where is Mama?" she mumbled, glancing at the basement door.

"Whatever you heard, it's not true." Tara's throat worked to swallow. "I don't gamble."

Tara was lying. Marigold pushed aside the image of Tara playing poker online. Sometimes the smell of someone's secret was so strong, it conjured up a picture as clear as her own face in the mirror.

"It's none of our business," Birdie said, and set a mug of tea in front of Tara.

Mama strode into the room, halting the conversation. She carried a glass spray bottle filled to the brim with golden liquid. Marigold knew it contained a charm of cinnamon, mint, and honeysuckle. It also was full of Mama's intentions; her best guess at what Tara needed and wanted. She was trying to help and yes, she was trying to pay their bills. Yet even now, Marigold could see the nearly invisible smoke from the scent wafting from the edges of the bottle and crawling up Tara's arms, entwined around her throat, forever altering her future.

Tara's eyes went wide. "W-what's that?"

"A special blend. Ray will get that job. All you have to do is spritz this into the air around him, and you'll have what you want." Mama smiled and held out the bottle.

Birdie's mouth tightened and she gestured to her sisters. Lou pulled Marigold out of her seat and pushed her toward the door. None of them looked at Mama.

"We're going to bed," Birdie said in a crisp voice.

Mama's smile faded. "If you'll give me a minute here, I could make some more tea."

"No need," Lou added.

Mama looked at her two eldest daughters and sighed at whatever she saw on their faces. "All right then." She turned and began explaining how to use the charm to Tara.

Marigold followed her sisters back up the stairs to their room. The twin beds were nearly touching, but there was a small space in the middle that was the perfect size for Marigold.

"Can I sleep in here tonight?" Marigold asked.

Birdie and Lou exchanged a glance, then Lou was shoving her field hockey equipment under the bed and Birdie was grabbing her own quilt and spreading it on the floor. Lou threw a pillow at Marigold, who caught it, grinning. Marigold swatted at Lou from the end of the bed.

"None of that now. We're all exhausted." Birdie surveyed Marigold's spot on the floor. "You'll sleep better in your own bed. It's a big day tomorrow, and all the research says we go into REM sleep faster when—"

"Birdie, no one cares." Lou flopped onto her bed.

"Hey some people think research is cool," Marigold said with mock seriousness, sinking down onto her cozy nest between her sisters.

"Oh man, I'm really in trouble if you two start telling me how to be cool," Lou said, smiling wickedly and clicking off the light.

The front door closed downstairs with a distinct thump. Tara was gone but Marigold couldn't help wondering what would happen to her. What about Ray and her daughter and the secret gambling? What kind of price would fate require for changing her future?

Marigold pulled the covers up past her chin, over her nose, until only her eyes peeked out. The image of Tara at her computer seared into her memory once again. She closed her eyes, willing her vision to shift. She listened to her sisters' breathing deepen. She smelled Birdie's sweet gardenia and Lou's spiced vanilla scents. Her limbs relaxed, her lashes fluttered. Slowly, the image of Tara faded. No use thinking about that anymore tonight. She was safe here in the warm darkness between Birdie and Lou, sharing the same breaths, the same smells, the same heartbeat.

Marigold always felt safest with her sisters.

The Secret Garden meets *Miss Peregrine's Home for Peculiar Children* in this charming adventure about a girl determined to infiltrate the enchanted grounds surrounding her grandmother's mansion with the help of some magically gifted friends.